Lethal Refuge

by

Vonnie Hughes

This is a work of fiction. Names, characters, places, and incidents are either the product of the author's imagination or are used fictitiously, and any resemblance to actual persons living or dead, business establishments, events, or locales, is entirely coincidental.

Lethal Refuge

Cover Art by *Kim Mendoza*

The Wild Rose Press
PO Box 708
Adams Basin, NY 14410-0706
Visit us at www.thewildrosepress.com

Publishing History
First Crimson Rose Edition, 2012
Print ISBN 1-60154-996-2

Published in the United States of America

Inching along the wall, Célie reached the window. She held on to the door jamb, a little island of security in a sea of fear. Then she stretched across and peered out.

A featureless face stared back at her.

She screamed and jumped back, bashing her elbow on the laundry tub.

Peaches lumbered to his feet, shaky and confused.

The face was still there.

No eyes. No mouth. No nose.

Peaches staggered over to the door and snuffled.

Mesmerised, Célie kept staring at that distorted face as she backed into a corner.

Then the face moved and a hand spread across the glass. The forefinger and thumb rubbed together.

Flashes of memory seared her mind.

She gasped, remembering that fearful morning when she'd discovered poor Occy's disemboweled body. Stunned, struggling not to vomit, she'd been hovering over what was left of Occy when she sensed she was being watched. For a few precious seconds she had stared back at the creepy figure silhouetted in the early morning gloom watching her—just watching her.

Then he'd rubbed his thumb and forefinger together covetously, as if he were contemplating the best way to eat her alive.

And she'd bolted.

And done her best to bury those memories.

Whoever that monster had been, he was outside the window right now.

Praise for Vonnie Hughes...

"The first thing I noticed was how strong a writer Ms. Hughes is... Well-written, this book kept me turning pages until the end."

~Long and Short Reviews (5 Books)
~*~

"With believable characters, a well-drawn background, and events rising naturally out of the preceding action, this is a well-written novel."

~Jay Dixon, HNR Reviews
~*~

"This book is extremely well written, and I loved the strong element of suspense in it. It was a treat to read and I was disappointed when I reached the end and had to let the characters go. I particularly enjoyed the fact that the emotional union did not come at the expense of good storytelling. Well done. You've done a great job!"

~Beverley Eikli, Hale Books author

Prologue

Célie Francis ran faster than she ever had in her life. Fingers of fog rolling in from the sea grabbed at her as her feet alternately flew and stuttered over the uneven pavement of the ocean road.

Where was he? How much time did she have?

The wash of the sea was a calm counterpoint to her harsh, frantic breathing. Above the sound of her thudding feet, the shriek of a bird pierced the air.

No, not a bird. Something was squeaking. Occy's old bicycle!

He had found her.

Faster, Célie, faster, shouted the little man on the treadmill in her mind.

I can't, she sobbed.

Fancy the consequences?

No, God, no!

Then run faster.

But her aching legs could not obey. And on the roadway, the relentless squeak, squeak kept pace with her. Frantically she zigzagged, seeking a haven in the fog. It was barely dawn on the lonely North Auckland cliffs above the Pacific Ocean. No help anywhere.

Have to hide. Have to hide. Her shoes slapped a rhythm.

Salty sweat stung her eyes. *Ignore it.*

The slap of her running shoes echoed, then died

in the mist. Died...

Her brain, tumbling in an endless whirl of fear and futile questions asked—why Occy? Why had he killed a man this time?

Up ahead loomed a deep grey cloud of mist. *Thank you, God.* She blasted into the fog bank and the squeaking receded behind her. *This is your chance,* the little man said.

Veering off the footpath, she streaked across a pristine lawn and crouched behind a lavender bush. Her chest heaving, she struggled to gulp another breath of sodden air.

Squeeeak. He was back. This was it. Eyes streaming, she curled into a ball on the cold ground and waited.

Something yellow zinged past her face and tickled her arm. A needle-sharp sting pierced her elbow, then another. Bees, irritated by her invasion, were trying to drive her out. *No, you won't. What's out there is a lot worse than what you can do.* As the pinpricks tingled and burned, she pressed her lips together so hard that the muscles on the sides of her face ached.

Louder now, the squeaking advanced and receded. He was casting up and down, looking for her. *Please, please...*

A sibilant whisper reached her through the clammy fog. "I know who you are, Célie. I know where you live."

Chapter One

Brand Turner, the North Shore Witness Protection Unit psychologist, checked the card in his hand. He stared at the unassuming house in front of him. Yes, this was the place. Average looking neighborhood on the south side of Auckland. Nothing different about it to draw attention. Weatherboards that needed a re-paint. Lawns that needed mowing. It blended into its surrounds as if it had been especially designed to do so. Which of course it had been.

He pushed open the squeaky gate and strode up the path to the WPU's safe house. He had to find Célie Francis—now renamed Melanie Pearson—before someone else got to her. Someone whose intentions were not altruistic.

As with all safe houses, there were no trees to provide cover for lurkers and Brand felt as exposed as a flasher on Main Street.

Just as he neared the corner of the house he heard a faint *chink* like metal brushing against a chain-link fence. He turned. A big bullmastiff trundled towards him, teeth bared—the biggest bullmastiff he'd ever seen.

Heart pounding like a jackhammer, Brand stopped dead. Anyone who said they weren't afraid of a guard dog like this was either lying or stupid. Or both.

The dog halted a few yards in front of him

taking up a foursquare stance, blocking the entrance to Ms Francis/Pearson's doorway—a canine Colossus of Rhodes.

It didn't slobber.

It didn't pant.

It just stared, its head on one side; no doubt working out which flank to rip up first.

Brand tried a jocular "Hullo there, Dog," and knew he sounded ridiculous.

The terminator curled a supercilious lip, exposing huge canines. It shifted from foot to foot like a javelin thrower getting ready for the run-up, then advanced with a menacing soft-shoe shuffle. No barking, just a businesslike, steady pacing.

Brand told himself he had faced worse than this. If he could face down a psychopath trying to eliminate innocent shoppers in a shopping mall, then he could deal with a dog. Of course he could.

Behind him, he heard a car draw up next to the sidewalk. A split second was all he had to decide— turn his back on the dog, or ignore what was behind him?

He spun around as the dog stopped pacing and glared at the car. Suddenly the animal lumbered past Brand, the wrinkled skin on its massive body gathering and stretching with each long stride. With a growl, it bashed through the wooden gate and lunged at the car. Someone inside shouted and slid the window up. Dog slobber streaked the glass as the terminator spread himself over the car door.

Brand raced towards the sidewalk, his mind clicking over at the rate of knots. So much for the safe house. Someone had already targeted Ms Francis.

The driver gunned the engine and Brand squinted to see the numberplate. But the maroon Mercedes dragged away with a throaty snarl and left the terminator staggering in the gutter.

As Brand's breathing steadied, he approached the dog. Carefully. "Are you all right, fella?" The car must have clipped its shoulder. One side lurched downwards while the three remaining legs fumbled to prop up the big, solid body. Gingerly Brand stretched out a hand as the front door of the house burst open and someone hurtled down the driveway towards them.

"You bastard! What did you do to him?" Pint-sized feminine fragility warred with naked fury.

Brand stood up.

The elusive Ms Francis. In spite of the new grunge haircut and less than stylish clothes, he'd know her anywhere. When he'd interviewed her, the lady's don't-you-mess-with-me attitude had failed to hide the deep fear beneath the veneer. And the eyes. Oh, yes. Who could forget those fabulous silver eyes?

Back to business, Turner. She's not for you. "It's all right, Célie," he soothed. "The terminator should be okay. A trip to the vet—"

She wasn't listening. Kneeling in the gutter she cooed, "Oh, Peaches. Poor baby. Let me see your sore leg." She kissed the slobbery muzzle of the mastiff while her long, thin fingers gently probed his body.

"*Peaches*?" Brand heard himself asking fresh air. "That's a hell of a name for a terminator."

"Mind your own business and call an animal doctor," she snarled. The dog whined and leaned against her.

"Well I—"

"No vet numbers on your cell phone?" she snapped. "That figures."

Ouch. Now she had him pegged as an animal-hater. If she'd waited for him to finish...

Then she peered up at him, blinking, and blushed a hectic red. "Oh, it's you, Doctor. Sorry," she mumbled.

The dog raised its head from her lap and stared

at him with serious brown eyes. Oh, *how* it wanted to slay him, but it couldn't dredge up the energy.

"Is your vet's number inside by the phone?" Brand asked.

"Yes." She was too absorbed in the dog to realize which way the conversation was heading.

"Then we'll go inside and call him." He leaned forward to ease the dog out of her lap, praying he didn't lose an arm.

"No!"

Brand had expected nothing less. The WPU had no doubt drilled into her their life-saving mantra: "Trust no one."

In spite of the hour he'd spent interviewing her three weeks ago, she didn't trust him. And she was right. But from her attitude that day, he considered the WPU mantra was unnecessary. He doubted Ms Francis had ever trusted anyone.

He held out his ID. She flicked him a look that said, *"Any idiot can make up an ID. And I do remember you. Just."*

He said placably, "So would you fetch the vet's number for me please."

"Oh, godammit!" She speared him with a filthy glance. Then she glanced down at Peaches. He could see fear in her tight facial muscles and anxious eyes.

"Here. Mind Peaches." As she eased herself away from the dog, Peaches, doing a Hollywood, played the scene for all it was worth. He whimpered and cast pitiful looks at Ms Francis.

Brand took her place in the gutter.

"Here." She rested the dog's head in his lap and he tried not to flinch. Those vicious teeth were perilously close to the family jewels. But Peaches didn't object. He began to dribble on Brand's Levis and shuddered in spasms. Brand looked up at the woman hovering at his elbow.

"He's in shock. Hurry."

Célie hurried. She raced up the cobblestone pathway and a few seconds later he heard her voice. "Hey!" she yelled, then the sound choked off.

Brand dumped the dog in the gutter and streaked up the path, crashing the front door back on its hinges. A huge figure was dragging Ms Francis along the hallway towards the back door. Her legs flailed as she grunted and struggled with her abductor.

Brand raced down the hallway and his impetus shot him clear out the back door.

"Oomph!" He collided with a sweaty human gorilla. The guy was huge. Twisting aside, he bolted after a second gorilla who was struggling to bundle Célie into a maroon Mercedes in the back street behind the house. Célie was not going gracefully. She head-butted her captor's chin. He lost his balance and staggered sideways.

Brand flung himself into the fray.

"Who the hell are you?" Célie's attacker snarled, lurching back to avoid Brand's right hook. Brand didn't waste time. He closed in and finger-jabbed the guy in both eyes.

But Brand knew he and Célie wouldn't last long against these two. He fumbled with the cell phone clipped to his belt.

Then as if he'd been signalled, their attacker whirled around and stumbled his way to the car, his eyes streaming. The second gorilla headed towards them at a shambling run, stamping over flowerbeds.

"Quick! Out of the way!" Brand yanked Célie aside and they watched as the second man dived into the Mercedes and gunned the motor. The car took off with an eldritch screech of mistreated tires.

"'M,'" Brand muttered.

"What?" Célie stared at him, her face taut with fear.

"That's all I could see. They've rubbed mud over

the numberplate." *And they hadn't expected anyone else to be at her place*, he thought.

"Thank you." Célie tried to smile. Then she exclaimed "Peaches!" and took off, running back through the house.

Brand caught up with her, his eyes swiveling in all directions. But all that was left of the gorillas were a few drops of blood on Célie's trainers.

She stood at the curb out front, talking to Peaches who was lying prostrate in the gutter. "Now look here, you ham actor," she was saying. "Enough. You did your best, but you're not hurt bad, are you, sweetie?" On the last words her voice softened to honey drizzling over warm toast and Brand's stomach tightened. The woman had the attitude of a demented bulldozer and the voice of a sorceress. His mind damn near shut down when she said, "Are you, sweetie?"

Pull yourself together, he admonished himself.

She looked up at him, those silver eyes unreadable.

"I came to warn you—" he began.

"Too late for that," she sniped. Then she pointed towards the house. "Tel-e-phone," she enunciated clearly, as if to a difficult child.

He grinned. She sure bounced back fast after a setback.

He jogged up the path and stepped through the front door.

Upstairs, a floorboard creaked. He froze.

Chapter Two

Another creak. Brand sprang at the staircase and thundered up the stairs. There was a thump and scuffle like the sound of someone dropping down on to the roof cantilevered over the back porch. As he crashed through the bedroom door at the top of the stairs, he heard footfalls thudding across the garden. Poking his head out of the window, all he glimpsed was a blur of movement beside the garage. A second later, a head bobbed up and down behind a boxthorn hedge two houses along. Looked like a guy in his thirties. The intruder or a neighbor?

Gone, dammit.

As his breathing wound down, he stood and glanced around the bedroom. Ms Francis was into minimalism. One bed, one chest of drawers, no knick knacks. Yes, that's the way he read her. No frills.

He peered into the built-in closet. Very few clothes. Had the intruder taken anything, and if so—why? He'd used the fracas as a cover to gain entry. It wouldn't have been easy because of the roof design, which was why it had been chosen for a safe house. What would someone be looking for in Ms Francis' bedroom?

He went back downstairs and picked up the phone. Dead as a doornail. No surprises there. He untaped Célie's telephone list from the wall. She wouldn't need that anymore. She was moving on. He checked the animal doctor's number and walked outside, using his cell phone to dial up Dr. Tim Makepeace.

"How long has your phone been out of order?" he asked Célie as he waited for an answer.

She stared at him blankly. "It was working an hour ago."

He glanced back at the house.

"Oh," she said. Just "oh," but he knew she'd connected the dots.

"Just as well you're here," she added.

Brand said nothing. Her comment seemed to have been dragged out of her so unwillingly that it couldn't possibly be construed as gratitude. But he didn't take offence. He knew there was fear, and then there was downright bloody-minded dread that caught you by the guts and wrenched. And from what he had gleaned when he'd interviewed her, he understood that Célie was a fighter who hated that out-of-control, nowhere-to hide feeling. Why else would she have gone anywhere near the cops?

Someone on the other end of the phone responded and he handed it to her to make arrangements for Peaches.

The vet arrived in ten minutes flat. And Brand saw why. The guy had the hots for Célie. He leapt out of his gleaming, girl-hunting convertible and rushed over to her. Célie had to point to Peaches lying in the gutter to get the man to slow down, stop gabbling crap like, "Are you hurt?" and take a look at the dog. Finally he came up with, "Ms Pearson, the dog has a dislocated—"

"Peaches. His name is Peaches."

Ooo-ee. Brand smirked to himself.

"Uh, yeah. Peaches. He has a dislocated shoulder that will have to be put back under anaesthetic. It might need pinning. I won't know till I see an x-ray."

"Your surgery—now," she barked at the vet.

Must have taken a few lessons from Peaches, Brand thought.

"Umm..." Makepeace glanced at his watch and Célie's eyes narrowed. "Tell you what. I'll call the emergency veterinary hospital. They'll fix it for you."

"*Emergency vets?* Strangers?" snapped one hundred and twenty pounds worth of vitriol. Hands on hips, Célie was one pissed-off woman. It was a wonder the paving stones beneath her tapping foot weren't shimmering in the heat.

Brand grinned and dialed his brother's number. "Sim? I've got a bullmastiff here that's been clipped by a car. Dislocation." Célie and Dr. Makepeace turned to look at him. He ignored them.

Sim came up trumps just as Brand knew he would. They always came to the party for each other.

"Okay. Thanks, Sim. I'll bring him over. See you in thirty." He clicked off.

"Who were you talking to?" demanded Célie suspiciously.

"My brother."

"Your *brother*?" She made it sound as though somebody like him didn't have brothers. "What use will *he* be?"

"A lot. Best veterinary surgeon in the country, if I say so myself."

"Oh." It was the first time he'd seen her speechless. Probably the last, too.

"Sim? Would that be—is that Dr. Simeon Turner?" Makepeace asked with awe. "I've been to a couple of his lectures and..." He caught Célie's eye and trailed off. "Oh, ah, you'll be in good hands now, Melanie."

Brand jumped into the back of Matilda, his Ford Explorer, to make a comfortable bed for Peaches. He had great sympathy for anyone with a dislocated shoulder. Very painful.

"Anything you need to collect before we go?" he

asked Célie.

"A few things." She cast an anxious glance back at the house.

The intruder was long gone so Brand didn't offer to accompany her. Makepeace could do that.

Brand hunkered down beside Peaches. Someone knew how important Peaches was to Célie and that Peaches was a force to be reckoned with, so Brand would stay right here. He might be exposed, but that cut both ways. Anyone who tried to get at Peaches or himself would have to come out into the open.

Célie pointed a finger at Makepeace. "Come with me," she said and headed for the house. The guy was so anxious to help, he almost fell over his own feet rushing to follow her. Brand swallowed a grin. Makepeace knew he'd goofed over the emergency hospital incident and was desperate to make amends.

Brand stroked Peaches' floppy ear, then phoned Detective-Sergeant Parlane to give him the good news.

"Two *what*?" the cop asked incredulously.

"Gorillas," Brand replied, pushing the envelope.

There was some heavy breathing over the phone and Parlane barked, "Cut to the chase, Turner."

Brand grimaced. Parlane took life seriously. "Two guys tried to kidnap Ms Francis," he explained. No comment from Parlane. "Thanks for asking and yeah, we're okay. I have to take her guard dog to the vet, then I'll...well, at this stage I'm not sure what to do with Ms Francis. Like we said, someone from the Unit knows every step we take. I'll work out something, but we have to get out of here *now*."

For once, Parlane didn't argue. "Agreed. I'm off duty in thirty. Let Mike Ellery handle it." End of conversation. Parlane was in a hurry.

Brand glanced around, then eased himself down on to the curbstones. He settled Peaches' head on his lap and waited. He could hear Célie and Makepeace pattering about the house, collecting this and that. He wished they'd hurry up.

At last, Célie slammed the front door shut. If they were under observation, then the watcher would realize that Célie was moving out. Perhaps the intention had been to scare her or drive her out. Or both.

Or maybe there was something else involved that only Célie knew about, because Brand agreed with Detective Senior Sergeant Parlane that Ms Francis was hiding something. Brand prayed it wasn't something that would get her killed before they discovered what it was.

He grinned as Makepeace staggered down the driveway under the weight of two big raffia bags.

"Melanie, why are you taking so much stuff?" the vet bleated.

Christ, the guy was a pathetic wimp, from his carefully careless hair down to his expensive loafers. Then he laughed at himself. *You're jealous. Grow up,* he told himself.

Célie hesitated. "Because I might have to stay overnight with ah...Dr. Turner," she said.

Makepeace shot Brand a venomous look.

Brand thought resignedly that "with...ah" meant she couldn't remember his first name. So much for rescuing a woman in peril.

"Will you help me get Peaches into the back of my Explorer?" he asked Tim Makepeace, who had dumped Célie's bags on the footpath.

Before easing Peaches into the 4x4, Brand executed a full circle turn. Everything looked like a usual day in the suburbs.

He took Peaches' top end. He figured that since Makepeace was an animal doctor, he was used to handling animals' rear ends.

Perhaps not. Tim recoiled as Peaches broke

wind then gave him a healthy boot with his hind leg. Good to know that end was in working order.

Célie nudged the vet aside. "Leave it. I'll do it."

Makepeace straightened up and looked at his watch. "I have to go. I'm late for an appointment."

"Okay. Thanks for your help," Brand said, since Célie didn't glance up from where she was petting Peaches.

Tim Makepeace jogged to his car and gunned the motor. And a very nice car it was too. Another Mercedes—a convertible this time. The local caryard was doing a roaring trade in Mercedes.

"I think you've lost a good man there," Brand said, just to be irritating. He still smarted over the fact that Célie couldn't remember his name, but he'd also seen the drawn, anxious look she'd cast at Peaches and he thought a little diversion was in order.

True to form, she bit, "Oh, shut up."

He grinned and shoved her bags in beside Peaches. "Hop in," he said. "The trip should take about thirty minutes."

"Your brother doesn't live on the North Shore, does he? Parlane says I'm not to return there under any circumstances."

"Do you always obey Detective Parlane?" he asked, downshifting as they approached the open road.

A grin snuck up and was quickly flattened. "Mostly. I know he's doing this for my own good."

She made Parlane sound like medicine. Privately, Brand thought that the safety of the public was not the first thing on Parlane's mind. The Cliff Road serial killer had been making headlines every day for weeks and Parlane admitted they had very few clues to go on. They were hoping for, but not expecting, a break in the case. The CIB, though technically in charge, was understaffed and running on empty. So far its sole contribution had been a political shove to hasten the forensic testing.

Brand checked the rear view mirror. The road behind them was clear. He glanced at Célie. "As you've guessed, I came to warn you that the witness program has been compromised," he said.

"Com-pro-mised," she mimicked. "God, you cops are something else."

"I'm not a cop," he said equably.

"That's right. You're the shrink who interviewed me. Why did they send you today?" She may as well have said, "Why did they send the office boy?"

"Because the Unit is out in full force all over the country. We're checking on all recent relocatees, trying to find temporary homes for everyone. A hell of a job."

"How 'recent' do you mean?" she asked.

"About three months."

"Ah," she said. "About as long as the Cliff Road murderer has been around."

"Hmm," he said in a non-committal tone. He flicked another glance in the rear view mirror and changed the subject. "How's Peaches?"

Célie glanced at the wing mirror on her side. "No one's following us," she said as if she played cops and robbers every day of the week. Unclipping her safety belt, she scrunched around to look at the dog. "He's whining to himself," she reported.

"You'd whine too if you had a dislocated shoulder. Had one myself once and it was agony."

"Oh? Got it playing cards, did you?"

Brand tried not to flinch. Someone had taken a chunk out of this lady long before the serial killer upset her world. It was his job to peel back those protective layers to find the scared woman underneath. And *if* the Cliff Road killer was captured, and *if* Célie would listen, he could help her restore her life. But Lord, he loved a woman with guts.

He waited a beat or two before answering. "Nah. Got my dislocation by being immature and making like Rambo on a bullrider."

That silenced her for two minutes. Then she started up again. "How long has your brother been an animal doctor?"

"About as long as I've been a psychologist. We're twins."

"Cool! So you prefer people to animals."

"Nope. Most days I'll take animals over people. Especially today."

She shut up till they turned into Sim's driveway, then she cleared her throat. "Umm...I'm sorry, Dr. Turner. I've forgotten your name."

As he switched off the engine, he had his petty revenge. "That's okay. Just call me Dr. Turner."

Her eyes narrowed. "Smartass," he heard her mutter under her breath. She swiveled her eyes this way and that, peering through the windscreen at Sim's scruffy backyard. She maintained a haughty silence till Sim trotted up to the Explorer.

"Where's the dog? You the owner?"

Célie jumped down from Matilda. "Yes. Melanie Pearson." She held out her hand. Sim ignored it and peered into the Explorer. He yanked open the tailgate to examine Peaches.

Célie looked from Brand to Sim and back again. And blinked.

Sim carried the dog into the surgery and Brand stepped back out of the way. For the time being, he had done his bit.

"What's his name?" Sim asked Célie.

Brand choked and Sim glanced at him, his eyebrows raised.

"Peaches," Célie said, raising her chin.

"Unusual," was all Sim said.

Célie obviously thought she needed to explain

herself. "Look, I know he's not pretty or anything, but with me he's all peaches and cream. He loves me, you know?"

"I know," Sim said kindly. No doubt he thought he was dealing with a woman in shock. Little did he know that over the past few weeks, Melanie Pearson/Célie Francis had suffered enough shocks to sink lesser mortals. But she was very upset about Peaches. Anyone could see that. She hung over the dog like a lover. Peaches loved her and Célie loved Peaches.

"He'll be okay. Sim will see that he is," Brand couldn't help saying.

She glanced up at him, animosity forgotten. "Thank you. If it weren't for you, Makepeace would have fobbed him off on to a student doing emergency weekend work."

Sim quirked his eyebrows at Brand. Brand knew that Sim was going to enjoy digging the information about Makepeace out of him.

"Just giving Peaches an injection now," Sim murmured, holding the scruff of the dog's neck. Peaches didn't even feel it, Sim was that good. Old Peaches drifted away to la-la land on a soft blanket of xlyazine.

"The x-ray will cost a fair bit. Got insurance?" Sim asked Célie.

"Yes."

Under which name, Brand wondered? This could get sticky. "If you prefer, I'll pay Sim now and you can repay me later," he offered.

She gazed at him out of those intense silver-grey eyes. "It's okay. Everything is arranged."

Good. Since she'd had time to arrange insurance, the WPU must have advised her on Day One to get a dog. At least she'd taken heed, even if she didn't seem to like taking advice. But she had desperately needed a companion she could trust, and in her circumstances a dog was her safest bet.

Peaches was x-rayed and nothing sinister was found. Sim wrestled the dog's shoulder back into place and they left him to sleep off the xlyazine.

As they left the surgery Brand said, "I must contact Ellery to get further instructions. We might have escaped, but I have no idea where to go from here."

Chapter Three

Two hours and three cups of terrible coffee later, they loaded Peaches into Matilda and headed towards Brand's house in the Waitakeres—the western hills outside Auckland.

"My house may not be the safest house in Auckland," Brand explained, "but it's not bad. It's on a dead end road, so any strangers in the district stand out. I've got an excellent security system, and when he's on his feet again, there's Peaches. You'll have to stay one or two nights until we can sort out a permanent safe house for you."

"How did whoever-it-was find out about me so quickly, d'you think? I've only been in the witness program for three weeks." She asked the question carelessly, but he wasn't deceived.

"Well, as I see it, the leak could have come from someone in the Unit management team, or one of the attached police personnel. It's also possible that one of the relocatees might bear a grudge for some reason. Doesn't make a lot of sense, but once you start dealing with the human race, a lot of things don't make sense." Knowing what he was about to say would keep her on her guard, he pretended to concentrate on his driving. "Yesterday I went to interview an old lady who'd just been relocated. She'd just been savagely attacked. She died in my arms."

"Oh, my God!" Célie folded her arms across her

chest.

"Yeah. She was a lovely person."

His fingers clenched on the steering wheel. He could still see in his mind's eye that poor widow who'd thought she was safe. Someone had shot her husband a year ago in an execution-style killing, and Mrs. Cameron had been the only witness willing to testify. They had failed to get a conviction so Mrs. Cameron was sent to ground. Considering the type of people Jock Cameron had dealt with, as soon as the leak was discovered, the Unit had made Mrs. Cameron their first priority. She'd been moved early yesterday morning.

And she'd been dead by mid-afternoon.

Brand cleared his throat. "Her state-of-the-art security alarm was disconnected and she'd been bashed about the head several times. Could be they were trying to question her and the attacker didn't understand the force of his blows on an elderly woman. According to the medical examiner, Mrs. Cameron was unconscious before the third blow was struck."

Brand glanced at Célie. She stared out the side window, playing cat's cradle with her fingers. As the car cornered, her chewed off curtain of hair swung forward, hiding her expressive face.

He cleared his throat. "Sorry, but you need to know what we're up against."

He wished he knew what she was thinking. Most likely she was wondering if she should grab Peaches and bolt as far away from Auckland as possible. Crammed up against the car door, she looked as though she was about to take a flying leap out on to the road.

He'd first met Célie on the door-to-door sweep after the first Cliff Road murder. Inspector Friedman and Parlane had ordered him to "Keep an eye out for behavioral clues that Ellery might miss."

Fortunately, considering the long hours involved, Detective Constable Mike Ellery and Brand worked well together. As Ellery had said, his expression sour, "Your insight and my boring, dogged persistence seem to combine well."

From those loaded words, Brand realized that Parlane probably hustled Ellery along, trying to jolly him out of his customary deliberate pace. Knowing the pressure Parlane was under to find the killer, Brand could see both sides of the story.

Brand's fingers beat a tattoo on the steering wheel and he struggled to keep his face bland. Mrs. Cameron's death wasn't the worst news he had for Célie.

Outside, the green countryside swished by, a weak, late autumn sun gleaming fitfully through the cloudbank. Brand kept the radio off. Radios discouraged talking.

"How many people do *you* have to check on?" she asked after a few minutes.

"All the local recent relocatees. I'm not in the 'inner circle.'" Brand's mouth twisted. "When the leak was discovered, they decided I could be trusted because I don't have access to the committee's client files." For once, Brand had been glad that Parlane's cavalier attitude towards him had been to his advantage. Brand had asked several times to sight the files he was not directly concerned with in the hopes of helping more victims. Parlane had always refused.

"My job is simply to interview and support the relocatees. It takes as long as it takes. Some people are moved two or three times," Brand explained. "I have to ensure that it works for them. Each to their own."

There was a short silence. "Are you sure this morning's stuff is not something to do with you, Brand?"

He damn near drove off the shoulder of the road as he negotiated a bend off the highway. What was she? A mind-reader? "Me?"

"Well—you went to see the old lady, and she died. You came to see me—and I almost wind up kidnapped. There's a pattern."

She was serious about this.

"I don't think so, C...Melanie."

"You should call me Melanie to keep my cover intact, Brand," she said primly.

Ms Francis prim? Hah! And he'd become "Brand," had he? Interesting, but he wasn't stupid enough to comment on it because she would put up the shutters so fast they'd be able to hear the slam in the next county.

He looked across at her. Her mouth pursed up as if she were trying not to laugh. He had to hand it to her. She bounced back after everything life threw at her. "Wiseguy, but you're right," he said. "It's just that you don't seem much like a Melanie. I rather like the name Célie."

The gamine face brightened. "So do I. Here's hoping one day I can come out from under and be myself again."

Brand couldn't help grinning. "Oh, I think you'll always be yourself."

They were silent for a time, then she was off again. "I miss my flatmate, Tara. And I miss my apartment. And my piano."

Brand's guts churned. Tara Smith. He still had to tell her what had happened to her best friend.

As they rounded the final bend, security lights lit up the courtyard of his mock hacienda. The alarm light over the front door had not been activated and the soft blue-grey dusk cloaked his home in its usual serenity. Brand relaxed a little.

"Wait in the SUV for me," he cautioned. "Just in case."

He almost wished he hadn't said it. She whitened under her tan and did as she was told. That's how scared she was.

He wasn't exactly thrilled either.

No one except his family and best friend knew the location of this place. His professional work was carried out through a couple of box numbers and cell phones. Central Police had all his details, or enough to satisfy them anyway. When Central had vouched for him, the new North Shore WPU had indicated that all they wanted was results. They were not interested in his private life. He was happy to keep it that way. The world was a dangerous place for shrinks whose clients consisted of threatened people.

Anyone determined enough could find out, of course. In today's world you could find out anything. Sure, he randomly changed his SIM cards and mobiles. His post boxes and home and car were all registered in his stepfather's company's name. But a hunter with a devious mind and unlimited funds could eventually run him to ground.

When he'd been seconded to the fledgling relocation program, he knew that from then on his life was in danger. Some of the criminals he'd interviewed and assessed wanted him dead. He'd winkled out their dark, desperate secrets and that made him dangerous. Most of those criminals were now tucked away from society, but they had friends and relatives who wouldn't hesitate to seek revenge if they could get away with it.

So he'd tried to keep a low profile—although according to his ex, Marina, he hadn't registered high on the social scale anyway—and he'd looked for a safe place to call home. When he'd discovered this place in the blue-green hills outside Auckland, the property had been overgrown, long deserted by its previous owner who had run out of steam and money pursuing the wilderness ideal. It had taken weeks to tame nature outside before he could begin on the house itself. It had been worth it.

Once the creeping vines were pulled away from the windows and several saplings had been felled to let in the light, the grumpy house had taken on a mellow look. He'd weather-sealed and whitewashed the plaster and replaced the front and back doors with stout, steel-centered timber-look ones. And Sparks Mullaney, his best friend, had installed an intricate security system.

Brand loved his place. He loved the way it smelled, the pine resin odor seeping in from outside to meld with the scent of the polished pine boards inside. He loved the way it felt—inviolate, secure against everything the elements threw at it. And hopefully inviolate against dangerous people.

Célie would be safe here, he was sure of it.

After a prowl around the yard, he deactivated the alarm. Nobody had been here since he'd left yesterday.

"Come on in!" he called to Célie. She jumped down from Matilda and sauntered across the yard, doing a good imitation of a confident woman.

Brand made up a bed for Peaches in the laundry with a bedroll, then they grappled the snoring dog out of the Explorer. Peaches wasn't feeling active. He rolled a bleary eye at them, then with a contented sigh, collapsed on to his comfortable bed.

Célie rubbed Peaches' head and laughed. It was the first time Brand had heard her laugh. And although it wasn't exactly carefree, it was a start. He'd like to hear it more often.

"He looks so relaxed," she said. "He'll be a new man when he wakes up."

Brand toted her gear into his spare bedroom. "This is yours, too," he said, showing her the ensuited bathroom he and Sim had installed. "Make yourself at home. The bookshelves in your room are stuffed full, and there's another bunch of books and DVDs in the main room."

He wanted her to feel at home but he didn't want to crowd her. She was the sort of woman best left to find her own way. He had some bad news to tell her, and he wanted her to feel safe when he disclosed what had happened to Tara Smith.

And then, after he'd ripped the heart out of her, he had to watch her lose that precious, fleeting feeling of safety.

Chapter Four

Célie stared at herself in the mirror. God, how she hated these rats-tails trailing outside her collar. A month ago her hair had been long and luxuriant. Nothing fancy. Wavy. Dark brown. But it had looked presentable. Now she looked as though she'd taken to it with a pair of sewing shears, which was what she had done.

When the Unit had found a house for her, they'd given her two hours to gather up her portable possessions and "do something about the way she looked." There had been no time to get to a salon. Tara had raced out and bought hair coloring and together they'd mangled Célie's hair into fawn-colored grunge.

Her clothes were dreadful too, she thought, grimacing. A cop had accompanied her to the local second-hand clothing store where she'd bought the two pairs of knocked-about jeans she'd lived in for the past month.

There was no problem with anyone recognizing her now.

She up-ended her bags and pulled out the sum total of her life. She'd had to leave a lot of stuff in the house she'd shared with Tara and she couldn't go back for it until this bad part of her life was over. During her time in the safe house, she had bought nothing except basic food items.

She'd been ripped out of a lifestyle she loved and

tossed into a sweet little furnished house—but Celie didn't go much for cutesy and pretty. She preferred a place where she could sprawl on an overstuffed sofa, legs dangling, chomping on Cheezels or whatever. Feeling like an unwanted visitor, she'd used the same coffee mug and plate every day.

Of course, that phase of her life wasn't meant to be permanent. Parlane and his gang would catch that maniac and then she could go back to her old life. God, she hoped that was soon. Her sense of dislocation was so acute, she felt as if she were grieving for a close friend who had died.

What if they never caught that freak? Sometimes cases like this dragged on for as much as twenty years until some cold case officer interviewed a person of interest who'd been on the periphery during the first investigation, or until forensic testing advanced enough to produce new evidence. She might be Melanie Pearson forever.

No. She wouldn't let that happen. Not after all she'd gone through.

Conscious of the tightness grabbing her throat, she peered out the window. She would *not* cry. Dusk had almost given way to dark. A morepork started up his lonesome, monotonous call and the sound of his plaint hovered in the evening air. Off to her right, she thought she saw a shadow moving among the trees. She blinked and the shadow disappeared.

"Pull yourself together," she muttered, turning away from the window. "It was probably a possum. What else would it be, way out here?"

She tugged the curtains closed and went back to her unpacking. "Some people have it a lot worse than this," she reminded herself. What a stupid platitude. It didn't give her a single crumb of comfort. It was like telling a child who hated mashed pumpkin that somewhere in the world a starving child would gobble it up.

Her hands stilled. Perhaps she should work out how to trap the killer herself. Could she set herself up as bait? Shivering, she muttered, "Don't do anything rash, Célie."

When she'd finished unpacking, she checked out the bathroom. Very nice. She'd have a shower and keep out of Brand Turner's way. She knew a loner when she saw one. It took one to know one. She was seriously invading his space.

An hour later she lay on her bed, flicking through some music arrangements she'd used, back when her life was real. She grinned. Parlane had had a hissy fit when he'd discovered she was "famous," as he'd called it. He'd gloomed on about how difficult it would be to keep her hidden. She wouldn't call herself famous, but she'd certainly arrived as a torch singer. Even had her own following. She'd been booked solid for twelve months until this creepy maniac had lined her up in his sights.

"Damn you to hell, whoever you are," she snarled, hurling the manuscript pages across the room. They fluttered to the carpet, forlorn.

Her career was gone. She couldn't show her face in public until the killer was caught. Even then, she'd have so much lost ground to catch up that she might never make it in the entertainment world again. All those years of grinding, unrelenting hard work had been for nothing. Boring studio shots with people she would normally cross the road to avoid; the endless polishing of the hardest phrases over and over so that on the night of a performance they soared faultless and thrilling.

She punched the pillow. There wasn't a damned thing she could do about the situation. She scrambled beneath the blankets and curled into a ball.

A long time later there was a tap on her door.

Brand stuck his head around it. "You any good at cooking?"

She sat up, half-drowsy. "Umm...not bad. What sort of cooking?"

"Whatever you can make from a big pack of ground beef."

She scrambled out of bed and pattered after him into the kitchen. He'd pulled the wooden shutters closed. Outside it would be pitch black by now, but in here the TV was chattering and most of the lights were on. It felt warm and good. Safe.

"Can I look through your cupboards?" she asked.

He leaned back against the granite benchtop. "Knock yourself out."

After some judicious research she announced, "I think it should be chili. That okay with you?"

"Terrific. I never make it from scratch. I just buy it in cans."

She pretended to be appalled. "You buy it in *cans*? You mean you never do the beans and onions and sauce and stuff yourself? Omigod." Clutching her hand to her chest, she staggered around, feigning horror.

He laughed at her antics and she found herself grinning like a Cheshire cat. She wasn't *that* funny. This guy was easy to be around.

"Okay, Sara Lee. Go for it."

She didn't whine about how he should be helping her because she knew what he was doing. He was keeping her occupied.

A short time later she plunked a bowl of chili in front of him.

"That was quick." He was watching the news on TV with the sound down low.

"Guarantee you'll like it."

"Hmm. I like a woman with confidence." He tasted some and looked impressed. "You're right. It's very good. No, better than that. Hold on." He savored another mouthful. "It's a nine out of ten."

"Always room for improvement," she agreed, sitting at the other end of the sofa, her legs tucked up.

They ate in a companionable silence, commenting now and again on the TV news. The news was followed by a blood-thirsty cop program. Brand got up and turned off the TV. "I'll make us some coffee," he said.

"Do you have any tea?" Célie asked. "I don't sleep so well after coffee."

"It's a wonder you've slept at all over the past couple of weeks, Melanie."

So he was making a concerted effort to call her Melanie. He was right. She should try to think of herself as Melanie Pearson but it was so very hard. With no family behind her to give her a sense of belonging, she had struggled to find her own identity. Now she had to dump that hard-won self-confidence and think of herself as someone else.

"Yeah. I've had a few nightmares, but my main problem is in getting to sleep. It takes forever. Then when I finally sleep, it's just for a couple of hours. Sometimes I read all night."

"Not good, Mel."

"Mel." She liked that. Better than Melanie anyway. Melanie sounded like a fairy in a light opera. God knew where the Unit chose their names from. The other choices they'd suggested had been even worse. None of them had suited her.

"We'll talk about your sleep problems later. But first I have something to tell you." Brand paused, the expression on his face somber and bleak.

Her stomach clenched. She had imagined things couldn't get any worse. Obviously they could.

"It's about Tara," Brand murmured.

She raised her eyebrows. Oh, Lord! Her flatmate was a darling, but she could be a bit of a loose cannon. Hopefully she hadn't pissed the cops off. Or maybe they'd had to relocate Tara too. Or—

She stared at Brand, trying to read his expression. Then she realized. "No, please no!" she yelled.

"I'm sorry," he said huskily. He took her in his arms and pressed her against his shoulder, as if he were trying to stop her from escaping.

Célie's stomach muscles clenched so hard they ached. "She's dead, isn't she?"

"Yes."

Please God. Not Tara. Not crazy, loyal Tara. Célie tried to wriggle free to vent her anger on him but he held her tightly.

"Stuff you all!" She punched at his shoulders but he rolled with the punches.

Helpless against the wash of despair bombarding her, she subsided in his lap and curled into a ball. And fell apart. Her body and mind felt as if they were splintering into a thousand pieces. She couldn't be staunch any more. Everything was too hard.

She hadn't broken down when the first newsflashes about the murders in their neighborhood had been blasted over the airwaves 24/7. She'd just resolved to take special care to make sure she was never a victim.

She hadn't broken down when she'd stood and looked at what was left of poor old Occy. She'd been too damned frightened.

She hadn't broken down when the Unit said they'd have to relocate her. Because she understood it was her only option.

But when Brand Turner focused those serious, hazel eyes on her and gently explained that her best friend was dead, his kindness unraveled her. He knew that Tara was important to her, and he hurt for her.

How had he figured out that Tara was her lifeline in a bitchy world?

She wrapped her arms around his waist. And cried.

Chapter Five

"It was *him*, wasn't it?" she asked a long time later when she'd gained a measure of control.

He nodded, his chin scraping the top of her head.

She took a deep breath and hiccupped. "Did he kill her because he thought she was me? Or was it because he couldn't find me and wanted to send a message?"

He hesitated. "I don't know, Mel. I left the scene straight away. I was checking your new address on my laptop when Parlane grabbed me and told me to find you quickly.

"When are you going back to—to the scene?"

"I'm not going back. The crime scene team is there. My priority is to make sure you're okay."

She sagged, defeated. Okay? She would never be okay again. Tara and Occy were dead. She was the last one left out of the three of them who just might have seen the killer. *I won't tell*, she promised silently. It wasn't as if she was sure, anyway.

Brand's hand rubbed up and down her backbone, comforting her a little. She reminded herself that he was simply doing his job. To him she was a "client."

"I phoned the team while you were packing," he said. "Mike Ellery has taken over from Parlane for a couple of days. Parlane is on leave."

"Good," she muttered.

"Yeah." Brand agreed. "Parlane gets me down, too. Anyway, Mike is searching for a new safe house for you. Do you have any preferences where you want to go? Somewhere not too far out of your comfort zone."

She wriggled around, banging the top of her head on his chin and stared at him in amazement. "Good God, Turner! I'm already *way* outside my comfort zone. I no longer have a job. I'm kept by the government. I can't go back to my old haunts. My best friend has been brutally murdered and my other friends don't have a clue where I've gone. How the hell can I get any further outside my comfort zone?"

"I know."

He sounded as if he really did know. She could have done with a man like this when she'd been going through all the bad times.

Then she took a grip on herself. *He sees you as someone who needs to be sorted out.* But he was so understanding, and he smelled so damned nice, she couldn't help wondering about the woman in his life. Because he'd have one, for sure. A high-maintenance elegant giraffe with a post-graduate degree and a silver spoon in her mouth.

She sighed and leaned against his soft sweater, worn out, lethargic.

Half asleep, she was roused by a buzzing sound in her ear. "Excuse me." He eased her away and shoved his hand underneath his sweater, pulling out a cell phone.

As he glanced down at his caller ID, a shock of hair fell forward and he forked it back with his fingers. Somehow the gesture was endearing and sensual at the same time. Her toes curled. *Get a grip.*

Brand cut straight to the chase. "Mike? I'll ring you back." He grabbed another mobile off the coffee table and punched in one digit. Then he carried on the conversation with Mike Ellery as if it had never been interrupted. It seemed to be a system he was used to.

He wasn't like most men she knew—impatient and antsy. He was slow and sure, but the guy could move when he needed to. And the intelligence that he kept rigorously suppressed made her feel safer somehow. Here was a guy who looked before he leapt. She rarely did, but that didn't mean she didn't appreciate those who did.

"Great. I'll tell her." Brand tucked the phone against his neck. "Mike has found you a room in student quarters at Coatesville."

"What sort of student quarters?" Her mind bolted from The Student Prince to dorm parties and back again.

A grin spread over Brand's face. "Ah, it's a religious retreat," he said, laughing at her dubious expression.

"Coatesville," she murmured. "I don't have a choice, do I? I hope they have a piano there."

"Sure to." He smothered the receiver so Mike couldn't hear. "Coatesville is under North Shore jurisdiction."

"Oh."

They looked at each other. There was a minute's loaded silence.

She'd much prefer to be under the City cops' jurisdiction. All their problems sprang from the North Shore Unit. All things considered, she might be better off if she quietly disappeared. *Hold that thought for later.* At the moment she had no choice. At least she had Brand on her side. He'd keep her safe. And one good thing could come of this. At the retreat, she might be able to get her hands on a piano. Her fingers had been itching ever since she'd left home. Tara and the piano—her lifelines. And she'd lost them both, thanks to a vicious madman.

No lip-trembling, Célie, she admonished herself. She concentrated on Brand's phone conversation. It sounded as though she would be moving out of here tomorrow. She noticed that Brand never gave Mike the slightest clue about the locality of his house. He just said things like, "We'll meet you tomorrow," and "No. She's fine here pro tem." Then he clicked the off button and dropped the cell phone on the table. She couldn't interpret the faraway look on his face.

"Is there—are there any developments?" she asked.

"Some," he replied.

"What?" She knew she sounded impatient, but what the hell? This relocation bunch acted as if it was their God-given right to play around with her life—as if this whole thing were an intellectual game and she was one of the checkers they shifted around the board to suit themselves.

Brand opened his mouth to answer when, from the back of the house, there was a scratching sound like nails drawn over wood. They froze, heads turning towards the doorway. Then to Célie's amazement, Brand vaulted over the back of the sofa and pressed a button on the wall behind them.

Bells clanged, sirens wailed, and there was a roar like a jet engine passing low over the house. Célie pressed her fingers against her ears.

Brand waited a few seconds, then pushed the button again and the alarm wound down to an eerie stillness.

In the silence, there was the gentlest of whimpers.

"Peaches!" they said in unison, and raced to the laundry.

At the same time, a cell phone in Brand's pocket rang. He tugged it out. "It's okay, Sim. False alarm. Thanks." He clicked out.

So his alarm was connected to his brother's place in some way. Made sense. His brother was the one person he seemed to trust.

When Brand had activated the panic button, Peaches must have thought he'd died and gone to Hell. He lay prone on the floor, his paws over his ears.

"Oh, sweetheart!" Célie plumped down on her knees beside him and cuddled as much of him as she could. He was a big boy and she couldn't quite get her arms around him.

"Careful of his shoulder," Brand warned.

"Sorry, Peaches."

But Peaches seemed fine. He gave them to understand that now the noise had stopped and he'd found his Mom, he was a happy dog. He lumbered to his feet, wincing, and lovingly slobbered first on Célie, then on Brand.

"He's back to normal," Brand said.

Célie grinned. Brand was *so* not a dog person, but he was trying hard.

"Your alarm system is very impressive," she said.

Brand rolled his eyes. "I've never had to use it before. Only tested it once for a few seconds. I didn't realize how loud it is. Sim got a shock, too. Almost as bad at his end, I think."

But Célie was no longer listening to him. "Damn," she muttered to herself.

"What?"

"No dog food."

"He won't want much after the anesthetic, Mel."

She blinked, still trying to assimilate "Mel." For half an hour she'd forgotten she was supposed to think of herself as Mel.

"I guess not," she said, "but he's a big eater. I have to be careful with his food because mastiffs gain weight so easily. I keep him fit in case—well, you know why."

Brand stood over them as she and Peaches lounged on his bedroll on the floor. "A couple of shops in the valley might still be open, but I can't leave you here on your own. I'm sure we haven't been followed but we still have to be very careful."

She watched as he rolled his forefinger and thumb together while he deliberated. Her stomach clenched. It reminded her of something or someone bad. Something from that day when all this had started.

"I'll be okay, won't I?" she asked. Now he had her doubting. "You said that only a few trusted people know this place, and they're not connected with the case at all. I'm sure I'll be all right for a few minutes. I need to be here. Peaches can't stand up properly yet."

"Got your cell phone handy?" he asked at last.

"It's on charge."

He fetched her phone and swapped it with one of his. Then he set up speed dial. "Here. Just press the latest number, see?"

Yes, she saw. She saw he was nervous about leaving her here alone.

"What's the problem, Brand? This place is a fortress."

"I just...oh, I don't know," he said, shoving his hand through his hair. "I have a strange feeling that something's wrong. That I've missed something. But if someone *has* managed to trace either your cell phone or mine, this will confuse them."

"Do you often get these feelings?" she asked, trying to lighten the situation.

"Sometimes."

"And are they right? Does something happen?"

He stared at her, his face pensive. "Sometimes."

She pulled a face. "Cheer germ. You're enough to make anyone scared. How long will you be gone?"

"About half an hour, max."

"That long!" She had imagined it would be ten or fifteen minutes. She'd been so anxious on the drive here that she hadn't noticed how far from the shops the house was. "Peaches and I will stay in the laundry." Remembering that shadow moving among the trees, she wasn't going to wander around the house on her own.

Should she tell Brand about the shadow outside? Nah. Ridiculous. There'd been nothing out there. It was her imagination running riot because she was so strung out.

Anyway, she'd be safe in the laundry because it only had a tiny window with safety glass in it.

She smiled at Brand, trying to sound confident.. "Here's what I want you to buy." She scribbled out a list of instructions.

As she handed it to him, he said, "Keep safe." Casting her an anxious look, he grabbed his car keys and left, double locking the front door after himself.

As soon as she heard the 4x4 start up, she scooted into the kitchen and grabbed a knife from the knife block. Just in case. Then she locked herself inside the laundry and checked that the outside door from the laundry that led to the garden was also locked. Of course it was. It had a monstrous double safety fastening with a deadlock. It would take Attila the Hun to axe through all that from the outside.

Heart thumping overtime, she lay down on the floor next to Peaches who was thrilled with all the attention. "We just have to wait," she told him. "We just have to wait."

The thick safety glass in the laundry window made it difficult to see outside. After a few minutes, Célie got up and turned off the overhead light, leaving a small downlight glowing. Now she could see a couple of smudged stars through the wavy glass. That was better.

As soon as the deep thrum of the 4x4's engine had faded into the distance, she'd become filled with an anxious disquiet. Peaches was no better. He slept fitfully, raising his head now and again to listen. Stretched out beside him, she propped her head on his flank. Peaches sighed and she smiled and reached up to rub his chest.

What was that? Her arm stopped in midair. She could have sworn she'd seen something move outside the window. "Don't be such a Nervous Nellie, Célie," she muttered. She glanced at Peaches. He lay supine. If someone was outside, Peaches would hear, wouldn't he?

Or would he? He was sleeping again, zonked out on xylazine.

She could go over to the window and have a look. Just to make sure.

But her legs refused to work. "Gutless, Célie. You are gutless, girl. Get up! Turn off the downlight and look out the window. Now."

Then Peaches stirred and stared at the outside door.

Her heart stuck in her throat. What had he heard?

But after a few seconds he lowered his head again and began to snore.

She swallowed hard. "I'm a wimp," she whispered to the sleeping dog as she scrambled to her feet. She clicked off the downlight.

Inching along the wall, she reached the window. She held on to the door jamb, a little island of security in a sea of fear. Then she stretched across and peered out.

A featureless face stared back at her.

She screamed and jumped back, bashing her elbow on the laundry tub.

Peaches lumbered to his feet, shaky and

confused.

The face was still there.

No eyes. No mouth. No nose.

Peaches staggered over to the door and snuffled.

Mesmerised, Célie kept staring at that distorted face as she backed into a corner.

Then the face moved and a hand spread across the glass. The forefinger and thumb rubbed together.

Flashes of memory seared her mind.

She gasped, remembering that fearful morning when she'd discovered poor Occy's disemboweled body. Stunned, struggling not to vomit, she'd been hovering over what was left of Occy when she sensed she was being watched. For a few precious seconds she had stared back at the creepy figure silhouetted in the early morning gloom watching her—just watching her.

Then he'd rubbed his thumb and forefinger together covetously, as if he were contemplating the best way to eat her alive.

And she'd bolted.

And done her best to bury those memories.

Whoever that monster had been, he was outside the window right now.

The panic button. She could press the panic button. Sim would phone—no, he'd phone Brand. Brand... The thought hit her with the force of a blow from an axe. Oh, she was remembering now. Brand had that same habit. When he was thinking, he gazed off into the distance, his forefinger and thumb rubbing together and Sim—Sim did it too! Well, they were twins after all.

Betrayal bit deep, but fear bit deeper. "Oh, God, please *no*," she prayed under her breath as Peaches scrabbled at the laundry door, trying to get to whoever was outside.

Had Brand Turner doubled back on his tracks? What game was he playing? No, that didn't make sense. He had had plenty of time to harm her if that was his intent.

From the rear of the house she heard a chink, the same sound that Peaches' identity disc made as he moved. But Peaches was right here beside her, the hackles rising on the back of his neck. She'd run out of time to call for help. Anyway—who the hell could she call?

Peaches growled softly and wheeled around unsteadily, ready to do battle, but his legs trembled and threatened to give way.

"No!" Célie grabbed his collar. "You're sick. What if they're armed?"

Peaches looked pained. *Do you want me to be a guard dog or don't you?* his expression said. He was no longer interested in whoever had been outside the laundry door. Now he quivered and strained towards the interior door into the hallway. Célie's hand shook on his collar as the clinking sound was accompanied by a scraping noise. She was sure it was much nearer now.

Her stomach pitched as she crept across to the window to see if the face was still there. Was she caught between two assailants?

There was nobody at the window. She should have trusted Peaches' instincts. It couldn't be Brand, because Peaches knew him and trusted him. But whoever it was had somehow got into the house.

Peaches, thinking for both of them, nudged her. *Time to go*, he was telling her.

"Thanks, Peaches," she muttered. "Here goes nothing."

Praying as she'd never prayed before, she levered open the heavy exterior door and stood back. She peered into the Stygian darkness. Nothing. Most of the stars were covered with a cloud layer. Even an owl couldn't see a thing in that gloom.

Then realization struck.

To escape, they had to creep alongside the house and cross an exposed space of driveway to get to the shelter of the bushland. Stars or no stars, under the auto security lights they were sitting ducks.

That sound came again. Chink...brush.

Her heart thudding so hard it was painful, she knelt down beside Peaches and curled her arms around his neck. "I'm sorry, darling," she whispered, "I know you're not well, but we have to run like crazy to get away from here."

She rolled up the sleeping bag and shoved it under one arm. Then she grabbed her purse and the knife and shot out the door.

Chapter Six

"Bad idea," Brand muttered as he hustled Matilda up the incline. Despite the fact that he knew Célie was safe—hell, he'd never have left her if he didn't think so—he'd had an uneasy feeling since leaving the store. He'd now been away almost twenty-eight minutes. The road plateaued off and he floored the 4x4. One more minute and he'd be home.

He rounded the last curve and heard it. The panic button had been activated. The cacophony shrieked in the still night air.

"Sweet Jesus! I knew it!"

As he accelerated towards the house, he scanned the area. All he saw was an empty, floodlit yard. The front door of the house was shut.

As Matilda rocked to a halt, spraying gravel, his personal cell phone rang. "Hi Sim. Yeah, there's real trouble this time. I'll get back to you." He jumped out and loped around the side of the house. And stopped. The outside laundry door stood open. "No! Oh, shit!" His heart dropped to the soles of his trainers.

The whine and clang of the siren and bells beat at his head.

Racing through the laundry, he shot into the main room and thumped the panic button. The siren wound down with a wail like bagpipes deflating. And he was left with the silence.

From somewhere a voice called "Brand! Are you okay?"

He peered through the oriel window. Steve Macklin. His nearest neighbor. Relief swept through him.

"Brand? Shall I call the cops?"

Brand yelled back, "Just coming, Steve! Trying to unlock the damned door."

He dragged the heavy door open and found Steve Macklin standing on the front steps, his cell phone in one hand.

"Thanks for coming, Steve." Steve wasn't very quick on the uptake, but he was safe. Neither Steve nor his wife knew Brand well. They took him at face value and he took them at face value.

"I heard the alarm go off twice tonight," Steve puffed.

"Sorry about that. The first time was just a maintenance check. But the second time...well, I don't know what happened. I left someone here but she's gone."

Steve might not be very bright, but Brand didn't dare say too much because Steve's wife, whom he called "Doll-face" was definitely not slow. And Steve passed everything by his wife before even sneezing.

"It was a friend—a patient," Brand corrected himself. It was pointless using the term "client" around Steve. Political correctness and Steve were not on good terms. "Thanks for coming, Steve. It will take me a while to sort this out. Let me drive you home. You've had enough exercise already, racing over here, and it's pitch black out there." And on the way he might find a clue to help him discover where Célie was.

Frantic for Célie's safety, he drove to Steve's place as if Mephistopheles had unleashed the hounds of Hell behind them. He practically tipped Steve out of Matilda on to the Macklin's driveway while Steve was still burbling about people escaping from locked houses.

Brand presumed that Célie had either opened the laundry door to someone she knew, or she'd fled because she didn't trust him. But he couldn't explain that to Steve. For a second Brand wondered what Doll-face saw in Steve, then he caught a glimpse of the guy in his rear brake lights. Shoulders from here to eternity. Right.

At home he re-checked the laundry. Even Peaches' bedroll was gone. If Célie had been kidnapped, why had they bothered to take the bedroll? More to the point, where was Peaches?

Sim! He'd promised to phone Sim back.

Sim picked up on the first ring. "Are you okay?" His brother sounded as though his characteristic sang froid had received a pounding.

Brand explained what had happened.

"I'll come over there if you want," Sim offered.

Brand thought for a moment. Two heads were better than one. Especially when the second head belonged to one of the few people he could trust. But Sim had a business to run and this brouhaha was Brand's own little mess to pick over.

"Thanks for the offer, Sim. I'll see if I can sort things out on my own. I may call you later."

"You're nuts, but I understand. I'm here if you need me." If anyone understood independence, it was Sim.

Brand checked Célie's bedroom for clues.

Nothing stood out.

Plenty of questions. No Célie. Only one thing to do. He fished her cell phone out of his pocket and dialed his own number. He waited. And waited. Then a mature woman's voice that was nothing like Célie's said, "Yeah?"

He thought quickly. "Can I speak to Mel?"

"No. She can't trust you." And the phone went dead.

He stood there, stunned. "She can't trust me?

She can't trust me?" He knew he sounded like a demented parrot, but Célie probably had that effect on a lot of people. He ground his teeth. He was putting his professional life on the line—cancel that—he was putting his *whole* life on the line to protect her from a killer, and she'd told some woman that she didn't trust him? What more did she want from him?

He sat down on the bed. The Unit would not be impressed to learn that Melanie/Célie had given her contact details to an outsider. And she didn't trust many people, so who would she have called?

Brand tugged at his hair. The accomplice must have been close by. They'd had only minutes to escape before he returned.

He'd known right from the start that Melanie/Célie was hiding something, and he knew Parlane thought so too. But now that Brand had taken her under his wing, he was responsible for her until the leak was sealed. Even if she was a pain in the butt.

"So start looking for her, Turner," he told himself. His stomach roiled. What if she hadn't left of her own accord? What if the strange woman was the killer's accomplice? Worst of all, lingering at the back of his mind was the black question—had she been taken to lure him out of hiding? There was no way he wanted to be the reason she had been kidnapped. He shuddered as he recalled the words of an amoral youth named Brian who'd escaped from detention recently. *I'll catch up with you, Turner. And when I do, you'll wish you'd never been born. I won't rush it like I did with those women. No, I'll take my time and give filleting a whole new meaning.*

Please God, don't let it be Brian.

Whoever it was, they couldn't have got far yet. Light bulb! Check for tire tracks.

He flicked on the extra security lamps and

grabbed a flashlight. On the chipped stone drive, all he could see were his own tire tracks. The 4x4 made impressions like a Sherman tank so they were easy to pick up. The stones told him that no other vehicle had been up here. But at the perimeter of the parking pad there were scuff marks leading into the bushland.

So they'd gone on foot. Either someone had been watching the house and had forced Célie at gunpoint to leave with them—it would have to be gunpoint because he couldn't imagine her meekly agreeing to go with anyone who was unarmed—or else Célie had walked out for reasons known only to herself.

He rubbed his forehead, feeling helpless. Shit, he hated being answerable to people he neither knew well nor trusted. When Auckland Central had been split in two and he'd been seconded to the new Northern Unit, he had looked forward to becoming one of the team. But he wasn't a natural team player and Parlane's mistrust of anyone who wasn't a cop had left him doubtful he'd succeed in his new role.

And now this.

He didn't know Melanie/Célie very well. Scratch that. He didn't know her at all. But someone inside the Unit wanted her dead, had her on the run. Now some strange woman said that Célie didn't trust him. Christ, if there was anyone Célie *should* trust, it was him.

Well, he wouldn't get any answers hanging around here.

He stuffed himself into a warm jacket and hefted his flashlight to check the batteries. Could be a long night.

Leaving a couple of lights on, he crunched across the driveway into the bushland.

Chapter Seven

Deep in the native forest, worry dogging him, Brand slogged through the wiry undergrowth. Where the hell was she? Should he go back and wait at the house? The cops would go ballistic if he fouled up a potential crime scene. And even *thinking* in terms of a crime scene chilled him to the bone.

No, he couldn't go back yet. What if she needed him? What if she was lost? What if she was at the mercy of someone dangerous?

He paced carefully, shining the flashlight around him in a circle before taking the next step. He saw nothing unusual.

But he heard plenty. Possums ch-ch-chaarred up in the high trees, and on the earth, small mammals shuffled and snorted in the fallen leaves. There was nothing dangerous in the New Zealand bushland apart from wild pigs and the occasional stag during the roar. Here, just outside city limits, there was nothing more sinister than a ferret or a hedgehog.

So he kept telling himself. He knew damned well that the most dangerous predator in the New Zealand bush was Man and he didn't dare call out to Célie in case someone else was hunting her too.

Ah! At last! He knelt down, shielding the glow from the flashlight. The dank smell of crushed leaves wafted up. From the broken grass stalks and scrubby bushes trampled down, he could see where someone had headed downhill towards the main road, then veered in a semicircle back towards his property. Lost. It was easy to get lost in bushland this thick, especially on moonless nights. There were very few lighted houses around for anyone to use as a lodestar.

He looked up at the night sky. It was getting cold. How long did Célie and her captor plan to keep going?

Anxiety gnawed a hole in his gut.

Head bent as he peered at the telltale tracks, he stepped over a fallen branch.

Something slammed down on the back of his head. The force brought him to his knees. Pain exploded through his head and neck.

"No, no..." He struggled to hold on to consciousness, but it drifted away and he gave in and rolled over on to the leaves.

****

Why was his bed so uncomfortable? He struggled to sit up and someone clashed a pair of cymbals together in his brain. Flinching, he eased back onto his side. All he could hear was the crunch of the leaves he'd disturbed and his own breathing. There was very little wind in the trees tonight.

Trees? Leaves?

He tried to think, but his brain refused to cooperate. "Get a grip, Turner," he said aloud.

He was in the bush looking for Melanie/Célie and someone had hit him from behind. Right.

He stayed motionless for a few minutes to regroup, then v-e-r-y carefully raised a hand to the back of his head. Mother of God, it *hurt*. He could feel the stickiness of blood. No surprises there.

Warily he cocked an ear and peered into the darkness. Nothing. As stealthily as he could, he scrambled onto his knees. Inside his head an entire orchestra clashed a series of discords.

Clenching his teeth, he raised his head and

50

peered through the undergrowth.

Nothing. Nobody.

Why had whoever-it-was left him here, incapacitated rather than decapitated? It couldn't have been the serial killer or he wouldn't have woken up with nothing worse than a pounding head. He wouldn't have woken up, period.

Rogue cop playing a double game? But nobody had followed them from Sim's place, he was sure of it. Nobody had had time to triangulate his position from his mobiles because they were brand new. And Sim was the only person who knew the numbers anyway. He would trust Sim with his life.

Perhaps someone had known all along where he lived.

His head buzzed and throbbed as he dragged himself to his feet, using a tree trunk for a handhold. "Get out of here," he told himself.

His mind spun around in circles. Maybe the attack on him wasn't connected with the case at all. Maybe.

Holding his hands to his head, he turned to retrace his steps. He had the strangest impression that if he let go, his head would fly to pieces. He was going home. He couldn't do Célie any good in this state.

Where the hell was the flashlight?

He put a hand in his shirt pocket and felt the familiar contours of his own cell phone, safe and sound.

That cleared up one question. It was either Célie or her accomplice who had bashed him. Great. But why...?

Stuff it all. His brain was fried. He would start again as soon as it was daylight.

****

Squinting into the sunrise, Brian Robinson jogged along the dirt track at the foothills of the

Waitakeres. The message left on his little sister's cell phone had said that this was where Turner lived. The tip-off had been accurate. He'd spotted Turner last night driving up the hill that loomed up in front of him right now.

Brian shoved his hand up inside his heavy T-shirt to make sure that Friend, his special knife, was still lodged in its homemade scabbard. After his arrest, Little Sister Annie had kept Friend for him in a safe place, just like she'd promised. It was easy to make Little Sister do as he asked. Brian grinned. The cops had never found Friend.

It had taken him a while to fashion Friend's holster just right so he wouldn't hurt himself as he jogged. But it was the best disguise. Joggers were two a penny around here. The hills had been a testing run since Arthur Lydiard's day.

Glancing around him, Brian slowed to a walk. He was hot and tired. Jogging was strictly for fitness freaks. There were no cars allowed here, but a steady trickle of exercisers flowed around him and towards him.

As he walked in what he hoped was the earth-eating stride of a power walker, he kept himself cheerful with thoughts of how he'd deal with Turner. God, the pleasure it would give him after all this time. He'd waited for it, planned for it and dreamed about it. Now the time was almost here.

First, he'd change into the clothes he'd stowed last night. Then he'd head up the side road he'd seen Turner take. Turner must have a bolt hole up there somewhere. Brian would find it. And then he'd do what he should have done a year ago. Get rid of Turner. Slowly.

He'd had to put up with the psychobabble crap that Turner had dished out day after day. Now Turner would put up with a few hours of Brian Robinson. If it wasn't for Turner, Brian could have talked his way out of the charges against him—well, enough to have ensured a short custodial sentence anyway. Or he might have received some pathetic "counseling" for six months. He snorted to himself. *Counseling*. Hell, he could counsel the counselors. As if he hadn't learned every trick in the book from the day he'd been born. He'd managed to manipulate everyone he'd ever met. Until bloody Turner.

His tongue flicked over his bottom lip. He'd show Turner just what a well-honed fleshing knife could do.

And then he'd find the stranger who'd left the message on Annie's answerphone. Find them and eliminate them. No loose ends.

He'd played that message over and over and he still couldn't work out if the disguised voice was male or female. How had whoever-it-was known that Little Sister had fled when she'd heard Brian had escaped from detention, and that he was now holed up in the attic of her townhouse?

His hands clenched into fists. He hated that someone knew things about him. It was *his* specialty to know about other people.

Then his hands uncurled.

He'd find the mysterious caller. With his I.Q., it'd be a cinch. He always found people.

Friend was going to be very busy over the next few days.

Chapter Eight

As usual, Brand woke at sunrise. For most of the night his head and neck had throbbed with jabbing little shards of pain. It had been a long night.

He discovered there wasn't much he could do about the wound on the back of his head. He couldn't see it and he couldn't reach it.

"Blasted woman," he muttered as he tried to sponge off the dried blood. He'd thought she'd begun to trust him. But then, what did he know of women? Not much, according to Marina.

He had to find Célie. He'd given up trying to think of her as Mel. Anyone named Mel would be sweet and bright and give him no trouble at all. But a woman named Célie had possibilities.

She might have bashed him on the head, or perhaps her henchman had. But either way, Célie was a babe in the woods when it came to dealing with a serial killer.

And if she had left under duress, Brand would have to deal with her unwanted traveling companion.

But first he had to deal with Mike Ellery. He keyed in Mike's autodial.

"God Almighty!" Mike sputtered. Brand had never heard him sputter before. "Parlane will have our balls on a plate!" Then he lowered his voice. "How many people shall I send? How far could they have got?"

Brand thought quickly. "No point in your men tramping all over the terrain and getting lost." *And,* he added to himself, *wiping out all trace of Célie.* "I might not be a cop, but in daylight I know this countryside like the back of my hand. Give me a couple of hours to try and find them before you notify the troops."

If a bunch of eager cops anxious to earn overtime freaked out Célie's abductor... Brand stamped on the thought. He was a good tracker and Ellery and Parlane were aware of that. He'd been involved with Search & Rescue for years but he'd learned most of his tracking skills from his stepfather, an avid wildlife photographer. Most of all, Brand had learned to respect the bush and love it in all its seasons. Which was more than could be said for a bunch of city cops who often thought that tracking in New Zealand's dense bushland was like a stroll through the botanical gardens.

He tried to smooth Mike's feathers. "Mike, I'm not sure what's going on here. I don't know if she left voluntarily or if she—"

"You've got your couple of hours and that's it!" Mike snarled. "I can't hold off after that because Parlane checks in every few hours when he's off duty. Control freak," Mike added. "On top of that, I've got reporters hanging around outside." He muttered something unintelligible and clicked off his phone.

Brand grimaced. It must be the pits working for someone as demanding as Parlane. And Mike didn't deal well with stress. Having the press on his tail would send his blood pressure rocketing.

Brand grabbed an apple, crunching it as he wrapped a piece of bologna sausage in plastic wrap. Peaches would be ravenous by now.

He poked the old Colt automatic his grandfather

had brought back from the Pacific in '45 into the back of his jeans. He had plenty of ammo and always kept the auto cleaned. He ripped open a packet of bullets and tucked a handful into his shirt pocket, then scanned the exposed front yard. Nothing moved. Birds sang undisturbed. Grabbing his binoculars, he checked the thick bushland on both sides of the house, but all he could see were fantails chasing insects.

Through his bedroom window at the rear, however, he was startled to glimpse a red knitted cap bobbing about amongst the tea-tree bushes. What the...? Oh, it was Doll-face.

Brand knew he was a fool to have mentioned Célie to Steve last night. Now he'd done something he had always managed to avoid—made Steve and Doll-face aware of him as a person. Hitherto they'd probably just thought he was an odd, reclusive neighbor. Now Doll-face had him pegged as a mysterious nutcase who dragged women to his lair. Damn.

He made a cup of coffee and as he gulped it down, decided to retrace last night's movements first. Then he would play it by ear.

As he crossed the driveway, every nerve end jangled a warning till he reached the cover of the trees. Then he settled down to follow yesterday's trail.

Scanning the track, he raised his eyebrows. Holy Hell! He'd staggered around like a drunk last night. He must have been hurt worse than he thought. He could see where he'd broken down several young seedlings when he veered away from the path that Célie and the dog had taken. But that was all to the good because he could clearly see their separate tracks.

And one other set of tracks. There had been somebody with them.

Or—no. He hunkered down. It looked as if the person was not *with* them, but was following a short distance behind them. The indentations in the soil were much heavier than Célie's and had almost obliterated hers in several places. There were scuff marks where it looked as though Célie had stopped abruptly and swiveled around. Had she heard her pursuer? In a couple of places the second set of prints veered off into the long grass and made deep indentations. Perhaps the follower had hidden when Célie halted.

Was it the woman who'd answered the phone call? He examined the cluster of prints again. The pursuer had been following carefully, placing his weight on the balls of his feet. Not a woman, or at least, not a small woman. Those tracks looked like a heavy-footed male placing his feet down very precisely, as if their owner was intent on making as little noise as possible.

Oh, Jesus. His stomach plummeted.

No one else had walked this way for many weeks. It was isolated; not a regular track, and it looked as though Célie had just slogged through grass and bushes alike in her determination to escape. It had rained a little yesterday and the likelihood of anyone else except Célie and her pursuer making those tracks was remote.

He set off at a jog, cursing himself for not continuing the search last night. He strained to hear any noises above the zing of cicadas. Then he came to a spot where Peaches must have decided to take a rest. The dog had spread out his front legs ready to hunker down. It appeared the person following them had stopped suddenly, taken unawares. The toes of their shoes had dug grooves in the leaf mold. Had Peaches tried to tell Célie they were being followed? Had he barked?

Brand pressed on, walking parallel to the track,

pushing through a mass of tea-tree bushes.

He nearly missed it. A few splodges of something rust-colored had seeped into the dirt several paces away from the track. His heart convulsed in his chest and missed a beat. He dropped to a crouch and examined the earth and foliage, then exhaled with relief. This was *his* blood. It was where he'd been attacked. Because of last night's disorientation, he hadn't recognized the place.

He pushed on, keeping to one side of the established track. He could tell by the scrape marks that Célie and Peaches were tiring. Peaches was dragging behind more and more. Poor Peaches. He'd had a helluva day and then he'd had a helluva night.

The most puzzling thing about all this was that the dog didn't seem to be fazed about their follower. Brand would have expected scuff marks and a beaten down patch of grass where Peaches had wheeled around, snarling, trying to attack the follower. Why hadn't Peaches reacted? Shades of Sherlock Holmes, Brand thought. The curious incident of the dog in the night-time.

Topping a rise, he stopped. It looked as though Peaches and Célie had spent the night here. Brand retraced his steps. Their follower had also spent the night here, a mere ten yards to one side of them. Why hadn't he attacked them while he had the chance? Had it been too dark to disable both the dog and the woman without alerting them?

Hurrying now, he saw where Peaches had wandered off on his own, taking an alternate path back towards the pursuer.

Brand's mind clicked over. Who had Célie bought Peaches from? He was an adult, fully trained guard dog. According to police records, five weeks ago Célie Francis hadn't owned a dog. Someone must have recommended a source. Or had Célie, being her usual self, struck out on her own to purchase protection without going through the approved channels? Damn the woman. It was an uphill struggle trying to save her from herself.

Then above the birdcalls, Brand heard the jaunty jangle of a cell phone.

He bolted towards the sound. Ahead of him, the Colonel Bogey ring tone choked off and was replaced with an almighty crashing as the cell's owner thudded downhill towards the scenic highway. His head pounding, Brand careened after him. Whoever it was knew where they were going.

Ratcheting up the pace, Brand plowed through and over vegetation like a steam engine on speed. Ahead of him he caught flashing glimpses of a hooded figure bent forward like a commando, clearing the scrubland in great, gulping leaps. He made even more noise than Brand and didn't hear Brand approaching until he swerved to avoid a puriri tree and caught a glimpse of Brand gaining on him.

The quarry hesitated, then ground to a halt. The instant Brand was in range, commando-guy crouched down and lashed out with his foot.

Seen that one before. Jumping back out of range, Brand grabbed C-G's ankle while he was off balance. Definitely a guy, but the face was covered with a dark stocking and the features were squeezed out of shape. Brand yanked the leg as hard as he could. C-G crashed flat on his back, whooping like a crane.

"Gotcha," Brand wheezed. But as he launched himself on top of C-G and pulled back his arm to swing a punch, sunlight flashed off the knife clenched in C-G's fist. Shit. Too late to draw back, Brand's fist connected with a satisfying crunch on C-G's jaw at the same time as the vicious bite of a blade sliced along his forearm. He rolled away, clutching his arm. C-G staggered to his feet and shook his head a couple of times, then rocketed off downhill.

Brand glanced at the long, shallow knife wound. It bled sluggishly but not enough to slow him down. He'd live. He took off after Commando Guy.

Way in the distance he heard something—a soft cry of distress, quickly muffled. Célie?

Without a qualm he abandoned the pursuit and hurtled towards the sound. As he threshed back uphill through the bracken, he hoped Célie would understand he was the cavalry. She was likely to string something across the track to bring him down, and then put the boot in.

He burst through the undergrowth into a clearing and there she was, leaning over Peaches. In her hand was a kitchen knife—*his* kitchen knife.

She stared at him, eyes drenched but ready to do battle. Then she lowered her hand.

"You!" But her tone lacked accusation or force. She looked gutted, full of despair.

He stopped short, his chest heaving. "What is it?"

Peaches never stirred, and Brand's stomach lurched. He took a deep breath and nodded towards Peaches. "Is he all right?"

"He's dead," she said dully. "See for yourself."

He stepped closer. And saw. Peaches' throat had been slit in the way of the human victims of the Cliff Road serial killer. Brand cursed himself for wasting time.

"Did he wander off while you were asleep?" he asked, already knowing the answer.

She nodded, tight-lipped. "I just found him. How could I sleep while Peaches was being k-killed? And why didn't they—why didn't they..?"

Because "they" were busy chasing him, Brand thought.

Célie's head bowed, and the knife slid out of her

hand on to the grass. He stepped cautiously towards her. "You were exhausted; that's why you didn't hear anything. You and Peaches had a huge day yesterday. And Peaches was still woozy from the anesthetic."

Relieved beyond belief that she was all right, he hunkered down beside her. "Have you got something we can cover him with?"

She sniffed. "Your bed-roll."

Okay. Anything in the name of kindness. He spread the thick blanket over Peaches, tucking the edges under the limp body.

"Thank you," she whispered, her voice as dry as kindling wood.

"I'll come back for him later. We'll give him a decent burial. Come on home now. I'm not sure what happened at the house last night, but I'm still your safest option."

"I-I went a little mad, I guess," she said, looking confused and doubtful.

He'd never heard Célie doubtful before. She was the most decisive woman he'd ever met.

In the distance a car engine started up. Six cylinders. There went his chance of catching her pursuer. He buried the thought. Célie needed help.

"What happened?" he persisted.

"I saw you at the window," she said. "You know—your silhouette through the safety glass."

He blinked. Huh?

"But your car hadn't come back." She turned on him. "I thought you'd left your car somewhere and walked back. After seeing the finger habit I knew it was you. *You!*" she spat. "And when I ran away, you activated the panic button as if it was a game..." She simmered, but her heart wasn't in it. She looked tired to the bone. He was glad it was he and not Commando Guy who had come across her first. In her present state she wouldn't have stood a chance.

But Brand was all at sea. She thought she'd seen him through the window before he actually arrived home? And she'd said something weird about a finger habit. "Célie—what finger thing are you talking about? I don't understand."

"What happened to 'Mel'?" she asked vaguely, pushing back her hair with a shaking hand. "Never mind. It wasn't you at the window last night, was it? I got it wrong. It felt wrong, but I was so scared I couldn't think straight."

Her face was as white as milk and she must have reached the end of her tether, otherwise she'd never admit to being frightened.

"Most people can't think logically when they've been scared out of their wits, Célie," he said. "And that came on top of the worst month of your life."

"More or less."

What the hell did that mean? That she'd had worse times in her life? Getting into Célie's mind was going to be a difficult journey. "Tell me about this habit you mentioned."

She tossed her head impatiently. "You know—it's that thing you do with your thumb and forefinger when you're thinking. You rub them together."

"Do I? Yes, I suppose I do. It's so ingrained I don't think about it. Sim does it too. And I've seen it somewhere else recently. A common habit, I guess."

"I saw it recently too," Célie said, sotto voce. "On the day I found Occy. All I could see was the outline of someone wearing a dark cloak. Then he raised his hand near his chin and rubbed his finger and thumb together. I ran."

"You didn't think it was a neighbor, come to see how Occy was getting along?"

"At five o'clock in the morning?" she asked scornfully.

"I guess not."

There was a short silence. "You sure laid me out

last night," he said, not yet ready to let her off the hook.

She blushed, the color looking clown-like on her pale face. "Sorry. I didn't know what else to do. Oh, I've got your torch, too," she added airily, as if that were of more consequence than bashing him on the head. Then she noticed his arm, and the expanding puddle of blood on the grass. "You're bleeding! What happened?"

"I think I met Peaches' murderer a few minutes ago."

"A few minutes! What...where...?" She glanced wildly around with unfocused eyes and tried to stuff her shaking hands into her jeans pockets. But her hands kept sliding out again and hung loose like wet washing at the ends of her arms.

Shock. Better get her back to the house. Better get himself back so he could swallow a pain-killer or three. He beat back a wash of nausea.

"Was that your voice on the phone?" he asked. If he concentrated on Célie, he could block out the pain.

She nodded. "It's one of the things I do—disguise my voice." She pulled a face. "In my real life I was a mimic as well as a singer." She shrugged. "Just part of the patter."

How could he have forgotten? During the house-to-house stage of the investigation, Mike Ellery had waxed enthusiastic about how Célie and Tara were "really talented birds." Mike had been especially taken with Tara. He had bored on about how she designed clothes for stage plays and TV shows, until Brand had said her name meant nothing to him but he thought Célie's name and face were familiar.

"Familiar? Of course she's familiar! She's on that Talking Heads program on TV—very witty. And she had a one-woman show at the Playhouse last month."

No wonder Parlane was stewing about the difficulty of keeping Célie safe, Brand had thought. "Did you go?" he'd asked Ellery.

"Yeah. Great stuff. Sings like a sexy angel. Versatile too. Did a vocal rendering of a Bach cantata and followed it up with an Edith Piaf song."

Brand looked at Célie. She didn't look much like a sexy angel this morning. She had fingered her hair into mismatched tufts all over her head. She looked as if she would burst into tears at any minute and her clothes were streaked with dirt and grass stains. He had to get her home. Now wasn't the time to hang around worrying about how Célie had fooled him.

"In future," he said, "when I get phone calls from strange women, I'll assume it's you. And for what it's worth, I didn't activate the panic button."

She stared at him in dismay. "Then who—?"

"Don't know. We'll worry about it later. Let's go home and have a shower and some breakfast. Here. Take this." With his left hand he tugged the .45 out of the back of his jeans where the sights had been biting through his T-shirt and rubbing his skin raw. "If I make a move towards you, shoot me with that."

She looked at him uncertainly, then, to his amusement, checked it over.

"Remember to release the safety catch."

She attempted a weak grin, then handed it back to him. "You're either very clever or very stupid," she said. She shuffled up to Peaches' body, pulled back the bedroll and stroked the brown fur. "Goodbye, Peaches," she whispered. She replaced the bedroll and clambered to her feet.

Scrabbling in her bag, she brought out a square of fabric and held it out to him. "Use this to bind up that cut."

"Thank you." He struggled to wrap the homemade bandage around his forearm with his left hand.

She clicked her tongue against her teeth. "I'll do it." Dropping her bag on the grass, she ripped the ends of the fabric square so she could tie off the bandage.

He wondered where she'd learned that trick. She was full of little surprises. As she bent down to reclaim her bag she muttered, "I'm starving," looking shamefaced that she could be hungry at a time like this.

Brand groped in his shirt pocket and handed her Peaches' bologna slice. "Here."

There was a short silence. "You brought this for Peaches, didn't you?" she asked.

He nodded.

"You're a very nice man," she said, a tear sliding down her cheek. "I'm sorry I thought you were a murderer."

He tried to grin and found the grin couldn't quite make it onto his face. "Now I know you're *really* upset when you call me a nice man. But I'm not worried. I know it won't last." In a more sympathetic tone he said, "I'm truly sorry about Peaches. Come on home now and tell me everything."

Chapter Nine

Célie watched as Brand checked the back of the house to find out where the intruder had got in.

He frowned. "Whoever he was must have access to the most sophisticated lock-picks imaginable to get through that lock. He'd have had to use a tension wrench for a start." Mumbling under his breath, he called his friend Sparks who promised to come out and fix it straight away.

After they'd showered then made a mountain of toast, they settled into the cracked leather sofa in front of the fireplace.

Célie knew that Brand was going to give her the third degree

He sipped his coffee. "How are you feeling now?"

"Fine." Everyone's stock answer.

They were curled up, bookends on the sofa. He had an Ella Fitzgerald cd running in the background and she relaxed a little. Just a little. She warned herself: *Be very careful, Célie. If he finds out you not only suspected him but also his brother, he won't be quite so chummy. This digging around in people's minds is what he does for a living.* She would fight to the last to stop him from dissecting her; clamp down so he couldn't disinter all the old emotions she'd worked so hard to bury and turn her over like a spade turned earth over in the garden.

Then she thought of Peaches. Brand had fetched his body and now he was buried in Brand's garden, where he would look out over the blue-green hills for eternity.

"Célie? Mel?" Brand asked, bringing her back.

She looked at him. "Make up your mind. What's it to be? I'm sick of this half-life." Leaning forward, she jabbed a finger at his chest and tore into him. "Do you guys understand what you're doing when you take people like me and turn our heads around?"

"Yes," he answered quietly. "*I* do. I can't answer for the whole team, however."

Her anger dropped a notch. She nodded. "Well, maybe you do, but Parlane and Ellery—they're different. They think from a cop's point of view. For them, the end justifies the means."

For the first time she saw uncertainty on Brand's face. She must have hit a nerve.

"I think you may be right. But Foster—"

"Foster! He's supposed to be the Unit leader, isn't he? I only met him once and I can tell you he doesn't see any of us as people. We're problems to be solved."

"Umm, I've always thought he was scrupulously impartial."

"Impartial!" she exploded. "We're talking about *people* here. People in trouble, damn it! How the hell can he be 'impartial'?" She mimicked Brand's voice perfectly and his lips twitched.

"Célie, the Unit needs someone like Foster. He's a cool customer, I'll grant you, but I bet he's working like a beaver for you right now."

"Cool? More like ice-cold. And anyway, I want a say in the decision-making," Célie muttered. "I'm used to looking after myself."

"Why?"

"Whaddya mean—why?"

"Why do you have to control everything? Let go. Let us do the jobs we're paid to do."

"Let go? Let go? Last time I let go I got saddled

with a pseudo-Italian boyfriend who wouldn't butt out, and before that I got dumped by the mother I trusted. Yep. I trusted her to handle everything and she did. She dumped me and ran." She sat back, refusing to meet his eyes. Bloody hell. She hadn't intended to say any of that. What would he make of her sorry little story? She cast him a furtive glance.

He wasn't looking at her. He was examining his hands as if he'd never seen them before. He looked up and she saw an emotion she couldn't define shimmer behind the hazel eyes before he said, "I know it takes a massive leap of faith to hand yourself over to others. But I want you to try. If you fight us every step of the way, you'll put yourself in more danger."

She opened her mouth and shut it again.

He switched gears. "Tell me, where did you get Peaches from?"

Lord, this man's mind jumped from place to place like corn on a hot griddle.

"I don't know. Truly, I don't!" she reiterated when she saw his look of incredulity. "On the first morning at my safe house, there he was, tied to the handrail of the back porch. There was a note taped to his collar that said 'He is trained for your personal security.' I presumed someone from the Unit sent him. Nobody else knew where I was."

He was shaking his head as her words died away. "They would have made themselves known to you. Professionals would never hand over a trained dog like a parcel without giving you instructions about its upkeep and training."

"Ah..." Célie felt hot color scald her cheeks.

"What?"

"Umm—it might be because I refused to answer the door. I'd only just moved in, and already someone was knocking on the door. I was crazy scared and uh..."

"I see."

Did he? He would naturally assume she'd been terrified, but what would he think if he knew she'd been so petrified that she'd locked herself in the bedroom and barricaded the door with the dressing table and bedside cabinet? Pathetic.

"Did you keep the note?" he asked.

She shook her head.

"Does the music bother you?"

She looked into the cool hazel eyes and smiled. "I'm sure you know how much I appreciate it. I had expected—"

"Alternative music, eternally rising to anti-climaxes but never quite resolving into real cadences? Mood sounds of birds in the forest? Whale calls?"

She exploded into laughter. "That's exactly what I envisioned."

He shuddered. "I get that when I get a sports massage. My masseur thinks it relaxes me. Actually it frustrates me and I can't wait to get out of his studio."

"Why do you need sports massages?" She grabbed at the chance to shift the conversation away from herself and on to him.

"I'm asking the questions, remember?" He smiled at her. "Try your avoidance games on someone else, Célie."

"So I'm to be Célie, am I?" A shame she hadn't been able to glean more information. She'd like to know what made him tick. Reading Brand Turner was not easy.

"There you go again."

She shook her head. "It's not avoidance. It's a question of lost identity."

Instantly he sobered. "I know. And I like your name. But the team insists on relocatees thinking of themselves as having been born again with their new identities."

"I think they've got that wrong," she said. "I have no identity." She felt her bottom lip tremble and stuck out her chin to fight the weakness. "I'm not Célie anymore and I'm not Melanie. I really, really need a piano."

He surveyed her with clinical detachment, and she castigated herself for thinking of him as anything other than a psychologist. He probably interviewed all his patients with the same cool politeness. "Célie, your identity is not tied to a piano. It's not what you *do*. Your identity is who you *are*."

"Yeah, yeah, yadda, yadda. I knew you'd say that."

There was an uncomfortable silence.

"Let's wait and see what Mike Ellery comes up with this afternoon," he said at last, his voice soft. "Now, I want to go over last night again. Tell me everything, no matter how small. What made you run?"

"Mainly it was the finger-rubbing thing. But also, through that reinforced glass in the laundry window, I could have sworn it was you."

"But you hadn't heard my car?"

"No. And then you said—*he* said—'Célie?' And he pronounced it the way you do."

Brand's brow wrinkled. "There's not many ways to pronounce it, honey."

She snorted with amusement. "You'd be surprised."

He shifted and stretched out his legs, surveying them thoughtfully. "You know, I'm beginning to think you were right when you said yesterday that this might be about me, not you." His voice sounded intrigued rather than concerned, as if it were an academic puzzle to be solved. "But why, I have no idea..." He trailed off, shaking his head.

"Someone is trying to look and sound like you,"

she agreed. "And they're using me. Two birds, one stone."

"The bloody leak in the Unit is more like a yawning pit. I refuse to hand you over to Ellery with no guarantees, because if the leak comes from within the police team itself, well..."

Célie shivered.

"And someone has gone to great lengths to find out where I live. Of course, I knew that one day I'd be tracked down. Not all that hard. One or two criminals I've interviewed have threatened me." He hunched a shoulder. "And one teenage boy I counseled told me he'd 'be coming for me,' but I took it with a pinch of salt. He told everyone involved with his case the same thing, even his lawyer. But I never expected that someone connected to a serial killer would come looking for me. I wonder what took him so long to find me."

"Maybe he's technologically challenged," she said, grinning, "and it took a while to suss out your details. But don't you think it's simpler than that? He followed us."

"That's the obvious answer, but we couldn't have been followed to Sim's. I made sure it didn't happen."

"I noticed. You took so many twists and turns I got confused."

He smiled faintly, and she watched him as he sat, staring into space. She could see the cogs and wheels in the sharp mind turning over. His private little eyrie high up in the hills had been violated and he was rattled, although he was good at hiding it. She understood his concern. How many other people would find out about it now? *Well, buster, now you know how it feels to have your whole way of life threatened.*

He stood up. "The point is, however it was done, someone knows you're here. Time to pack our bags."

Surprised, she stuttered, "What about Mike Ellery?" She had assumed his concern was for his own safety. Obviously she was wrong. The thought that his concern was for her, rather than himself, touched her deep down where nothing much had touched her for a very long time. It had been half a lifetime since anyone had cared enough to go out on a limb for her.

"I think it would be better if the Unit and the cops don't know where you are for the time being." He blew out a breath. "I'm worried about the other relocatees."

Yes. That was Brand Turner all over. Worried about others. She raised an eyebrow. "By the way, it's just a thought...why aren't there any women in that Unit?"

He stared at her. "You're worried about feminism at a time like this?"

She shrugged. "No. Just thinking they must relocate lots of women—maybe as many women as men. So why don't they get counseled by women?"

"Would you rather have a woman to talk to?"

"No." She grinned. Now she'd confused him.

But he just looked steadily at her and she knew her sidetracking hadn't fooled him one bit. He prowled over to her, his expression serious. "First, we'll go to Sim's place. Do you trust Sim?"

For a moment she hesitated. He stared at her—hard. "I think so," she answered quickly.

"Do you trust me?"

"I don't know. I guess so."

He pulled a face. "Damned with faint praise."

"Well, you're one of 'them,'" she excused herself.

He held out his hand to pull her to her feet. "Do you trust Ellery?"

"Maybe."

"Do you trust Parlane?"

She didn't answer, just looked at him.

"Me neither. Strange character. He'll do what looks best on police records, and that's all."

Well, that was interesting. She had been going to say maybe, but he had second-guessed her, and for once, guessed wrong. She felt a certain loyalty towards Parlane. He was the first person she had spoken to after fleeing from the murderer through the fog. Rattled and terrified, she had found his astringent calmness soothing. He had believed her improbable story even though he'd shown his impatience with young women who fouled up his crime scenes.

"Who do *you* trust, Brand?" she asked, wondering if he'd answer her. She'd told him her most private secrets, but she knew very little about him.

"My brother. My stepfather and my mother. My friend Sparks Mullaney. In that order."

"That's all?"

"Since I began this job, it is. None of my other friends know what I do for a living. I've let them presume I'm still in private practice. Once or twice someone has asked me where I live now, but I just say it's so far out of town that I only get home on weekends. They're intelligent enough to know a roadblock when they meet it." He paused and looked thoughtful. "One of my friends is a reporter."

"Good heavens! I bet he's persistent."

"He is. He's a good reporter." Brand laughed.

"What?" she demanded.

Brand was still grinning. "He was becoming a pest so I more or less told him the truth."

"What does 'more or less' mean?"

"Told him I was working on this hush-hush project and daren't give him any details. Of course he laughed his head off."

"Clever. You know him well. Now if I told Tara—" She broke off. She would never tell Tara anything again. Tara was on a cold slab in the mortuary and she'd never again hear Tara's crazy, infectious giggle, or hear her airy voice saying, "Oh—Celly? Just borrowed a pair of your jeans." Célie's chest tightened as she fought to keep back the hot tears boiling inside her.

Brand took her hand. "Célie."

That was all he said, but it resonated deep within her. Surely she could trust this guy? He comforted her. He put up with her snarking. He had followed her into the bushland to rescue her and been injured in the process. He'd been as upset over Peaches' death as she was, although he'd tried not to show it. And he'd even buried Peaches in his garden. Okay, taking chances with trust was not her style. She'd found out the hard way that the few times she'd trusted people without her usual caution, she had been pulverized by some cretin who liked playing games. But this man was...different.

Then she pulled herself up short. Whoa! Brakes on. She'd thought she could trust Giorgio and what an idiotic idea that had been. Only *she* could be stupid enough to trust an Italian gigolo named for a perfume. First he'd hit on Tara, and then when Célie had given him the heave-ho, he'd disappeared with their rent money. They thought they'd hidden it where no one would find it. But of course Tara's panties drawer was right up his alley.

Yup, Célie Francis. You're a great judge of people. Look at all those years you wasted trusting that your mother would come back for you.

"You have to trust somebody one day, Célie," Brand said softly.

She gaped at him. "What are you? A mind reader or something?"

"No." He touched her cheek with one finger. "But your face is very expressive."

"Oh, Lord! I hope not!"

He laughed.

She looked down at her feet. "I was having an argument with myself about trusting you."

"Argue with yourself a lot, do you?"

She shrugged. "Sometimes."

"Who won this time?" His tone sounded light but his eyes were serious, as though her answer mattered.

She smiled. "You know me. Argumentative to the last. It was a draw."

Unexpectedly he leaned forward and dropped a quick kiss on her forehead before changing the subject. "Okay. Moving on. Let's get out of here. The watcher is gone for the time being but he'll be back. First, can you fix last night's handiwork? I can't make the bandage stick."

"Oh." He constantly left her with nothing to say. He was good at dropping subjects just when she'd settled in for a good argument. She didn't enjoy feeling the ground being cut from under her. Best to say nothing. Hey, she must be growing up! She knew she often mouthed off without thinking, but for some reason she didn't want to hurt Brand's feelings. He might seem inviolable, but she guessed that underneath that easy-going exterior, lub-dupped a fragile heart. He hadn't achieved all his insight on human nature from textbooks.

"Let me see that arm, too," she said. Crumbs, she sounded like Florence Nightingale. What the heck did she know about fixing bashed heads and knifed arms? *Oh, get on with it,* her conscience nagged. *You owe him.*

She knelt on the sofa and angled his head so she could see the back of it. And drew in her breath. She'd made an excellent job of mashing his scalp. Five star. Her stomach heaved. Settling her shoulders, she screwed her fingers up then stretched them out like a piano player about to attack a difficult concerto. "Got a first aid box here?" Her voice came out brisk and calm. Just as well he couldn't see her face.

"It's in the main bathroom." He went to stand up.

"I'll get it," she said. "You stay here." How on earth had he survived the night and morning in this state? He'd been racketing around with his head split open since late last night. Not to mention the run-in he'd had this morning with Peaches' killer. *Goddamit, Célie. You went too far this time.*

In the bathroom she took a couple of deep breaths before opening the first aid box. She refused to let him see how squeamish she felt. He'd done a helluva lot for her, and all she'd done so far was take, take, take. *Time to pay your dues, girl.*

She patched him up as best she could. He didn't say anything when she swabbed both wounds with an antiseptic rinse but she felt him tense up. Not surprising. The head wound—the one she'd caused— was much worse than the shallow knife wound. His head must be throbbing like crazy. She pressed a padded gauze square into place and strapped it down with hospital tape. She remembered that tape very well. She'd spent a couple of weeks covered in it a long time ago.

"There," she said at last. She wadded up the dirty cotton balls and clicked the first-aid kit back together as if she did this sort of thing every day.

"Thank you," was all he said, but she knew he was damned glad she'd finished her ham-fisted ministrations.

"I think I'll take a couple of ibuprofen," he added, struggling to his feet.

Apologizing wasn't her strong suit, and she swallowed the words a couple of times before she bit them out. "Sorry. I'm really sorry." She didn't get any further because the antiseptic was making her eyes sting. Even her throat was clogged. That stuff was strong. Brand was paler than his shirt and her hands were still trembling, so after handing him a couple of ibuprofen, she took one herself.

"Time to leave," Brand said, obviously making an effort to pull himself together.

They stuffed the bare necessities into several shopping bags and Brand phoned Sim on their way out the door. Célie tossed their bags into the back of the Ford while Brand wrote a note for Sparks Mullaney.

As he eased the 4x4 into first gear, Brand asked her, "Who gave you your mobile? Did the team give it to you, or did you buy one yourself?"

"Mike Ellery gave it to me."

"Oh? Usually Foster does that. But you were moved in a hurry. Doesn't matter anyway. We'll buy new ones on the way to Sim's place."

When they stopped to buy a couple of Cokes at a corner store in the suburbs, he purchased new mobiles and SIM cards and before taking the Peninsula road to Sim's, he dropped the old SIM cards into a roadside dumpster.

"Later we'll purchase another couple of phones and cards," Brand said. "It never hurts to have more than one cell phone. Confuses the issue for anyone making inquiries. Doesn't hold 'em off forever, but it delays things."

Startled, Célie wondered how often he'd done this sort of thing.

"Of course if the Unit thinks we're still together, they'll approach Sim anyway," Brand said. "But I think they'll leave it awhile to see what we're up to."

"When they asked for my next-of-kin details, I said I had no one," Célie said. "It's the truth," she added virtuously.

Brand grinned. "That's a first."

Célie stuck out her tongue.

"I feel sorry for Ellery," Brand said. "Parlane will crucify him. Since the attack on Friday, the police have become accountable for your safety once more."

Célie was surprised. "I thought that once we'd become buried in the witness protection program, we're on our own. That's what Mr. Foster intimated. All he gave me was a phone number for emergencies. He sounded as if he didn't give a damn."

"That's just Foster's way. But now your cover's blown, and with the attacker still at large, you're back under police jurisdiction."

She began to understand how many people were involved in keeping her safe. She hadn't thought about it before. Fear tended to make one selfish.

"The die is cast now and we can't phone Mike. He'll be sitting in a booth at Starbuck's cracking his knuckles and gulping short blacks," Brand said.

"When will you contact him?" Célie asked.

"I don't know." Brand concentrated on edging the 4x4 past a lumbering truck. "I need to find out whether this is about you, or if it's about me as well. Best to wait and see if the cops come looking for me. Prior to this my background hasn't mattered. In a few hours Ellery will be scratching around, trying to see what he can dig up about me. I'll be interested to see what happens."

He made it sound like a chess game.

"What about this?" She gestured towards the 4x4. "Is it registered in your name?"

"No."

Oh, well. That was that. She hadn't expected him to tell her his whole life story, but this guy had more corners than a politician's closet.

Chapter Ten

Make yourself at home," Brand said as he dumped Célie's belongings on a freshly made up bed in one of Sim's spare bedrooms. "Sim?" he yelled.

Sim wandered in with two huge German Shepherds at his heels.

"Found places to sleep?" he inquired. Then he indicated the two Shepherds who smiled, long tongues flapping. "This is why we won't have any intruders, Mel."

She hadn't met them on her first visit and she was charmed.

"Don't be deceived by their smiles," Brand said. "I've seen them in action."

Célie crouched down to make friends with them. Much better to have them on her side, than against her. God, how she missed darling Peaches. When all this was over she was going to buy herself the biggest, sloppiest dog she could find. She'd go to the pound. She didn't want some snooty pedigree dog, just a mutt of her own. But perhaps it never would be over, she reminded herself. Maybe this transient lifestyle would be hers forever. She couldn't hold the tears back any longer. Scrubbing at her cheeks, she tried to choke down the rock in her throat.

Three minutes later she wiped her eyes and looked up. The men were gone. Nothing like tears to clear the men out of a room. She'd heard them leave but hadn't been able to stem the tide. One of the dogs had stayed behind. She was sprawled across its tail, and it lay quiescent, panting.

"Oh, sorry." She scrambled to her feet. But it didn't seem to hold a grudge. It lumbered to its feet, made a vague swish with its tongue in her direction and trotted off.

She began to unpack her possessions—somehow every time she shifted she had less—and looked around the room that was to be hers for the time being. Which could mean anything. It might be two days or a week. God, she craved stability—always had, and hadn't got it until she and Tara found the house on the North Shore where the sea met the pale cliffs. On a still night they could hear the wash, wash of the waves against the sand. They'd signed a one-year lease as soon as they'd seen it. Stability. They'd both needed it.

Somebody else would have moved in by now. The real estate agents called it "a desirable property." Her sun lounger would be stuffed into the garden shed. The Welsh dresser that Tara had adored would be full of someone else's china, and the sun would no longer slant in through the windows on their hard-to-come-by squishy footstools.

More hot tears gathered but she beat them back and stoically began placing her things wherever she could find a space. There was no going back.

****

"I don't know where we go from here, Sim," Brand said as he sipped yet another mug of Sim's appalling coffee. If he and Célie stayed here for a while, he'd make sure he bought some decent coffee, some Arabica or perhaps Blue Mountain. This pseudo-Brazilian stuff curdled his stomach lining.

"You sure this whole thing is just about Célie?" Sim asked. "What about that young guy who said he was coming to get you?"

Brand noticed that Sim had quit calling her *Mel.*

"Yeah. I thought about Brian," Brand admitted. "Especially since he escaped from detention last month. But this whole scenario is way too complex for him. Of course he might have got help. I've been wondering if the traitor in the Unit offered him a partnership. Someone seems to want me off the relocation team, and someone also wants Célie dead. I've been working on the premise that it was one and the same person, but now I don't know. Between you and me, Célie's flatmate was found hanging by her hair from the umbrella clothesline, which of course was one of Brian's little specialties. Parlane reckons Tara must have surprised her murderer as he was prowling around her place."

"How so?"

"She'd been designing for a festival and went to the Bahamas on a photo shoot. But the weather was so foul it was canceled. A courier came to deliver a parcel or she might not have been discovered so soon."

Sim grimaced. "Poor girl."

"Yeah." Brand shook his head. "Thank your lucky stars you didn't see her, Sim." Brand thought of Tara's lolling head, her bare feet dragging on the ground, and her hands hanging lax, smothered in blood. She must have clutched at her stomach, either in a vain effort to assuage the agony, or to prevent the viscera escaping. Not content with slitting her stomach as if he were about to stuff a belly of pork with capers, the murderer had given an enthusiastic twirl of the rotary clothesline so that Tara's intestines were grotesquely draped in a haphazard radius on the grass below.

"Do you think she was killed by mistake for Miss Francis?" the CIB detective-inspector had asked. Everyone knew he had too many cases and not enough investigative staff to cover half of them. He'd looked helpless, as if he was on a runaway freight train to nowhere.

"Nah, don't think so," Parlane had replied. "I think the guy did exactly what he wanted to do, but also it's a warning to Miss Francis."

"Jesus." Brand had turned away from Tara's body and tried to figure out why Parlane had gone down that road.

"Do you agree with him?" Sim asked Brand.

"Don't know. Maybe."

Sim snorted. "So how can I help you and Célie?" he asked, propping his elbows on the old oak table. Sim loved anything that was solid and sturdy. Most of his house was crammed with borderline antique furniture and Brand surmised that this was Sim's rock—his stability. After an uncertain childhood built on shifting sands, they each sought stability in different ways. They looked identical, but in many ways they were as different as the North and South Poles. However, they were the same where it counted most.

What could Sim do to help? Brand forced himself to relax. He hadn't realized he was so strung out. It was good being with Sim. "First, is it okay if we swap vehicles?"

Sim sniggered. "It'll do you good to drive around in my old 4x4 that stinks of dog vomit."

Brand grinned. Sim's 4x4 wasn't the world's cleanest vehicle, but it was appropriate for a vet who carried God-knew-what. Brand rubbed his head, weariness adding to the pulsing headache. "I need a plan. I can't just drift, hoping something'll break from the police end. What's worse, I have to turn up for work on Tuesday armed with a damned good explanation of why I've got Célie under lock and key in direct contravention of the rules."

"How about those yobs who tried to kidnap Célie?"

"Well, that little fracas could be construed as a

misunderstanding. Or a warning. Definitely not attempted murder."

"What about the breaking and entering at your house last night?"

"There's no evidence that the lock was forced. He was a professional. So the cops will say I left the door unlocked and there was no intruder. No crime was committed. And the rest was a figment of Célie's overwrought imagination."

"I'd call the murder of a dog a crime."

"You would, and I would, but I don't know how much importance the cops will attach to it."

"What about your assailant?"

Brand shrugged. He had no intention of telling Sim that he'd actually been attacked twice, and that one of his assailants was Célie. "I'm still standing."

Sim's expression darkened. "It's a damn shame there aren't laws that prevent crimes rather than deal with the consequences once they've occurred."

"Tell me about it. In casework I meet people who are time bombs ready to explode, but all I can do is advise and stand back. I could name you half a dozen people right now that I'd classify as powder kegs. Most of their acquaintances think of them as sane, normal folk until they do something odd or dangerous." Brand shrugged. "It doesn't help that the cops think I'm an effête twinkie because I dabble in minds, not blood and guts."

Sim said carefully, "Has it occurred to you that you might be in the wrong job?"

Brand looked up from where he was flicking his coffee mug with a fingernail. "Frequently. But I also have a thick file of thank-you notes from grateful ex-patients and relocatees and that counts for a lot." Then he laughed. "I have a suspicion I'll be axed as soon as I put my toe in the door on Tuesday anyway. I want to find out if they've discovered anything else in the past couple of days. And it won't prevent me from fighting them all the way. I'm damned if I'll just hand Célie over for them to play with. Somebody involved with the Unit has a contact to the Cliff Road serial killer. Whether it's someone from the relocation team itself, or a cop selling information to fund his dentist's bills, I don't give a cuss. What matters is that Célie is kept safe."

Sim raised his eyebrows. "Well, well." He gave a low, appreciative whistle. "About time. I was beginning to think you had half the polar icecap in your veins, brother."

Brand felt himself flushing. "Oh, shut up, Sim. It's not like that, you know it isn't—" He broke off. Célie was standing in the doorway.

"Come on in, Célie." He'd shut up now and let Sim do the talking. Because Sim knew him too well. And because he needed to regroup after that little bombshell.

Was the reason he didn't want to hand Célie over to the police that he feared for her welfare, or was it that he wanted to keep her close to him? Was he endangering her life while he played getting-to-know-you? But how could he hand her over to people he didn't trust?

Determined to bury himself in work, he got out his whiteboard. He made a list of people who knew where Célie was—himself, Sim and Célie. Next he made a list of people who might guess where Célie was. Then he made a list of people who had reasons for needing to know Célie's whereabouts.

Then he made out similar lists for himself.

He sat back and looked at the lists for a long time. He was comfortable with lists. From them he could extrapolate possibilities, both remote and probable. Convergent thinking had worked well for him in the past.

Not today. There were very few lines he could connect between the lists.

"Think, Turner," he told himself. Someone wanted either to frighten Célie or kill her. That person had eliminated Peaches so he could get closer to Célie.

Why? What information did Célie have that could implicate the Cliff Road killer?

Information?

He threw his whiteboard marker on the table and called, "Célie?"

"Right here." She was standing at his shoulder, looking at the whiteboard.

"What was it you and Tara and Occy thought you saw?" he asked.

All the color bleached out of her face and he made a grab for her as she swayed on her feet.

****

"Célie?"

"I'm fine, I'm fine," she muttered irritably when Brand lowered her onto the sofa. She'd just felt a bit woozy for a minute. Nothing to get excited about. It must have been Brand asking her what they'd seen. Or perhaps seeing those names on his whiteboard had brought home to her the reality that she would never see two of those people ever again. Two people she had loved.

She struggled to sit up on the deep sofa, pushing aside the squishy cushions threatening to drag her back down.

Brand had asked her what they'd *seen*—she and Occy and Tara.

And then there was one.

She swallowed hard.

After she'd described the scene at Occy's, the cops had pressed her for information. They'd known she was holding something back, but Brand was the only person who'd realized it wasn't something she *knew*, but something she had an impression of; something out of place. She had no intention of pointing the finger at an innocent person.

Looking up into Brand's hazel eyes, she saw nothing but concern. No blame.

She took a deep breath. "I...uh, we—"

"Tell me when you're ready. Here, drink this."

He held out a cup of tea and her stomach heaved.

"Bad idea, huh?" he said wryly, putting the cup down on a table.

She tried to smile, but knew it was a weak, pale attempt. "I need to tell you now," she blurted. After weeks of swallowing it, of vowing to Occy and Tara that they'd keep quiet about what they'd seen, here she was, steaming to divulge their secret. Because it had all become too hard—way too much responsibility on her own.

Brand sat down next to her on the sofa and held her hand. She guessed he did this with a lot of his patients, oops—clients! He had the sort of eyes and hands people trusted. Calm eyes that said they'd seen terrible things but still believed there was goodness around, and callused hands that said they'd done good, hard work and would come back for more.

She took a breath. "It's about something we— that's Occy, Tara and myself—saw on the day of the first murder."

"The Cliff Road murders?"

She wondered why he was being so pedantic, then glimpsed the small recorder clipped to his sweater. So much for imagining he wanted to get up close and personal. He just wanted her voice to come over loud and clear. She tugged her hand out of his.

"Yes, the Cliff Road murders. It was on March 4th. We didn't make a note of it at the time, but later when the police were swarming all over the place, Tara and I remembered the date. Occy didn't, of course. Dates meant nothing to him. But like us, he wondered if she had something to do with the murder."

"*She?*" Brand straightened up and stared at her.

Célie nodded. "She was running along the beach, frantic. We'd seen her once or twice before, beachcombing and mumbling to herself. We presumed she was a bi-polar sufferer with demons of her own."

Brand's eyes narrowed. He looked as if he was grappling with an alien concept.

"*Now* do you see why we said nothing? Parlane and Ellery gave the locals a really hard time. So when it came to telling the cops about a sick woman staggering along the beach at dusk—well, we doubted she could cope with Parlane's style of interrogation so we decided not to mention it."

Drained, she lay back on the cushions.

Brand toyed with the whiteboard marker and she could tell he was assembling a new plan of attack.

"Okay," he said at last. "What does she look like?"

"She wears a man's long raincoat and black rubber boots. Her hair is short and wild—sticking out all over the place. She smells a bit."

"What of? Do you mean she's unwashed?"

"Noo-oo. It's not unpleasant. Reminds me of my childhood.

He leaned forward. "In what way?"

She hesitated. "I'm not sure. It's...comforting."

Brand raised his eyebrows. "What color is her hair?"

"Grey."

"Age?"

Célie shrugged. "Not sure. About fifty."

"*Fifty*? A fifty-year-old female serial killer? Unusual." His stunned tone said, *not bloody likely*.

Célie pinned him with a look. "There. I told you

so. Knew you'd think it was improbable. But you've got it wrong. We didn't think of her as a murderer. We wondered if she'd witnessed something that frightened her, or perhaps been pursued by the murderer."

"What else can you tell me about her?"

"Not much. Don't know where she lives. As well as talking to herself, she walks with a sort of shambling gait. We were sure she was mentally ill."

"Uh huh."

She grinned wanly. "Don't have to have a degree to know the woman is ill."

"Did she see you?"

"Oh, yes. That's why..." She trailed off.

"I mean, did she see you and *comprehend* she'd seen you? Not just look straight through you," he persevered.

"I think so. But she looked sort of lost—very upset. Her eyes were roving everywhere and she was hurrying along, tripping over stones."

"As you surmised, she may have happened on the scene of the murder."

"Yes. Also, Occy and I wondered if her illness was progressing faster, that she was sliding downhill. We knew the police were looking for a man and we'd have looked damned ridiculous if we'd mentioned her. Parlane would have blown a fuse."

Brand turned off the recorder. "How well did you know Occy? I've been wondering what two go-ahead young women had in common with a forgetful old recluse."

"We were all running away from something," Célie heard herself say before she could stop herself. Damn, he was good. But he didn't pursue it like she thought he would. Advance, retreat, advance, retreat. He was very clever.

"What was Occy running away from?" he asked.

"I think he was trying to escape from Social

Services and his grandson—people who kept trying to fit him into neat little boxes. He wasn't so much running from old age as jogging happily along with it. He just didn't like being patronized when he arrived somewhere and couldn't remember why he had gone there in the first place." Dear Occy had been such a sweet little man. He wouldn't have put up much of a struggle against the murderer.

"So you and Tara helped him out, now and then."

"Uh-huh. If we saw him wandering about unable to find his way home, we'd give him a meal or a cup of tea and walk him to his door. We never went inside his house unless he invited us in. It was a pigsty. I cleaned up for him once and it took him weeks to forgive me. He valued his privacy. I thought I was doing the right thing but he was deeply offended." She laughed a little, recalling the gentlemanly lecture Occy had given her about invading other people's space. Then she hid her face in her hands, remembering Occy as she'd last seen him, his slashed throat gaping in an obscene smirk and his belly bisected, the entrails coiled up on the floor beside him.

The sofa dipped as Brand moved and gathered her against his chest. She burrowed her face in his woolen sweater. They stayed like that for a long time.

A long while later she raised her face and said simply, "Thanks."

Chapter Eleven

Sorting through the last of her belongings, Celie stacked the clothes in the old chest of drawers in her room. When she'd finished, she felt a little better. Doing things always made her feel better. Having time to think was much overrated.

In the living room she heard the rise and fall of the brothers' voices. She couldn't quite hear their conversation and she didn't want to. For today she'd had enough of surmise and intrigue and fear. She would read. Reading soothed her. When she checked out the bookcase she found an eclectic assortment of novels and autobiographies, and to her amusement, several Boys' Own Annuals. Cool. She'd see what Captain Dromorne and his World War II flying aces were up to.

She glanced at herself in the mirror and grimaced.

There was no problem with anyone recognizing her now. Not one person, from her most ardent fan, to the peculiar woman on the beach, would recognize her.

She shrugged and settled down with Captain Dromorne.

Half an hour later, Brand's voice called, "Hey! Chili maker!"

She closed her book. Good. She had finished Captain Dromorne's exploits and moved on to The Black Ooze. But TBO was nowhere near as exciting as Captain Dromorne.

"Sounds as though you need a chef!" she yelled back.

"Just a short-order cook will be good enough, thanks."

She went out to the kitchen where Brand was wrestling with a frozen chicken. "What am I supposed to do with this? Sim dug it out of the freezer, but it's like a rock."

She fielded the chicken and doused the frozen lump under the hot water tap. "Where is Sim?"

"He went shopping. It was better for him to do it because when someone local sees me, they assume I'm Sim. A few times I've become involved in some complicated conversations. Like at what age to spay a cat and stuff like that."

Célie snorted with laughter and looked around the cluttered kitchen, searching for a dish towel or a roll of paper towels. *Think, Célie. Where would you expect to find them in a man's kitchen?* Ah. Right behind a dead houseplant. Of course. She patted the chicken dry with a paper towel. "You're not really alike. There are differences."

He flicked a sideways glance at her. "Such as?"

She pretended she hadn't noticed that intimate look and peered at the oven temperature dial. "Oh...your hair grows differently—same color, but yours waves and his—that's it!" She snapped her fingers and spun around to face him. Excitement speared through her. "That was why I thought it was you at the laundry window! It wasn't just the finger thing. It was the hair, too."

He looked mystified. "Somebody has hair like me? I would guess there'd be a couple of million guys with hair the same."

"No, no. It's the way it falls, just here." She stood on tiptoe to show him what she meant. And came up against his hard chest.

He slipped an arm around her. "Where?" he asked, grinning.

For a moment she stayed still, reveling in the closeness. She wondered what it would be like to kiss him. He'd be a good kisser—generous... She shook her head to clear it and wriggled away. "Ha ha. Wise guy."

He let her go without a struggle. He hadn't meant anything by it. Just a friendly cuddle to fill in the evening. Fantastic. She'd finally decided to trust someone and he was just using her to pass the time.

"Anyway," she muttered, "that's what I saw through the safety glass. The guy's hair flopped forward over his forehead, like yours does. And he sounded like you."

"Well, it wasn't me," he snapped.

She wasn't sure if he was annoyed because she'd pulled away from him, or because he was sick of repeating that the man who'd freaked her out wasn't him. Whichever, this was the first time she'd seen him look impatient. Most other men she knew wore their impatience like a cloak.

Her father, for instance. He was always saying he'd never wanted kids and that they were all leeches. He'd never hit them, but she and Nadine walked on eggshells around him just the same. Then one day something broke. Célie had often wondered whether he'd lost his job, or if the sight of their mother lying on the couch with a bottle in her hand yet again had set him off.

He'd slouched wearily through the front door, stared at them all sitting in front of the TV and yelled, "Get out! I'm sick of you all. Bloody drones." To their shock he had shoved the three of them outside and slammed the front door in their faces.

And then there was her impatient stepbrother, Clyde, though calling him a stepbrother was putting a respectable face on it. Unable to survive on her own, her mother had shacked up with Clyde's father to gain a roof over her head. And young Clyde had hated Roberta Francis and her two sniveling daughters with a vengeance. That's what he'd called them—'the sniveling sisters.' Had Célie been the only one aware of the impatience and anger boiling beneath the surface of Clyde's sullen expression?

Like father, like son. Clyde's father had a propensity for impatience that rocketed into violence in the blink of an eyelid. Célie had been in school when Roberta Francis fled with Nadine. She'd had no idea where they'd gone, and they never came back for her. That was when she discovered just how impatient Clyde's father could get.

But in a way, the impatience of the three men closest to her had been a blessing. When she'd half-crawled, half-stumbled into the accident and emergency department of Auckland Hospital one rainy Sunday morning sporting an array of bruises and a couple of cracked ribs, a host of people sprang into action. Social Services traced her paternal grandfather and her father was forced to assist towards her upkeep.

And in her grandfather she'd met a man who had all the patience in the world. He mightn't have loved her, but he'd done his duty by her. And thanks to him she'd received her first piano lesson.

In some ways Brand Turner reminded her of Poppa. It was a pity Brand had an agenda that did not include Célie Francis. Ah, well. She gave a mental shrug. Life was like that. She'd learned not to expect anything, and that way she was never disappointed.

"Any vegetables?" she asked Brand.

He looked at her for a minute. "Where did you go just then?"

"None of your business."

"No, it isn't. I'd like it to be, but it has to be in

your own good time, Célie."

Something warm and hopeful bubbled up inside her. She stamped down on it. He was talking professionally. "Vegetables?" she repeated.

He opened the refrigerator and bent down to pull out the vegetable bin. She admired his delectable, tight backside as he dug around, trying to find anything resembling a vegetable. Before he straightened up she switched her eyes away. Grabbing a cleaver from the set of kitchen implements in one corner she looked for a chopping board, then set to work to dismember the half-frozen chicken. Using the hatchet reminded her of something. She stopped and turned around to face him. "Umm, Brand, I've just remembered. I've still got your kitchen knife."

He looked amused. "You brought it with you?"

She felt herself blushing. "Yes. I don't know why."

"I do. You don't trust me."

"Well...I almost do. If I was going to trust anyone, I'd trust you," she admitted.

"In connection with the murders or in a general sense?"

"Both."

He looked confused but pleased. However he seemed to understand she was not prepared to go any further. "If it makes you feel comfortable, keep the knife." Then he changed the subject. "It doesn't look as if Sim is big on vegetables. I hope he buys some while he's out."

"Will he mind if I ah...clean up a bit?" She didn't know how else to say it. The chicken spat away in an oven pan, but if they were to prepare vegetables, especially a salad, then the bench-top needed a scrub.

"You're not here to do housework, Célie. You're here to relax in safety."

"Got to do something," she muttered.

He smiled. "I know. Go for it. Sim will understand and he won't be offended."

Shoving the memories aside, she scrubbed out her anger and grief on Sim's bench-top. And when Sim returned fifteen minutes later, his eyes opened wide. "Good Lord! Is *that* how it's supposed to look? Umm, Célie...what about the floor tiles?"

She scowled. "Don't push your luck, Sim Turner. If I feel like it, I might clean them. Otherwise—no."

He sighed. "It was worth a try." He turned to Brand. "I got it," he said, and he and Brand went out to Matilda and began ferrying shopping bags and boxes into the house.

Célie pounced on some sweet potatoes and scrubbed them, then tucked them in the oven next to the chicken pieces. She ripped open a salad pack and began rinsing and chopping and dicing. Yay! Such small pleasures would have meant little to her a few weeks ago. Now doing something productive was almost as soothing as working at her piano.

She was shutting the refrigerator door when she heard it—the deep, throaty groan of an electronic keyboard. Knife and chopping board clattered to the bench as she raced towards the sound.

"You have a keyboard!"

Sim and Brand were standing in the dining alcove wearing twin grins.

"Brand remembered it," Sim explained. "I collected it from Mum's place on my way to the supermarket."

She looked at them, smiling. Oh, they were such nice guys. How had she ever imagined they were murderers?

"Thank you." She pecked Sim's chin and grazed a kiss over Brand's cheek with a little more care.

They'd placed the keyboard on a coffee table and she grabbed a chair and parked herself in front of it.

As she went under she said vaguely, "Keep an eye on the chicken. I might not notice."

****

A long time later Celie surfaced. Manuscript paper had appeared at her elbow along with a couple of pencils, and inspiration had flowed and flowed. She'd written a new song that had been on the tip of her tongue for days.

She flexed her fingers. And sniffed. The chicken was way past done! She leapt up but found the two men dishing up dinner together, working alongside each other with a swift competence that said they'd done this many times before. As Brand split open the sweet potatoes, Sim dropped a gob of butter on each one. Then Sim sprinkled Italian dressing over the salad and Brand tossed it.

She leaned against the doorway watching them, wondering what her little sister was doing now. One thing was certain. She wasn't companionably making dinner with Célie.

As they ate, Brand asked, "Will you sing for us?"

She smiled. Would she? She could hardly stop from breaking into song, even as she ate. "So long as my voice is not too creaky. It hasn't been oiled for a few weeks. Let me do some exercises first."

And she found to her delight, that rather than rendering her voice toneless or unpolished, her enforced break had given her middle voice a clearer quality which complemented her earthy lower register. Perhaps she had needed a break. She tried not to bore her listeners by singing for too long, but they egged her on.

"Do that changing your voice thing, Célie," Brand encouraged.

So she did her signature imitation of Edith Piaf and followed it with a sultry, breathy Marilyn Monroe version of "Diamonds are a Girl's Best Friend."

96

Sim raved but Brand just watched her, smiling now and again. She knew he was thinking of that phone call.

For the first time in weeks, she went to bed happy and relaxed.

But her confidence lasted only as long as the first nightmare. Usually when the nightmares began she was able to pull herself out of them before they dragged her under. But tonight's was a doozy. Though well aware it *was* a nightmare, this time she could not escape its clutches. A hooded, cloaked figure pursued her across rock-pools slick with seaweed, and every time she slipped, he got closer. He was surefooted and seemed almost to float across the tops of the rock shelves. His chilling whisper came closer and closer. "I know who you are, Célie. I know where you live."

She screamed, "No, you don't know where I live! Not anymore!"

A cool hand touched hers and she whimpered and fought the bedsheets, frantic to escape, until a gentle voice said, "Ssh, Célie, it's all right. It's me—Brand."

Cracking open her eyes she peered into the darkness and threw herself in the direction of his voice. He caught her as she tumbled out of bed and they rolled onto the floor together.

"Oomph." The breath squeezed out of Brand's lungs as she landed spread-eagled on top of him.

"S-sorry."

"No need to be sorry. His voice turned husky. "I don't mind at all."

Yes, she could feel that he didn't mind.

She smothered a nervous giggle. "So I see—er, feel." He had broken her fall by raising one knee. Her mouth hovered above his, but in the darkness she couldn't see his face. She felt the rise and fall of his chest and her fingers brushed over the hectic heat of his skin. What was he thinking?

His arms fell away. Damn it all! He was just going to get up, say goodnight and walk away.

She tightened her arms around his neck and leaned closer. "Kiss me, Brand. I dare you. You know you want to."

There was a short silence. "I want to do a lot of things, Célie. Doesn't mean I'm going to do them." He sat up, taking her with him. Not bad for a man who pretended the words "weight lifting" weren't in his vocabulary. "And next time you ask me to kiss you, I might oblige. But tonight you're using me to escape from a nightmare."

She felt herself flush. She was damned fortunate he hadn't taken her at her word and jumped her bones. Afterwards she would have been royally pissed off with both of them.

He was a cool one. If it weren't for his impressive erection she'd have thought he didn't want her. He was still hard as iron underneath her bottom and she was tempted to—*no, Célie. Don't go there. You're very lucky he's the sort of guy he is.*

"You're right," she said, scrambling out of his lap. "Just as well you're thinking for both of us. But if you want me in future, you'll have to beg. I never ask twice."

"That's my Célie," he said, getting to his feet. "Never a kind word."

Then he walked over to her bed and pulled back the covers. "Here. Hop in and stop giving me a hard time." He smoothed the hair back off her face and pecked her on the forehead. "Goodnight, Miss Francis. See you tomorrow."

She noticed he didn't quite shut the door behind him. Still on duty.

She grinned. Ah, she liked this man. So-o-o mature compared to Giorgio whose temper tantrums had shaken the earth when she arrived home from a gig worn out, too tired to play.

"Célie," he would cajole in his carefully cultivated Italian accent, "you cannot mean no. Giorgio needs you. Feel how Giorgio needs you." And he would roll on top of her as if she'd been a mattress.

She had put up with that for...how long? Almost a year. Silly girl. All because she'd had a taste of companionship and didn't want to be alone any more.

For a long time after her grandfather's death she'd protected herself by holding aloof from others. Then one day she'd signed a lucrative three-month contract with the Playhouse and had gone out for drinks with a bunch of friends in the industry. For once she'd let her guard down, and there was Giorgio with his beguiling ways and beautiful voice. She had let herself succumb because after all the struggling she'd finally arrived as an entertainer. She'd felt she owed it to herself to have a little fun.

Well, okay. There'd been no fireworks. Giorgio had wanted someone he could freeload off, and she'd wanted a no-strings-attached soufflé relationship. For a couple of months they'd each got what they wanted. Then things went pear-shaped but Giorgio clung. How he'd clung! It had taken her another eight months and some expensive therapy to get rid of him.

And therapy was where she'd met Tara. They were both on the run from life, but when they'd shifted in together to the house above the cliffs, they stopped running. They'd melded together well, and for four months the beautiful old bungalow was a sanctuary filled with laughter and companionship and plain hard work.

Then a sadistic psychopath came calling and took it all away.

She leaned over and clicked off the bedside lamp

that Brand had left burning. She didn't need it. She was a survivor.

****

Brand stood under a cold shower cursing himself for having considered, even for one second, taking what had been offered. She was hurting and he would not add to her trauma. A quick lay sounded good in theory, but he wasn't made for that and neither was Célie. Oh, she gave off the vibes of being tougher than tough but nothing could be further from the truth. Inside all that angst was a hard-working, conventional woman. She must have busted her buns to reach the heights of the local entertainment world while she was still in her late twenties. In spite of her cool, throwaway attitude he knew that hours and hours of practise and self-discipline had gone into developing the lyrical voice and advanced keyboard skills.

Propping himself against the shower wall, he tried to convince himself he'd done the right thing. If doing the right thing left him with a hard-on a cold shower wouldn't eliminate, what the hell was the point? He shuddered, then turned on the hot water to give himself a break. It was the only break he was going to get until someone found the Cliff Road murderer.

Chapter Twelve

On the northern side of the city, a woman rocked backwards and forwards on the edge of her bed. It was okay to rock. She was alone.

Of course she hadn't been able to do it in the old days when they'd gone out in public together. "Don't do that!" He'd snap. "People are looking at you."

As if. A long time ago people used to say they made an attractive couple. But now they were getting old and He refused to admit it. His job was far more significant than most because He made a difference, He said. He was still climbing the ladder and he needed to look good, which translated to— *'keep out of sight and don't stuff it up for me.'*

Sometimes He disappeared for days on end and left her locked up. She had a small window to look out at the sea. Oh, the freedom of the sea! If she could only sail away...but nobody could escape themselves, could they? Anyway, the two little rooms were just fine. She had her own sofa and she could run the shower for hours if she wanted. Most important of all, she had her own bed. Ugh! She'd hate to go back to sharing a bed with Him again. And the TV was great because she got cable.

Her daughter didn't come to see her any more. Good riddance. The girl had moaned on and on about how He'd cancelled the doctor's appointments she'd set up. Who cared? She didn't want to see a doctor anyhow. The doctor might lock her up, like last time.

On one of her good days when He had let her out to walk along the beach, she'd had a couple of spare keys cut at the hardware store on the corner. So for a while she'd been able to leave whenever she wanted to. She laughed. He thought He was clever, but she was the clever one.

When He visited her to bring food, he always emptied his pockets and tossed the contents onto the tray on top of the TV. He carried bunches of keys like a jailer. Well, he *was* a jailer—her jailer. Two of everything. He was a creature of habit and *so* predictable. She snorted to herself. What did they call it? Anal-retentive. That was it. It hadn't been difficult to snaffle the key.

She grinned to herself. He panicked if she showed signs of erratic behavior so she sometimes gave Him what He expected. She would grab the rug off the sofa and huddle next to the TV, muttering. While He raced to find her medicine in the bathroom she'd nick a few coins off the tray—not too many. She had to be careful because sometimes she *really* forgot things and couldn't remember if she'd already stolen some coins that day.

She began to pace. The black feelings were coming back. They skittered across her skin like cockroaches.

She wouldn't be in this predicament if it weren't for Him. Something to do with those pills He gave her, she was sure. For some time now she hadn't swallowed them unless he stood over her, making sure she did so. They made her fall asleep and when she woke up she couldn't remember anything. And something bad must have happened during one of her journeys to the beach after she'd taken those pills.

One day the door had crashed open and He'd rushed in fuming and shouting. "You stupid bitch!" He'd hissed. His fingers had bitten into her skin and the pain had brought back fuzzy, frightening memories. Spurred by fear, she'd wrenched free to run and hide behind the sofa.

But instead of hurting her any more He just sat down on the sofa and put His head in His hands. She hadn't dared to move. After a long time He got up and walked around to where she was crouched. "Give me the key," He said. She'd pretended she didn't know what He was talking about. Her little bit of independence was precious. But He'd yelled, "*Now*, you stupid cow," so before his fist shot out she'd pulled the key out of her pocket and thrown it to Him.

And now she had to be very, very careful because sometimes He turned up unexpectedly— even in the middle of the night.

The woman paced over to the mirror and stood in front of it, mimicking His clipped, bitter words. "Turn the bloody light off! It's three in the morning..."

She smirked. She still had the duplicate key. How she loved the powerful feeling of gliding through bushes like a ghost, peering in through the seaspray-sticky windows of the houses above the cliffs or walking along the beach with its tang of ozone. Sometimes, though, she couldn't remember leaving the house and clambering down the cliff path to get there.

She could always find food. She was quite clever at taking things when people weren't around.

That old man who lived right down by the beach—he had cupboards full of food. She watched him sometimes because she thought he was a bit like her. He didn't have a very good memory either. He would put things down and then wander around looking for them. But she hadn't seen him for ages. The last time she'd managed to escape, she'd found his house was all locked up. Perhaps he'd gone away.

Just like those young women who lived along Cliff Road. She'd watched some of them for hours—sunbathing on green lawns, chatting on their cell phones and trying on each other's clothes.

But they'd gone away too.

It was weird really. The people she watched—they just went away. "Poof! Like that!" She snapped her fingers and laughed.

Chapter Thirteen

Brand lay in bed, arms akimbo, his head resting on his palms. By whatever means he could, tomorrow he would wrest from Parlane a list of everyone connected to the administration of the Unit. Of course Parlane would kick up a stink about it. He'd mutter his usual comment about Brand not being an official member of the team, "just a shrink who was foisted on us from Central." And he'd threaten to arrest Brand if he didn't bring Célie to them.

But Brand had one card up his sleeve. He could go over Parlane's head and speak to Inspector Ralston at Auckland Central. Brand and Ralston had worked together many times in the past. Ralston had seniority over Parlane. But it was fair to give Parlane a chance first.

Also, Brand was sure that Lilah, the new Unit profiler, would back him up. Lilah was...different. Her stark, empty face puzzled him. He wasn't sure if she wore a chilly mask to stop her emotions spilling into her work or whether she simply didn't care about the victims. It could be that her interest lay only in whoever she was profiling at the time—a true professional in the coldest sense of the word. Clinical detachment was not always a cloaking device. Sometimes it just...was. He knew Lilah was contemptuous of Parlane's insistence on a secret society mentality. More than once he had heard her mutter that she was far too busy to waste time sealing her reports with colored tags as per Parlane's instructions. She was a great believer in getting on with things, and Brand guessed she'd advise Parlane to hand any pertinent information over to him if it would move the case forward.

Brand eased out of bed and stretched. Wherever the leak was, it had caused three deaths and there might be others as yet undiscovered. It was time the North Shore Unit searched its own backyard. Not his.

He poked his nose around the door of Célie's room.

"How about a run?"

"*Can* we?"

'Don't see why not, provided we don't go too far. Nothing has happened since we got here so I think we're safe for the time being.'

'Cool!'

You'd have thought he'd offered her a basket of chocolates and caviar. In two minutes flat she was dressed in shorts and a T-shirt and was yanking on her Nikes.

"Sunglasses?" he asked.

She walked to the window and peered out. "Why, it looks nice out today even though it's almost winter." Then she added, "The weather hasn't meant much to me for the past few weeks."

He grinned. "Must be the company that's got you going today."

She rolled her eyes. "Don't you wish."

She was back to the old Célie, for which he was grateful he told himself. They set off on a five-mile loop he had run a couple of times before. He kept a wary eye out for passers-by, but they were alone here on the headland.

Sim had kicked up a fuss. He thought they were mad. "Why on earth would you run for pleasure?

Necessity I understand, but pleasure?"

"Funny. I'm sure that half an hour ago I heard some amazing grunts coming from your home gym," Brand had retaliated.

They jogged down the driveway and Célie grinned as she settled into a rhythm beside Brand. "The way you two argue makes me laugh. You don't mean anything bad by it, but for twins you have very different interests."

Brand grunted. "Only on the surface."

"Understood. That's what I like. You're the same deep down where it counts. Do you have any other brothers and sisters?" she shot out in between breaths. He had cut back his speed in deference to her slower pace, but obviously it was still too fast for her. He worked on slowing his pace by degrees so she wouldn't notice. If Fighting Francis thought he was making the run easier, she'd up the pace and kill herself before she'd admit she was pooped.

"No more siblings. We were enough."

She labored up the second hill where the track veered away from the road and hung over the sea below. "You're lucky. It'd be great to have a brother or sister to share things with." Her voice sounded wistful.

"You don't have any?" he asked, keeping his tone casual. Her profile had said nothing about siblings.

"Oh, somewhere I have a sister. And a mother. They left."

"Left?" Unconsciously, he picked up speed on the downhill, his legs working in conjunction with his brain. They'd *left* her? Where? What did she mean?

"Yeah. They left me with my mother's boyfriend and his son."

Oh, hell. This could be construed as interviewing a client. Yeah, and he'd be kidding himself if he used that rationale. His interest was personal. Pure and simple. "Did that work out okay?”

"No. But later it did."

He frowned, wondering what she meant. And how long it had taken for her world to improve.

"Hey, you've speeded up!" she called out as he broadened the gap between them.

Damn. Now she'd change the topic. He eased back.

Sure enough: "Do you realize I haven't run since the day the killer chased me? Well over a month now. That's why I'm so unfit." She stopped and doubled over, hands on hips, huffing and puffing. Something whined over the top of her head and she glanced up as Brand swept an arm around her. He shoved her down on the grass and flung himself on top of her.

****

Célie's heart stuttered. Not bees this time. She lay prone under Brand, squashing her face into the cold grass. Overhead a seagull screamed. No other sound except their breathing.

Brand raised his head, trying to see where the bullet had come from.

"Careful," she hissed.

"It came from straight in front of us at the top of the hill," he whispered. "If we stay like this, he can't get a clear shot because of the rise of the ground."

"I'm damned if I'm going to lie here all day," Célie griped. She felt him snort with laughter into her hair. Darned if she could see anything funny in their predicament.

"We haven't got a choice. He's waiting for us to stand up."

"Or she."

"Yes. Or she."

Silence for a few seconds.

"There is one way." Brand's breath tickled her ear.

108

"Yeah?"

He hesitated a beat. "Yeah."

"Come on, come on, what is it? At this rate we'll be dead from the cold long before we get shot."

"We could roll, soldier style, back downhill. To get a clear shot he'll have to break cover and we might be able to identify him."

"Dodging bullets as we do it, huh? There's not much point in recognizing him if we're dead. Who're we going to tell then?"

She felt Brand shake with laughter again. The guy laughed at the strangest moments. She had the feeling that his senses hyped up when danger came calling. Not your average psychologist.

"Ready?" he asked, and began rolling like a kid over and over back downhill the way they'd come. She followed, cannoning into him a couple of times as she picked up speed.

Still no sound. Brand continued rolling, and the next time she bashed into him he rolled her right over the top of him and tumbled them into a cluster of castor oil bushes beside the track.

She opened her mouth to speak.

"Ssh," he said, listening intently.

Then she heard it too. Thud, thud. They crouched, knees protesting, behind the wine-red bushes. Célie had a sense of déjà vu.

Then Brand's shoulders relaxed. "It's okay," he whispered.

It was another early morning jogger chugging up the hill towards them. Brand cautioned her to stay still and rose to his feet. Célie, peering through the bushes, saw the jogger almost jump out of his skin. He flicked Brand a look that said, *Wacko hiding in bushes*, and gave them a wide berth as he continued plodding upwards.

At the top of the hill a figure wearing a long coat stood outlined against the sky waiting... The jogger was between them.

"Now!" Brand urged and they bolted for home. In three minutes they were back amongst traffic and people.

"I hope he doesn't shoot that poor jogger," Célie gasped as they turned into Sim's driveway.

"Nah. This guy's careful. But he might ask the jogger if he saw someone lurking in the bushes."

Célie threw herself down on Sim's garden swing and laughed. "In that case he'll have a tale to tell, won't he?"

If she hadn't been watching for it she would have missed the expression on Brand's face, but she was learning to read him. "What?"

He didn't answer straight away—just looked at her with amused resignation. She held her ground and he gave in. "He's getting desperate, shooting at us in the open. What I want to know is how he found us. Not just found us, but found us so quickly."

Célie twisted a strand of hair around her finger. "Okay, laugh at me playing amateur detective if you like, but what about a tracking device?"

Brand hunkered down near the garden swing and plucked a couple of grass blades. His face gradually altered from skepticism to speculation. "Considering we're dealing with cops and a covert organization here, anything's possible." He thought for a minute. "I'm not sure what to look for because I've only seen LoJack. It has to be someone using a laptop or a fairly sophisticated cell phone since they're on the move."

"How did he know we were going for a run?" Célie asked, puzzled.

"He didn't. If there's a tracking device then he knows where we are. But he can't get near the house because of the dogs. There's one way in and out of this area—the road we took. Driving, walking or running, sooner or later he was bound to find us. I was stupid to bring us here."

Célie shrugged. "You came to someone you could trust. But is it you or me he's after?'

"I guess if he could remove both of us at once he'd be thrilled. Although it would generate such a fuss I'm amazed he attempted it. Must be getting desperate." He stood up. "I don't know what I'm looking for but I'll try to find this bug."

She draped herself over the sun-warmed concrete steps and watched him as he stared contemplatively at the 4WD, his hands on his hips. She'd seen that look before. He was figuring out all the angles. After a few seconds he lay on his back and wriggled underneath the 4x4.

Three minutes later he shimmied back out. "Can you find a knife or something? The unit's magnetized and I can't unstick it."

He'd found it already. Just like that. He was wasted as a psychologist.

She scurried inside and pulled a bread and butter knife out of the kitchen drawer. A flat-sided knife would be better than a sharp one, she guessed.

"Here." She crouched down.

He was back underneath the Ford and his voice was muffled. "I thought while I was here I'd look for other things too. Stand way back."

"What other things?" Even as she asked she realized what he meant, and stepped back several paces. Not that that would save her if anything lethal was planted under the Explorer. She dithered until he eased back out again, a little oblong metal box in one hand.

"Anything else under there?" she asked, unable to stop the fear leaching into her voice.

"No. My imagination ran riot for a moment. So far, apart from today, this character has stuck to the script. But," he pulled a wry face, "the joke's on me."

"Huh?" She tilted her head on one side.

"When I bought Matilda, I purposely bought an Explorer without in-built GPS. I have a dislike of being traced."

Célie stared at him. "Brand, why are you so paranoid? I would never think of something like that. I mean, the idea that someone would bother tracing you through your GPS is weird. It's just a driving aid."

"When you've worked with as many kooks as I have, you learn to look over your shoulder."

She pursed up her mouth, trying not to grin. "I don't think you ought to talk about your patients like that. Not very professional."

"Hell, I wasn't talking about my clients. I was talking about the cops and the Unit."

Speechless, she stared at him. He grinned in appreciation. "I feel vindicated. Whoever it is had to install this little gadget to find us because Matilda *doesn't* have GPS."

She read the brand name on the side. "StarTrack."

"Yeah. It's a realtime tracking system."

"You don't say."

Brand laughed at her less-than-enthusiastic response, then looked down at the little rectangle in his hand. "What shall we do with this?"

"Put it in a bucket of water," Célie suggested with an evil grin.

"Hmm. I was thinking of something more devious."

"Ooh! Such as?"

"Attaching it to a bus or something like that."

Célie could feel the bubbles of laughter fizzing up inside her as she visualized all sorts of scenarios. "Way to go!"

Hearing the hiss of tires she tensed, ready to run. A family sedan drew up outside Sim's surgery. Children tumbled out of the car calling out to each other and she relaxed. It was ridiculous to allow the killer to rule her life to this extent—that she could look at an ordinary family car and get herself in a tizz. This murdering creep had her where he wanted her. He was consuming her life.

She straightened her shoulders.

No. She refused to let that happen. She would *not* allow that thug to drag her down into a miasma of fear. She'd stood alone against evil creeps before and she could do it again.

She smiled at the family who had brought a giant lop-eared rabbit to see Sim. The rabbit was lucky. He had five family carers and Sim for a vet. He'd be okay.

"Poor Peaches," she murmured to herself as she wandered over to scratch behind the rabbit's fawn-coloured twitching ears.

"What's wrong with him?" she asked one of the kids, a boy in his early teens.

"It's not a him—it's a her," the boy said with all the scorn of a teenager for a dimwitted adult. "And she's pregnant."

"Oh."

Brand gave a shout of laughter.

"Shut up," she said out of the corner of her mouth. "How was I to know?"

He clung to the doorpost and laughed even harder. "If you could have seen your face!" he sniggered. "You know what they say about rabbits."

Célie threw him an old-fashioned look.

Brand was still laughing. "That's why I keep well away from Sim's patients. I'm hopeless at that sort of thing."

She looked at him. In the morning sun, his thick dark brown hair glinted with golden chips of light. His T-shirt stretched over a great chest and his little bitty running shorts left little to the imagination. Even so...she imagined. It never hurt to imagine.

****

Brand sat at the table, a cup of coffee at his elbow, a notepad in front of him. He glanced up now and again to look out the window at the blue sky threaded with scudding clouds. His mind ran over and over this morning's fracas in a never-ending loop. Just as he was about to give up, his brain snapped to attention. "I have to go back to where we were this morning. I need to look for the cartridge case—if he hasn't already picked it up. I don't think he had a revolver. I think he would use a .45."

"Why?" Célie asked, frowning.

"Because I own a .45. You know, the one I showed you."

She nodded.

"For some reason this character wants me to take the rap for..." He trailed off.

"...for killing me," she finished. "Two birds, one stone."

"He must think I know a hell of a lot more than I do," Brand said, shaking his head.

He fetched the .45 from his bedroom and laid it on the kitchen table. Then he turned to stare at her, trying to gauge her mood. She did not seem upset. On the contrary, he had an idea that sometime this morning she had made a decision. He hoped she wasn't planning on going it alone. What would he do without her, his lodestar? *You'd go back to your old empty life; that's what you'd do.* He had to give her up someday, but he wasn't allowing some scumbag who belonged behind bars to harm her, not while he had a breath in his body. Of course she'd be moving on when all this was over. *But not yet, Célie. Please.*

He could see the bright mind turning over behind those silver-grey eyes.

"How would this guy know you own a .45?" she asked.

"No idea. But someone knows a lot more about

me than I do about him," Brand said tersely. "And I don't like the feeling."

"Understatement of the century," Célie commented. "Where do you hide the .45?"

He gave her a what-do-you-want-to-know-for? look.

"Well?" she demanded. "I know you wouldn't leave it in plain sight. Whoever pressed the panic button didn't have much time between my escaping and your arrival. Would they have had time to look around?"

Brand shook his head. "No. I figure they had only three minutes—four at absolute tops—to dash in and out."

She grinned suddenly. "If I'd known earlier that you had that thing—" she nodded towards the .45— "I'd have been more circumspect in my dealings with you. Even so, you are *not* going to look for the cartridge case on your own."

He raised his eyebrows at her proprietary tone. The lady was trying to take over and he wasn't sure he liked it. As his stepfather always said, if you handed over the reins, you got lost in the shuffle. Brand was used to being on his own and making his own decisions. This sharing stuff was new.

On the other hand, Célie seemed genuinely worried about him which was uh...nice.

He compromised. "I'll ask Sim to come with me when he's finished surgery. We'll leave the dogs to guard you."

She nodded as if giving him permission. Something new, an emotion he wasn't familiar with, stretched itself deep down inside him like a lazy cat. He told it to lie down and be good.

Just before sunset he and Sim began to comb the grassy area where they estimated the shooter had stood. They searched for a half-hour and found nothing. Brand stood on a knoll and surveyed the area, frustrated at hitting another dead end. "One good thing is that if he's watching us, and wasn't aware that we're twins, he just got a big shock."

Sim grinned. "That'll shove a spoke in his wheel. From now on he won't know which one of us he's following."

"Up till now the bastard hasn't *had* to follow us," Brand said, and explained what he'd found stuck underneath Matilda.

"Hell. We need to be ultra careful, bro. I drove that thing to the supermarket and to Mum's place yesterday."

"Sim, I think this character already knows about Mum and Tyler. Remember all the fuss about the .45 three years back?"

Sim looked thoughtful. "Is that why you think he used a .45? To incriminate you?"

"Well, he can't have missed all the hoo-hah about the bloody gun, can he?" Brand asked irritably. "The press yammered on about it for days, calling our step-dad a hero because he stuck up for himself. Remember, the cops considered charging him for using the Colt in self-defence. I had to re-register it in my name and the only people who could know that would be people with access to the weapons register."

Sim looked at him. "Cops?"

Brand nodded. "Cops."

It was pointless to continue searching for the cartridge case. It had grown too dark to see anything smaller than a cat. As they walked home, far out at sea a lighthouse winked at the sliver of a moon and all around them the sounds of a dying day wound down to a peaceful evening.

Sim sighed, sounding weary. "I've got your back, Brand, but for God's sake wrap this thing up soon. I've only got one brother and I aim to keep him."

"Ditto. Wish I hadn't brought this thing right

into your backyard." Brand booted a pebble along the path in front of them.

"Of course you came to me," Sim said, sounding affronted. "Who else could you trust?"

"Got a point there," Brand muttered. Thank God for Sim.

"Have you checked out that young nutter who liked to stalk women? The one who escaped from his minders?"

"Not yet. But Brian keeps hovering at the back of my mind. When they sent him to the halfway house after his hearing, he spat a stream of vitriol in my direction, probably because I spent so much time with him and dug so deep." Brand rolled his shoulders, trying to ease the heavy feeling. "God, I hope the cops catch him soon. His amorality is a fearsome thing."

"Would he have connections to this thing of yours?" Sim asked.

"I doubt it. But slice and dice *is* his specialty. Somewhere, someone is suffering because of him, you can be sure of that."

"God, Brand! The types you work with!"

"I know. When this contract expires I don't intend to renew it."

"Good." Sim looked up at the clear night sky and breathed deeply. He changed the subject. "Hopefully Célie has done kitchen duty again." Then he caught himself up. "Hell, I'd better rephrase that. If she hears me say that, it'll be me she slices and dices. That's one stroppy woman."

Brand laughed. "That reminds me. Célie is wandering around with one of my kitchen knives in her bag."

"Then I'd be obliged if you took it away from her."

They stopped outside the kitchen door. "No. I can't do that. If it makes her feel safe, she should keep it. I haven't been very successful at keeping her safe so far."

"Crap. You've done just fine. She's alive and she's on an even keel and that's all that matters."

Brand didn't agree with Sim, but he didn't argue.

The two German Shepherds and Célie were examining something in the oven. She turned as she heard their voices and said, "Don't beat yourself up about keeping me safe, Brand. I'd have been kidnapped by now if it wasn't for you."

Brand wondered about that. She might have been able to handle the two gorillas on her own. Even if they had overpowered her, it would have taken time. She was no pushover and she would have created such a huge stink that the two attackers might have had to cope with some irate neighbors. That third character lurking upstairs in her house—he would have been like smoke in the wind and left his henchmen in the lurch if the neighbors had called the cops. But Brand wasn't so sure about her night in the forest. She had come very close to being more than kidnapped.

He tried to ignore the domestic scene in front of him, the cute rear waving about as she peered inside the oven and the two dogs, their tails stirring as they consulted with her about the casserole. *No. Don't look, Turner. Keep it light and bright.* He shook his head as if he was clearing water from his ears. "Is that really Ms Francis who told me not to beat myself up? I must have become hard of hearing. Will the real Ms Francis please stand up?"

"Oh, shut up, Brand."

"Thank goodness. I thought for a moment you'd knocked out Célie and stuffed her in a cupboard. Glad she's back." He wasn't sure why he wanted to needle her, but he thought it had something to do with the way she'd been so quick to his defense. She must not see him as a hero because he wasn't hero material. And if she thought their association was a lasting one, she'd better think again. What he wanted and what would happen were two very different things. He was no good at keeping independent women happy and Célie was long overdue a dose of happiness. His mother and Marina had been the most important women in his life and he had failed them.

Marina had left him for someone "who knew what women wanted."

And every time their father had retreated inside himself and refused to communicate, their frightened mother had scurried around like a mouse on a treadmill, unable to settle to a task or to rest. No matter how hard he'd tried, Brand hadn't been able to help her.

She'd much preferred Sim's detached watchfulness. Sim had learned to protect himself from their parents' problems at an early age by becoming emotionally detached.

Brand tried to concentrate on what Célie was saying.

"Didn't you find the cartridge?" she asked.

Sim shook his head. "Dinner smells good."

"Yeah, I enjoy playing the little woman now and then," Célie said, right on cue. "But tomorrow night it's someone else's turn."

Brand and Sim smirked at each other.

"What? What did I say?" she demanded.

"Nothing," they chorused meekly.

The phone rang. "Saved by the bell," Sim muttered and almost knocked the cordless phone off its stand in his haste to get to it.

Brand watched his brother's face settle into lines of concentration as he listened to the caller.

"What?" he asked, as Sim hung up.

"Emergency. Someone's bringing in an injured

dog. Hold my dinner." He rushed outside to turn on the surgery lights, the German Shepherds at his heels.

Brand followed. "Be careful, Sim. Make sure the call was a genuine one."

Sim looked at him. "You're developing paranoia. Don't worry. He's one of my regulars."

"Oh." Sim was right. He was seeing a murderer under every bush.

Sim shrugged into a smock and pulled some instruments out of the sterilizer.

Brand backed out of the surgery. He was no use here and he had work to do. He had to nut out a strategy for dealing with the cops tomorrow.

Chapter Fourteen

Next morning Brand sat in front of Foster, Ellery, and Parlane in Foster's small, dim office adjacent to the district court. Brand could feel the irritation rolling off Parlane in waves and he didn't give a shit.

Foster sat well back from the desk, silent and watchful. Usually he took his cue from the cops, even though he was the notional head of the Unit, but today there was a worried crease between his brows as if he were puzzled.

Parlane attacked in his usual manner. "What right do you have to take a witness out of a safe house and keep her from us, Turner?"

Brand paused before he said his piece. "The right any citizen has when they know the police are grossly at fault." His voice was cool, measured, and designed to irritate the hell out of Parlane.

He succeeded.

"Shrinks!" Parlane said with disdain.

"What do you mean, Turner?" Foster asked.

Brand settled back in his seat. "Well, I'll be damned," he said to Parlane and Ellery. "You haven't told the other Unit members what's going on, have you? Hell, you don't even trust each other!" He snorted.

"What's happening?" Foster demanded.

"There's a leak in the Unit, John," Brand explained. "Parlane was forced to tell me after I discovered the body of one of our relocatees at her safe house. She'd been murdered."

Foster's jaw dropped. "Oh, God!" Then he caught on. "A leak?"

Parlane glared at Brand. "Look, it's a question of need to know."

Brand couldn't take the bullshit any longer. "*Need to know?* You hypocrite! While you've been covering up a leak, one woman has died and another is on the run. And for all we know, there are others in imminent danger. What price your 'need to know' now, Parlane?"

Ellery spoke for the first time in the voice of a reasonable man goaded beyond his comfort zone. "We thought we could contain it—sort it out before too much damage was done."

"Like an oil spillage?" Brand queried.

"Something like th—of course not!" Ellery denied quickly.

"And in your arrogance you didn't inform John, the manager of the Unit, what was happening. Because he's not a cop. Not one of you." Brand's cold tone said it all. "Did you consider that the leak might come from one of the lay members in the Unit and not the police?"

The comical, confused looks on Ellery and Parlane's faces showed they hadn't considered that. Brand stirred some more. "Is your department so corrupt that you assumed...?"

Amazingly neither Parlane nor Ellery leaned across the table and decked him. They looked at each other in silent communication.

Then Ellery looked down at his PDA and twiddled a pen in his long, white fingers. "There was an indication that the leak might be local."

"Define local," John Foster challenged.

Ellery raised his head. "From within our own department."

"What sort of indication?" Brand demanded.

Ellery looked at Parlane. Parlane nodded and allowed Ellery to explain. "We employ several lay office people. Last month there were two attempts to access some files that are off-limits to non-police personnel. Headquarters in Wellington notified us."

"They came from *your* office?"

"Yes," Parlane answered, his face screwed with distaste.

Brand was skeptical. What were the chances that Parlane and Ellery were off-loading the whole problem on to civilian staff? "Whom do you suspect?" he asked.

John Foster leaned forward, anxious to hear the answer.

"A clerical worker. Inspector Friedman questioned her then asked her to leave. She protested her innocence of course."

"But you're not sure she's the culprit?"

"No," Mike Ellery said, shifting in his chair. "But she *was* poking around where she'd no business to be."

To Brand it sounded like normal curiosity that had gotten out of hand. Just the same, he intended to question the woman. How could he find out who she was?

John Turner leapt to his feet. "All this has been going on while I've been placing people in new homes in good faith? Sweet Jesus! Why on earth didn't you—"

"We only found out a few days ago," Parlane interrupted.

"A few days ago!" John Foster's voice trembled with anger. He slammed his hand on the desk. "Don't you care that a few days can mean life or death to these people?"

"Of course I care!" Parlane shouted back.

Now that was not the full truth, Brand thought.

Parlane cared passionately about the reputation of his police squad, but he gave not one brass razoo for the people on the witness program. To him they were numbers. Entry in, entry out. So long as the numbers balanced, Brand was sure Parlane didn't give a toss about them as individuals. And he suspected Ellery was the same.

He stood up. "Here." Unclasping his briefcase, he pulled out a sheaf of papers. "This is an account of what's happened to Célie Francis and me since I went to warn her that her new identity was compromised."

He handed them each a copy. Of course he hadn't disclosed every detail. If the person disseminating information was one of the three men sitting opposite, they'd know the details anyway.

"When you read this, you'll see why I don't intend to hand Célie over for further relocation. Not until we find out where the leak comes from. The way things stand, I wouldn't hand a canary over to any of you," he told them.

Three faces glared at him. He didn't give a damn. He agreed with Célie that they played with people's lives as if they were puppet masters. When they heard his next demand, they'd get even shittier. He closed his briefcase with a snap that overrode the rustle of papers, then settled himself in his chair. "In the normal scheme of things I wouldn't dare to make a request like this, but since my life is in danger..." He paused. "I want to see a complete list of every person on the management committee, both police and Unit members. Including those on the periphery that I don't usually deal with."

"That information is off-limits to you!" Ellery exclaimed.

Parlane said nothing. Deep in thought, he rubbed his thumb across his bottom lip and stared right through Brand.

It seemed that Foster was a speed-reader. He flicked over the pages of Brand's report and into the awkward silence he muttered, "Oh, my God."

"Makes interesting reading, doesn't it?" Brand said.

"Before you get carried away, you should read right through this," John Foster said to Mike Ellery.

Brand sat and waited while Ellery and Parlane plowed their way through the report. Parlane finished first. He went right back to staring hard at Brand.

Ellery kept referring back to previous pages, and the papers fluttered like birds' wings.

Parlane cleared his throat. "Don't suppose you got the numberplate of the maroon Mercedes?"

"Do you think I'd be sitting here if I had?"

Parlane shrugged. "Just thought you might have got one number or one letter perhaps."

"An *M*, but that's all," Brand said shortly. At the time he'd been too busy saving lives to worry about numberplates. He'd castigated himself ever since it had happened. Now he knew why so many witnesses said, "It all happened so quickly. I didn't have time to look at the numberplate."

Parlane tapped something into his PDA. "That *M* will narrow the field anyway." He looked down at the papers on his lap. "As you are so suspicious of us all, I presume this report is not as ah...comprehensive as we might expect."

Brand nodded. "That's right. But there's enough there for you to get your teeth into." He'd avoided mentioning anything that might jeopardize his and Célie's safety. Like the .45. Leaving things out of the equation was not so bad. But once you started outright lying, life got too damned complicated.

"What you're saying, Turner, is that this Cliff Road serial murderer found out about Ms Pearson/Francis' whereabouts from the leak in the system. Is that right?" Foster demanded.

"Yes. And I'm not thrilled at being framed for her murder."

"How's that?" Foster rubbed his temple, looking perplexed.

"I think you'll find that a few little details Turner omitted from his report confirm that," Parlane said.

Brand said nothing.

Ellery sat back in his chair, his legs spread out in front of him. "So," he said in amusement, "you expect us to give you the names of every single person associated with the Unit, just like that!" He snapped his fingers.

"Just like that!" Brand said, snapping his fingers right back. He was sick of them treating him as if he didn't count because he wasn't one of "them." When he'd signed their work contract he'd agreed to a non-disclosure clause. He hadn't seen anything unusual about it and indeed, he couldn't have got the job otherwise. It had never occurred to him that one day he might be driven to desperate measures such as seeking the help of the Press. It wouldn't hurt to let them know he was willing to risk his working reputation if he could use the Press to save Célie's life. Were they aware one of his friends was a reporter? "Yes, I want that list before I leave here today," he said.

Parlane's eyes narrowed. "Or else? You're very cocky all of sudden, Turner."

"Being shot at tends to make a man rather demanding," Brand responded, his tone biting. "And in case anyone thinks to supply me with a little fairy story of names that don't exist, I'm wired." He unbuttoned his jacket. "This will verify what I asked for, if I need to prove it to a higher authority. Or even the Press," he added.

"Thought of everything, haven't you?" Parlane

said, a hint of amusement in his voice. He was probably laughing up his sleeve at a psychiatrist trying to play cops and robbers.

"I've had to."

John Foster sounded sympathetic as he said, "I'm not surprised you don't trust us, Brand. But don't count me amongst your enemies."

"The jury's out on you at the moment, John," Brand said. He'd always thought that John Foster was too pukka sahib to be true, but up till last week he'd have trusted him. Now, however, trust was in short supply.

Mike Ellery looked at Parlane and Foster. "What do you think?" he asked them.

Foster nodded. "Of course he should see the list," he said impatiently.

Parlane nodded and shrugged. "As long as he doesn't interfere with our investigation."

In other words, Parlane didn't expect Brand to make any headway with his inquiries.

Ellery huffed and stood up. "Okay to use your computer, Foster?" Without waiting for an answer, he left the room. But he was only gone for a couple of minutes.

Brand glanced down at the page Ellery handed him. "Hasn't got your name on it, or Parlane's."

Foster raised his eyebrows. "I'll get you my list."

"What are you going to do with these names?" Mike inquired.

"Insurance," Brand replied. "I intend asking Inspector Ralston from Central to investigate the North Shore cops in the Unit. Someone from outside the Unit with some clout is the obvious answer. The sooner the better."

An expression of horror contorted Ellery's face.

"Set a thief to catch a thief, is that it?" Parlane said, his tone dangerous. Then he let fly. "I rue the day we took you on board, Turner. You've been nothing but trouble. You came highly recommended, but in eighteen months I haven't seen any positive results from you."

Brand said nothing. He let the silence stretch. He knew what most of the Unit did not—that Parlane had seriously compromised the search for the Cliff Road murderer. One of his interviewees, a frightened teenager, had complained to her parents that Parlane had tried to intimidate her—which, no doubt, he had. Brand could still remember the skepticism on the faces of Mary-Anne's parents as he had trotted out placatory phrases such as, "We don't think Mary-Anne understands how valuable her evidence is. Detective Sergeant Parlane is desperate to nail this murderer before he strikes again."

The parents hadn't laid a complaint—Parlane had been dead lucky there—but they'd been icily polite. Then the wind had whistled around Parlane's ears as they'd whipped sweet Mary-Anne out of her Cliff Road apartment and back to their own household. They'd refused to allow the police to speak to her again.

"I'm sorry you think I'm not much use to the Unit, Colin," Brand said, not sorry at all. He knew it annoyed Parlane when people he considered non-police called him by his Christian name.

"That's not quite true, sir," Mike Ellery commented. "Brand has been very helpful a time or two."

A time or two. That covered the twelve-hour days, six days a week quite well.

Parlane glowered. Mike Ellery fidgeted, and Brand sat back in his chair and gazed out the window.

Outside, normal people scurried about their lives. Winter had arrived and a vicious wind battered the naked branches of the plane trees lining the avenue. Brand wanted to be out there, protecting

Célie, finding clues. But he'd been forced to come here first. If he had delayed, the police would have bust a gut to pick him up and the danger to Célie would have rocketed out of control. He struggled to maintain a bland expression and squelched an urge to shuffle his feet.

Foster returned with his list. There were five names on it—his own, his two assistants, a lawyer and the M.E. Brand held the two lists, one in each hand, and scanned them.

"So apart from the cops, is this all the Unit consists of?" he asked, startled.

"That's all the time and money the government are prepared to put into it," John Foster said. "We get reciprocal manpower from Central any time we want. And we get by. Or we have till now." He glowered at Parlane and Ellery.

"Do you expect to take those away with you?" Mike Ellery asked, narrowing his eyes.

Keep calm, Brand told himself. This was about to get sticky.

"Yes, I do, because I want Célie to see them."

"Célie, is it?" The insinuation in Mike Ellery's tone would have riled Brand no end under different circumstances. He chose to ignore it.

"Yes, I think Célie has every right to read these lists. After being attacked, stalked and shot at, and having her dog killed, I reckon Ms Francis has the right to go to the Press and ask for help from the public. But we're hoping it won't come to that, and that you people find the Cliff Road killer first."

Parlane cleared his throat, "You know damn well it's a police matter if someone's shooting at her, Brand."

As far as Brand could remember, it was the first time Colin Parlane had ever called him by his first name.

"Normally, yes. But it might be a member of the

police force who's doing the shooting."

"If it is—and there's no way I believe that—then it's only one person. The rest of the Unit would ensure her safety."

"They haven't so far."

Parlane gazed down at his shoes as if he could see the secrets of the universe on his scuffed Kenneth Cole loafers. "What I want to know," he said, "is how this...traitor contacted the Cliff Road killer or whoever is chasing you two."

"Could it be one and the same person?" John Foster asked. He shrugged. "Just an idea. If it's not a cop, then theoretically it could be one of my assistants. We're cleared to access the same information you are."

"Which one did you have in mind?" Brand asked, grinning.

He knew both women well and Helen Argyle, nicknamed Helen of Troy behind her back, was fiftyish, prim, and straight as a die. The second woman, Toni Cooper, was a researcher with a PhD in a couple of obscure fields. Although single, she repulsed all approaches by any male under seventy and kept to herself. The only person Brand had ever seen her warm to was Lilah, and God knew, the profiler could do with some warmth.

Brand looked at Foster. "I still can't get over the fact that you run the Unit with so few people."

"Actually," Foster said, "there was somebody else for a while."

There was a charged silence. Distant traffic noise filtered through the door and windows. Brand, Parlane, and Ellery all leaned forward in their chairs as if to draw closer to John Foster.

"Who?" Brand asked.

"He was a criminology student doing his dissertation on relocatees. Brilliant mind but an unfortunate manner."

Brand's lips twitched.

"You didn't bloody well tell *us!*" Purple splotches speckled Parlane's neck and face as he glared at Foster.

"I'm within my rights to employ whom I like, provided I stay within salary parameters. Chip signed the disclosure. After all, he expects to get a job with a department like ours when he's completed his dissertation," Foster defended himself.

"Just the same, we should have been notified," Ellery objected.

"You listen to me, you two." John Foster jabbed a finger at them. "I'll back my team any day. That's why I'm willing to cooperate with Brand. Have them investigated, but..." He paused. "As he suggested, I want Brand and someone from Central to do the investigation. I no longer trust your lot."

Brand jumped in before Ellery and Parlane worked up a head of steam. "The logical thing to do is to investigate the two ex-employees first. Do I have your permission, Parlane, to speak to the woman you fired?"

"Go ahead." Parlane ground the words out. "She no longer works for us so I can't stop you."

"Yes. Doesn't mean she'll disclose anything of course."

"And my student?" John Foster asked.

"Can you arrange for me to see him soonest? I'll phone Ralston now and explain things." What Brand meant was, "I'll get in first to avoid interdepartmental squabbling."

He walked away from the table and faced the window to make his call. Detective Inspector Ralston was unavailable as usual, so Brand left a message emphasizing the urgency. He turned back to the others and asked, "By the way—who got the dog for Célie?"

"Dog? What dog?" John Foster asked.

"Didn't know she had a dog till I read your report," Parlane answered.

Ellery looked straight at Brand and said, "Nor me, till you told me about him when you phoned on Saturday. She asked me about a guard dog on the day she was relocated. I didn't have time to look into it right away."

"You didn't have time," Brand repeated.

Ellery flushed. "I forgot."

"Well, someone remembered. They left a well-trained security dog tied up outside her door."

"Who would have done that?" Parlane asked, puzzled.

"Maybe one of your staff remembered and did Ellery's job for him," Brand commented.

"Anyway, what's the importance of a dog?" Foster asked.

"Remember the 'curious incident of the dog in the night-time'? Why didn't the dog bark? Think about it."

"Hmm," Parlane said.

Brand could practically see the man's mind spinning with ideas.

Brand's cell phone rang.

Ralston.

"Where the hell have you been, Turner? I've been trying to get hold of you. Something's come up."

"Sure has," Brand muttered.

"What? You in strife over there? Told you to go easy on the North Shore cops." Ralston sniggered. There was no love lost between the two divisions.

"Nothing I can't handle. How can I help?"

"It's the damndest thing. Someone is looking for one of your relocatees."

"You can say that again," Brand muttered.

"Huh? Anyway, it's the woman's long-lost sister. I've checked her out. She seems kosher, although a little flakey. I didn't know how to tell her that her sister's under wraps. I'd brush her off but this is a mercy situation. Her name is Nadine Francis and she's looking for Célie Francis because their father has terminal cancer—liver and pancreas."

Chapter Fifteen

Brian Robinson was puzzled. He'd lost sight of Brand Turner. The guy had disappeared. His house bristled with alarms and Brian wasn't game to attempt a break-in. Not his bag, anyway. Most of the time he just walked into places, often at someone's invitation. Usually a woman's.

He stood, hands on hips, surveying the bushland he'd spent hours stumbling through. Give him city streets any time.

Someone was playing games. Was it the person who'd left that message on his sister's answerphone? Was it Turner himself? Or was someone playing him off against Turner? Whoever it was would be in for a big shock when Brian got things sorted.

"I'll find you and you'll tell me what's going on," Brian said aloud.

A slight rustling in the undergrowth had him spinning around. He yanked Friend out of the scabbard.

"Who's there?" he shouted.

From around the side of the house jog-trotted a woman wearing a red knitted tea cosy hat, its pom-pom bobbing about frenziedly. She carried a shotgun. Glaring at Brian she hefted the shotgun, ready to fire. "Who the hell are you?" she snarled. "Don't tell me there are two of you!"

****

Célie paced up and down the hallway. The two German Shepherds accompanied her.

For once, music failed to interest her. She wondered how Brand was faring. Had Parlane and Ellery "detained" him because he was hiding her? If they had she was on her own, although that wasn't her main concern. She was used to being on her own. But Brand's impeccable work record would take a dive if he was accused of harboring a...what was she? A fugitive? A person of interest?

If she and Sim received news that Brand had been detained, she'd wait until Sim became engrossed in his work at the surgery, then she'd disappear. She'd have to leave a note saying she had a safe place to stay so as not to worry Sim. Sim must never know she had nowhere to go because he was too much like his brother. He'd come looking for her and end up endangering himself. Although he lived by the same set of principles as Brand did, Brand thought faster on his feet and stood a better chance against cops and serial killers and God knew what else.

Anyway, being on her own with her back against the wall was familiar territory. Of course the last time her life had been in real jeopardy was when she was seven years old and Clyde's father had taken out his anger on her. Since then she'd learned a lot. All the same, right now she wished she had someone to turn to. Must be getting soft. Huh! Where were her much-vaunted powers of independence and self-reliance now? Down the gurgler with the death of her best friend, that's where.

Oh, Tara, I miss you. She stopped pacing and clutched the sofa cushion, burying her face in it as her stomach churned. Brand hadn't told her how Tara had died, but if it was anything like the way Occy had met his death, she didn't want to know.

Better to think of Tara as she had been—full of energy with a tongue that swung from sweet to sour in three seconds. What would happen to her friend now? Tara had had no relatives. Would there be a funeral for her?

She resumed pacing, faster this time. *She wouldn't be able to go to Tara's funeral.*

"You've won, you bastard!" she muttered. "You've got me terrified, and you've killed my best friend and I can't say goodbye to her." Her voice rose. "Are you happy now, you raving monster?"

She wasn't just frightened for herself. She was frightened for Brand, too. Brand had done more than befriend her.

He'd frustrated her kidnappers.

He'd kept her hidden.

He'd attacked the killer.

What punishment would the killer mete out to Brand if he caught him? This killer didn't stick to a pattern. Even Brand found it hard to follow the convoluted reasoning of the CRK.

And that was the scary part. What would happen next?

Her cell phone rang. She looked at the display. Brand. Even so, as Brand had instructed she let it ring and go to message bank. Then she reclaimed the message.

"Célie, I'll be away all day because I need to interview a couple of people. I've got a list I want you to look at, to see if you recognize any names. I'll text it through in a minute. But something just happened." Here Brand coughed and hesitated as if he wasn't sure what to say. "A young woman phoned the cops at Central looking for you. She says she's your sister."

Célie dropped the phone. No! Nadine was looking for her? Well, she hadn't looked very hard until now. Her legs shook as she bent over to pick the phone up.

"And Célie?"

"Yes," she whispered, shocked to the core, forgetting she was talking to a machine.

"Your father's very ill, honey. They need you. Call me?"

She keyed in Return Call. Brand answered straight away. She didn't give him a chance to speak.

"*They* need *me*? Where the hell were they when *I* needed *them*?"

"I understand, Célie. And I want to help—of course I do." He sounded harassed. "But it's important that I interview these people as soon as possible. When I get back we'll talk about your family."

Célie felt her self-control begin to splinter. She was being pursued by a murderer and *now* her family decided to make contact? Great timing. "Can't Nadine read a telephone book?" Célie shrieked. "Doesn't she read newspapers? Shit, I'm splashed all over the internet! Where has she been for twenty years? Where has *he* been for ten years? What about my mother?"

"I don't know. But we'll find out. I promise you, we'll be very, very careful when we contact them." He had that hateful, soothing, let-me-take-care-of-it-for-you tone in his voice.

She gritted her teeth. "Forget it. I'm not going to see them."

There was a short silence. "Okay. Your decision. I have to go. Keep safe, honey. Rely on Sim. See ya." And he was gone.

She flicked the End Call button. He was fond of sprinkling "honeys" around. Almost made her gooey. "Come on, Célie," she muttered aloud. "Concentrate." She was playing her old game, diverting her thoughts away from her family. And it wasn't working because thoughts of Brand were just as disturbing as thoughts about her family.

Twenty years. Twenty years and nearly every day of those years she'd needed her mother and sister. Her grandfather hadn't been able to take the sting out of their desertion. He had been a sweet man with a fund of common sense and a strong sense of duty. But nothing could make up for the incontrovertible fact that her mother and sister had dumped her like so much garbage and split when she was seven years old.

But thanks to Poppa and Social Services her father had been forced to pay for her upkeep until she was eighteen. Then she'd snatched the first job she could get, finally able to breathe again, free of the yoke around her neck.

Once, during her one-woman show at the Playhouse, she had imagined she'd seen her father in the audience. She'd caught the flicker of a pale coat as a middle-aged man near the front stood up to leave. But she'd dismissed the idea as ludicrous. Why would he come?

She stalked into the kitchen and poured a glass of water.

By God, she'd worked way too hard for her security to risk becoming embroiled with that rag-tag bunch of misfits known as her family. Gulping down the water, she sneered. Now Nadine expected to crook her finger and her little sister would come running. They'd probably read the tabloids and decided she was raking in the money. That would be it. Their father had conned Nadine and her mother back to his bedside and they'd been making plans.

Of course when she was younger, Nadine would have had to do as she was told. But couldn't she have tried to find her sister when she grew up? Perhaps their mother had forbidden her to. Who knew? Who cared?

Célie stomped around Sim's kitchen. She'd do some cooking. Cooking was good. She glanced at her watch. Two o'clock. Jeez. Time went by slowly when you sat around waiting for a serial killer to pounce. "Stuff you," she muttered to the serial killer. "Thanks a bunch for cutting up my life." Then she decided that "cutting" might not be the best word under the circumstances.

She swallowed down the ever-present little frisson of fear and began wrenching open cupboards and peering inside drawers. Didn't Sim keep any cookbooks? She'd go over to the surgery and ask him. The dogs would go with her.

As she crossed the driveway to the surgery she glanced towards the road. Brand's 4x4, Matilda, stood in the driveway. Today he'd used Sim's old Toyota. Beside the back door of the surgery the tracing unit sat submerged in a bucket of water. She grinned and, unhooking the hose off its reel, added another splash of water just for luck.

Skreeek! The loud shriek of grinding metal and shattering glass pierced the air. Out by the road a man shouted and she caught the flash of sunshine on pressed steel.

The accident was right outside Sim's gateway.

She should help.

She hesitated.

Her heart thudded a frantic rhythm. Sim and Brand had warned her not to react to anything unusual and on no account to go anywhere on her own. "Stay inside till I get home," Brand had said firmly.

For form's sake she'd disagreed of course. "How boring is *that*?" she'd sniped.

Again, she tried to peer down the driveway, her eyes squinting against the glary sun. Couldn't see a thing. Her nose tingled with the acrid smell of burning rubber. "Oh, for heaven's sake, Célie. What sort of terrified woman are you, not to help at the scene of a wreck?" she muttered. She just had to be careful. Slowly she jogged down the driveway, the two German Shepherds frisking beside her. But at the gateway the dogs stopped. The big one slowed, trying to block her from moving forward, while the smaller one began barking in sharp, bone-searing shrills of caution.

The surgery door slammed open and Sim rushed down the long driveway towards her, his arms flailing like windmills. "No!" he yelled.

The urgency in his tone had her skidding to a halt.

Behind her, a motor revved up to a grinding scream. She spun around, startled. A maroon Mercedes mounted the footpath, and like an unstoppable juggernaut it rocked towards her. She picked up her feet and bolted back towards the house.

The car hit one of Sim's gateposts with a sickening thud and hovered, wheels spinning. As Célie reached the safety of the doorway, the driver reversed into the road. Tires screeching, the car sped off.

Chapter Sixteen

Tracking down Chip Edstrom, the eager student that Foster had mentioned, was not hard. Brand ran him to ground in the university cafeteria. Most criminology students wore their ID cards clipped on lanyards around their necks for easy access to locked-off areas. Chip had his head buried in Genge's Forensic Casebook, oblivious to the clink of plates and the raucous laughter around him.

"Chip?"

Chip carried right on reading.

Brand tapped him on the shoulder and tried again. "Chip Edstrom?"

Chip laid his book on the table, keeping a finger on the paragraph he was reading.

"Uh huh?"

When Brand explained the situation, Chip was like a puppy on the trail of a biscuit. "Oh, wow!" he exclaimed, not at all offended at being investigated. "The Cliff Road Killer! I've been following the case of course. Cool. Look, the way I see it, we label them 'serial killers' and give them credit for doing what people have been doing for centuries. The modern psyche demands that we hang the mathematical tags 'serial' and 'multiple' on them, but I reckon..."

Chip reminded Brand of himself as a young, eager student about a century ago.

Chip waffled on. "They are not all predators, you know," he explained earnestly. "Some of them are reacting to tremendous historical abuse with a set of values that..."

Brand tuned out. He was wasting his time. He could imagine Chip talking someone to death, and he could imagine him bludgeoning someone with endless theories, but there was no way Chip Edstrom could ever cut someone's throat.

"I'd like to talk this over with you some time soon, Chip," he said, "but I'm running out of time."

"You be careful, sir," Chip warned him. "And if you need any assistance, just call. I'd be thrilled to help out."

For a moment Brand was tempted. Another educated lay mind to bounce ideas off would reduce the loneliness. He was the only one trying to approach the problem from an angle other than law enforcement. But there were too many people involved in this thing already.

The civilian data processor whom Inspector Friedman had dismissed was understandably reluctant to meet with Brand. He had to do some fast talking to convince her that he was "researching staffing levels" and that he would value any insight she could give him about her experiences in the Unit. She finally agreed to meet him outside a downtown mall where she was browsing—"Not to buy anything," she said with acerbity, "since I was fired without a reference and I've got no money."

By the time they met she had calmed down some and discussed her months with the Unit with a sort of wry acceptance of life's foibles.

Brand realized right off the bat that she knew very little about the relocatees. Although she had managed to dig out details of the Unit's committee and its purpose, she had been unable to access any information about the relocatees. He could do nothing for her, nor she for him, so he bought her a coffee and left her to brood over her own stupidity.

But the profiler had the greatest surprise in store for him. Parlane hadn't said Brand couldn't talk to Lilah, so he walked into her laboratory carrying a cup of caramel latté as a bribe.

"Don't harass me, Turner. I'm doing all I can, considering the measly budget."

"What? Have they scaled down the budget already?" He set the latté down beside her.

She scarcely glanced at it. "Not yet. But they never allowed for such an ongoing investigation in the first place. I'm working nine hours a day on this and being paid for seven," she snapped. "But there's something you need to know if you're sleuthing around on your own. We haven't released this information yet, because the M.E. still has to finish the final autopsy. Also, he's waiting on a batch of skin analysis results."

Brand stared at her. Her normally pale face was pink and she sounded excited, as if something about the investigation intrigued her.

"Brand, Bob Anderson thinks there are two people involved in the killings."

"What?" He stared at her, his head in a whirl. "Two of them?"

She nodded vigorously. "The first three killings were identical in method, but the old man and the girl on the clothesline are different. Not so much ferocity."

Brand was glad Célie couldn't hear Lilah's cool assessment of the evidence.

"The incisions on the old man and the girl were made with what Dr. Anderson calls 'shaky control.' He thinks the first three murders were committed by a left-handed person. But the second two are puzzling. It's as though they've been carried out by someone pretending to be left-handed. The initial impact was strong enough, but it seems as if the perpetrator was unable to sustain an even control.

Dr. Anderson wants to do a re-enactment."

"Why, exactly?" Brand asked.

"He didn't tell me. It's something to do with the girl—"

"Tara. Her name was Tara." Brand felt a cringing distaste at the way Lilah's professional cool would not allow her to acknowledge that Tara, until four days ago, had had a name and a living, breathing identity. Maybe that was how Lilah coped with her job. But he wondered how she'd feel if one day some people stood over her body on a slab and called her "the girl."

"Yeah. Tara. Anyway, Bob is going to contact me when he's finished. Shall I call you?"

"Yes please. At the moment I'm flying blind. Psychology isn't much use when there are dead bodies around."

Lilah smiled her thin smile and said, "Profiling isn't much use when I'm stuck in a room with a real live basket-case either."

Hmm. Lilah wasn't exactly endowed with tact or the milk of human kindness, but she was all he had to work with.

He thanked her and headed home to Célie. How would she react when she heard they were trying to evade not one killer, but two?

****

Brand turned into Sim's street but found his entry blocked. Two police cars, a fire engine, and an ambulance jostled for space in the roadway. What the hell? His heart plummeted. "Please say this has nothing to do with us," he muttered under his breath.

After checking his ID, the cops waved him into Sim's driveway. One of the gateposts leaned at a crazy angle. This *did* have something to do with them.

He rushed into the house and was met with a

deathly hush. Célie was tinkering at the keyboard, and Sim was sitting in an armchair sipping a strong-looking whisky, staring into space.

Whisky? Sim never drank anything stronger than beer. What had happened?

"Ah—any ice in that, bro?" Brand asked tentatively.

"Nope." Sim's voice was different than usual. Sort of flattened.

Brand dropped his briefcase on the floor.

"What happened?"

Célie didn't even look up. She had escaped into a world of her own.

There was a pause. "Someone tried to get at Célie," Sim eventually replied, then took another gulp of whisky. His face creased with distaste, but he held fast to the glass like a lifeline.

"Shit! I was sure she was safe with you and the dogs around."

"It's bad, Brand. The police have just left. There was a car crash out there," Sim nodded towards the road, "and Célie raced out to help. I did too, but when I realized Célie was outside the property, I yelled at her to come back. Just as well I did." He took another swallow of whisky. This time it seemed to go down more smoothly.

Brand strode to the kitchen and came back with some ice and a peanut butter jar, the only glass he could find. Then he grabbed the bottle of Glenfiddich and splashed a healthy dose into his makeshift glass.

"And?" he prompted Sim.

Sim told Brand what had happened.

"Did anyone see who was driving?"

Sim shook his head and swallowed more Glenfiddich.

Brand stared into his drink. She'd been in the worst possible danger *and he hadn't been here, goddamit. He hadn't been here to help her.* "So, do the police have an APB out for a dented maroon Mercedes?" he asked huskily, trying to dislodge the boulder in his throat.

"Guess so."

"Which police?"

"North Shore."

Parlane and Ellery would have heard by now— or would they? They weren't concerned with traffic accidents. He'd better call them.

"Have they identified the young woman yet?" he asked Sim.

Sim shook his head. "No. The car wasn't registered."

"They'll be able to check the engine number anyway."

"I guess."

Sim had obviously just had his first brush with a day in the life of Célie and didn't like it very much.

Brand knew he needed to calm down before he spoke to Célie. He must try to disguise the blazing anger shimmering beneath his skin and inside his head. Judging from her closed-in expression, she would need careful handling.

He phoned Parlane, who was unobtainable. Brand left a message.

Meanwhile his head spun with ideas of where he and Célie could go to hide out.

Célie sat staring at the keyboard, a million miles away. She had cut herself off. This time, instead of using diversion, she had run away from the problem.

He walked over to stand beside her. "Talk to me, Célie." He heard Sim get up and go into the kitchen. Good. If he had to be cruel to be kind, Sim didn't need to hear.

"Talk to me, dammit," he ground out.

She turned her head and stared straight through him. Her wispy brown hair stuck out as if she'd been massaging her head, but her hands lay still on the keyboard.

Damn it to the pit. She had been coming out of her shell and had begun to trust him, but this had set her back on the rocky road to withdrawal again. Fear rose in him, boiling over into irritation. "Don't you dare disengage! Don't do this to yourself. You're a fighter, remember?"

"This is not about *me*!" she flashed, suddenly coming to life with claws unsheathed. If her nails had been any longer she would have scratched his face. Her hands wavered in the air then dropped back on to the keyboard. "Don't you understand?" she demanded. "I thought you would." And her face showed a bitter disillusionment.

His stomach tightened. He had let her down. She expected him to understand that she grieved for the innocent stranger who had died to entice her into the killer's orbit.

He'd misunderstood.

All he'd seen when he walked in the door was Célie in pain, so he'd tried to force her to face what had happened—to short-track her out of the pain. Why couldn't he get it through his thick head that a strong woman used her own resources when the chips were down? So much for his "expertise." It wasn't sympathy Célie needed. She needed to grapple with things her own way.

He straightened up and turned away, unbuttoning his collar. The bloody thing was choking him.

Morosely he told himself he'd walked right into this emotional tie to Célie. He needed to pull back from her—*now*. He couldn't save her life if he was always worrying about her, rather than searching for the pattern in this débacle.

Because there was a pattern. Human beings couldn't help themselves. It was part of the human condition to establish one. A casual onlooker might perceive only randomness, but always beneath the randomness there was a hidden kernel relating to the person's past experiences or emotions. He would find this one.

Then Célie would be free to live her life again—to glow onstage, to charm her audience, to make friends she could trust and maybe to contact her family. Ultimately she would leave him far behind. That was as it should be.

And he would never work for the Unit again. He would go back to working with misunderstood teens and broken marriage casualties. After this experience, attention deficit disorders would be a mere hiccup.

He hefted his briefcase and, leaving the cool silence, walked away to his room.

Chapter Seventeen

Célie stared after him. Oh, rats! What had she done? Brand had rushed in, taken one look at her and realized she wouldn't accept his help. And he hadn't known what to do.

For once in her life someone wanted to help her with no strings attached and she'd shoved him away. She'd ruined it by raging on about the girl who had died. Of course she knew he hadn't forgotten the crash victim. A guy like him—well, he couldn't help but worry about all victims.

So Célie Francis wasn't one hundred per cent at the moment. So what? She fought her own battles. He'd wanted to take on the world for her and she'd given him her usual, *No need, mister. I'll look after myself, thank you. Don't get too close.*

She shouldn't have chilled him. He had called her a fighter—and he'd said it with respect in his voice, and a certain despair. He must be worried shitless.

Time to eat crow.

She unfolded her legs and stalked across the hallway to his room. The door was shut but she didn't knock, just barged in.

He had pulled his tie off and thrown it on the floor. Sitting on the bed with his head in his hands, he didn't hear her come in.

"Brand." She sat down beside him, feeling the bed give under her weight.

He refused to raise his head, so she shuffled closer and slid her hand up his spine to massage his neck muscles with her fingers. They were corded as tight as a lock-box.

"Don't." His voice was muffled. "I mean—" He raised his head and screwed around to look at her. "I'd rather you didn't do that."

She smiled to herself. He even tried to be polite when he was pissed off at her.

"Why? You need a massage. You've had a hard day. Tell me about it."

Jeez. She sounded like the little woman when her man came home from the saltmines. *Hi honey, I'm home*!

"*I've* had a hard day? Then what have you had?" he demanded.

"A weird experience."

"A...?"

"Okay. A very frightening, weird experience."

He broke. Lunging at her, he wrapped his arms around her and scrunched her so tightly against his chest that she hoped her ribcage could stand the pressure. She buried her nose in his shoulder and smiled smugly. At long last she was seeing the real Brand. The Brand she'd known was there. The Brand he kept hidden from the world.

And it felt good to be needed. She couldn't think of a time when someone had needed her.

Of course she doubted Brand would come right out and say he needed her. He kept trying to distance himself from her. Three steps forward and two steps back. But he wanted her all right. Maybe it was the ethical doctor-patient thing—correction, client thing—or maybe it was something else. Something deeper. She'd find out. Because she wanted to. For once she didn't want to keep someone at a distance. Brand Turner with his degrees in criminology and psychology and God knew what else was a man she wanted to know—inside out. She didn't kid herself he'd want her for long. She'd never gone to university, never had the security of a family—all those things that Brand had had. Her very public persona would drive him nuts.

But just for a little while, she could be his.

She disentangled herself and prowled over to the door, kicking off her shoes as she went. Then she snibbed the lock.

Brand stared at her, bemused. He looked like a man who wasn't sure if he was in heaven or hell.

She grinned at him and stripped off her T-shirt.

Brand's eyes almost popped out of his head. All he said was "Uh..." It sounded smothered, as if his tongue was stuck to the roof of his mouth.

Célie sashayed over to the bed and clambered up behind him. Leaning forward, she snaked an arm each side of his neck and began to unbutton his shirt.

He found his voice. "No, Célie. It's not right—"

"That's true. I told you you'd have to beg next time. But I've decided I don't like seeing grown men on their knees. Much better lying down. On a bed." She patted it for good measure.

He stared at her like a hound dog drooling over a pet rabbit he'd been ordered not to touch. Then he shook his head to clear it. "This is not a good idea—"

He was right. It could only complicate things. So what? He was worth it.

"Hey, it's a great idea! Don't rain on my parade, Brand."

She had his shirt off and her busy hands were working their way down...down. He held his hand over hers to stop their progress, then she felt him cave in. He pressed. Hard.

Ha! Got 'im!

"Oh, hell, Célie,' he groaned and rolled her onto her back, pinning her to the bed. He shut his eyes and brailled her face and body with his long, lean fingers. The fingers lingered in a couple of crucial spots. Célie squirmed as she felt the tension climb and climb. She could feel the hot, hard bulge lodged against her stomach. Oh, yes. He really, really wanted her. Every bit as much as she wanted him.

Mmm. Brand Turner was *very* good at this. She purred as his tongue explored the curve behind her ear and one hand slid down to cup her breast. Oh, they should have done this sooner. Curling an arm around his neck, she pulled his face close, desperate to kiss him. She'd been wondering forever about his kiss, especially since they'd come so close a time or two. "Kiss me," she demanded.

She felt him shake as he laughed into her throat. "That sounds like my Célie. Full of orders and demands. Yes, ma'am."

But he hesitated, and her eyes which had drifted shut, cracked open to see what was wrong. He was gazing into her face as if memorizing every feature. She opened her mouth to say, "It'll still be the same tomorrow, Brand," but something in his expression stopped her.

"Brand," she whispered, shaken, shaping her hands to his face as he lowered his lips to hers. But after just a gentle touch, he pulled away. Disappointed, she followed.

"Ssh. Let's take this slowly," he murmured. His tongue tapped along her upper lip, then slid back and forth along her lower lip.

She melted. This was a lover who wouldn't swallow her whole. He sipped in little samples, then went back to make sure he hadn't missed anything. She admired his self-control, even as she felt hers slipping its leash.

Then he slid his tongue inside her mouth and withdrew. In. Out. In. Out. Oh—holy shit! Her legs writhed beneath his. It had never been like this before. She didn't deserve him. She really didn't. But she wasn't going to stop him.

She sucked in her stomach as his fingers fumbled with the brass button on her jeans.

"What?" he asked, looking up.

"Nothing."

"Nervous?"

She gulped and nodded.

"I can stop. I think." The arm he had propped himself up with began to tremble. He could no more stop than she could.

"No! Don't stop, Brand." In a panic she reached down and yanked the button undone. Then she guided his hand to the zip. But after he had eased the zip down, he used the heel of his hand to press on her mound in gentle circles and he seemed in no hurry to pull off her jeans. Hah! She'd soon see about that.

She rubbed her hands down his back, pressing here and there with her long piano-honed fingers, teasing the muscles beneath the skin. Then she clasped his buttocks and raised herself from the bed to rub her breasts against his chest.

His breath hissed in between his teeth as he dragged at her jeans in a sudden frenzy. Good. She held her body off the bed to make it easier for him and came into contact with his magnificent erection. Yum. Her stomach contracted with wanting and every pulse point in her body tingled.

Brand had given up being a gentleman. He ripped his jeans and shorts off together and pounced on her. Célie giggled and muttered, "Oh, yes, *please.*" With each shaky breath he took, she felt the hard, warm length of him pulsing against her skin. Then he shifted to one side and very gently slid his finger inside her. She bucked, every sizzling nerve end burning with need. God, he *must* be able to feel how ready she was, so why not...?

"Condom," he gasped.

Oh! How could she be so stupid?

He wrenched himself away and staggered over to a chest of drawers. In the half-light she had a gorgeous view of taut buttocks. Sigh.

"Somewhere here," she heard him mutter. Just as well he was thinking for both of them. Her lack of restraint with this man shocked her. One-night stands were something she *never* did, but right now she didn't give a damn. She would worry later in the cold, hard light of day.

"Yes!" he called, as if he'd discovered the Holy Grail. She gurgled with laughter when he leapt back on to the bed, frantically trying to rip open the foil with his teeth.

"Stop! You'll rip it. Here, let me," Célie said, taking it from his fumbling fingers. She wondered if she dared put it on him. What would he say?

"May I?" she asked, dangling the ribbed condom in front of him.

"I-I... Please."

He sounded as if he'd never had a woman do that before. Fine. They were even. She'd never done it before either. But oh, she enjoyed it. At last she had the right to hold him in her greedy hand, and she made the most of it—smoothing, smoothing, until he snatched her hand away and ground out between his teeth, "Enough, Célie. Otherwise it will be all over."

Pushing her knees up, he knelt between them and bent his head. Célie tugged at his hair. "Not this time. All of you. Now. Please." She drew out the "please" like a little girl begging for ice-cream. Good Lord, was that her?

Just the same he tested her again with one probing, thick finger and she murmured in enjoyment.

"Guide me," he murmured.

She took him in her hand, but he didn't need any guidance. He slid in, smooth and strong, and she raised her knees higher, wanting him deeper, deeper.

"Yesss," she sighed, echoed by his "Oh...yeah."

He paused, and she gazed up at him anxiously. But he was simply allowing her time to adjust. Then he withdrew and plunged in again and again and again...

Célie's excitement shot off the Richter scale and she climaxed in a spectacular heave that nearly tilted them both off the bed. Brand hung on for dear life and climaxed a few seconds later.

****

Ten minutes later, as she drifted back down to earth, Célie couldn't subdue the helpless tremors shaking her body.

"Are you cold?" he asked, trying to drag the bedcover over them both.

She shook her head. "No. Still recovering."

He grinned like a school kid. "It *was* rather spectacular, wasn't it?"

"Definitely. You are very talented, Mr. Turner."

"Ms Francis, you are not lacking in talent either."

They laughed softly together, until the sound of footsteps outside the door had them holding their breaths.

"Dinner in five!" came Sim's voice through the door.

"Dinnertime already?" Célie gasped.

"Quick. You have first shower. If we go in there together, we'll never make it out again." Brand flung her a sexy grin, and Célie realized that for one glorious half-hour she had forgotten about serial killers and poor dead girls.

As they scrambled for their clothes, she heard the house phone ring. Sim's voice hummed in conversation, then he said clearly, "Go to hell!"

Brand dragged on his jeans and dashed out of the bedroom.

"What? What's happened, Sim?"

Célie strained to hear their conversation.

"Don't worry...going anyway..." was all she could hear Brand say. Then he strode back to the bedroom and began yanking on his clothes.

"What happened? Have you and Sim had a fight?"

The easy-going Brand of five minutes ago had fled. She heard him curse under his breath.

Drat the man. She would *not* let him carry all the worry and fear.

She wrapped her arms around him and held on, forcing him to slow down. "What happened?" she asked quietly. "Tell me."

He looked down at her, doing the inscrutable psychologist thing again. "It's nothing I can't handle."

She pulled back from him. Hell, if she'd had her black kick-ass boots on, she'd have stamped her foot, or better yet, kicked him in the shins. "What is that supposed to mean?" she demanded. "Bloody men! Do you all take a course in being cryptic when you're in diapers?"

He sighed. "It was a threat. Some guy on the phone told Sim to get rid of us or else Sim and his property would suffer 'irreparable damage.'"

"Bastard," Célie snarled. "Is Sim upset?"

Brand grinned. "Nah. He told the guy to piss off. Just the same, pack your bags again. We're leaving."

Chapter Eighteen

"Where do we go from here?" Sim asked at the dinner table. He had politely ignored their eruption into the dining room with *great, mind-blowing sex* written on their foreheads.

"*We* don't go anywhere, Sim," Brand answered. "I've put you in great danger, so Célie and I will leave early tomorrow. I've booked a rental car."

Sim looked horrified. "But where will you go?"

His expression said that someone had better keep an eye on the children.

"Haven't the foggiest idea. I'm thinking. I'm thinking," Brand said.

"Not noticeably," Sim muttered under his breath.

"I heard that, bro." Brand decided Sim was right. It was high time he blanked out the euphoria and got down to business. "Most importantly, I need to tell you both what I learned today." He drew a deep breath. "The profiler told me that the M.E. thinks there are two killers."

"Two?" Sim and Célie said in unison.

Brand nodded, watching Célie carefully. She looked thoughtful rather than terrified.

"Two people working together or separately?" she asked.

Brand shrugged and shook his head. "At the moment, it's just a theory."

She blew out a breath. "As if dodging one killer

is not enough."

"Holy crap! Thank goodness the cops pulled in the CIB," Sim exclaimed. "The locals will need all the help they can get, theory or no theory. You two need to be *very, very* careful."

No kidding, Brand thought. "I've wasted most of today," he said. "I interviewed face-to-face the people Parlane allowed me to. But I intend to dig deep into everyone on those lists he and Foster supplied. Sure, they can refuse to answer my questions, but..." He shrugged. "I can find ways around that."

Sim raised his eyebrows.

Célie, however, knew what he was getting at. "Of course you will," she said. "You're good. You'll have them telling you things they don't realize they've told you.'

Brand didn't reply. For a minute he regretted winkling her secrets out of her, then he told himself to get realistic. He'd needed to know her secrets in order to keep her safe.

"I could do with some help," he said. "The research must be methodical and exhaustive, right down to everyone's associates and family connections."

"You could start that on my old dial-up internet tonight," Sim suggested.

Brand nodded. Dial-up might be slow, but the desktop computer Sim owned was better than his own laptop because he and Célie could work on the desktop together.

****

Two hours later they were cross-eyed from staring at thousands of internet entries. Google and Dogpile were exhausted. And none of the names on the lists rang any bells with Célie, although one had attracted Sim's attention.

"So *that's* what she's doing," he said in surprise. He was referring to John Foster's brilliant young

158

assistant.

"You know her?" Brand asked, raising his eyebrows.

"Used to," Sim mumbled.

Célie glimpsed the haunted look on Sim's face and jumped in. "Well, we've learned some interesting things tonight. We've found out that a local breeder of bullmastiffs is named Parlane. Parlane certainly isn't a common name. And we've discovered that John Foster is so highly qualified he's wasting his time running the Unit." She yawned. "Since we have to be up early, I'm off to bed."

If Sim hadn't been there, she and Brand could have played with a few innuendoes, but poor Sim had put up with quite enough from the pair of them. He would be glad to be rid of them.

That night she didn't have any nightmares at all.

****

They left next morning in a big U-drive car that had been around the block several times. But it was gutsy and powerful enough to outrun any old maroon Mercedes. Brand had decided that the Hilton near the international airport would be a good place to go to ground. The area teemed with people and they'd be hidden amongst the ebb and flow of tourists.

"Great place," Célie enthused, running the palm of her hand over one of the big squishy leather chairs in the living room. She prowled outside to the balcony and peered down into the courtyard below. "Ten stories up. Should be safe, except from Spider Man."

Brand grinned. "The best part is that I intend to demand recompense from the Unit accountants. That'll put a twist in their knickers."

Célie snorted.

"Thank God for wireless internet," Brand said, fitting his laptop into the slot on the worktable set up for internet access. "Ten times faster than Sim's antiquated system, but at least we were able to make a start at his place."

"Did you notice how he behaved when he saw the name of John Foster's assistant?" Célie asked.

Brand glanced up. "Yeah. Took me by surprise. I had no idea he knew Toni."

Célie wandered from room to room. "This is a nice cage, but it's still a cage."

Célie looked the way Brand felt.

Insecure.

Hunted.

"What about a workout in the hotel gym?" he suggested.

Her eyes lit up. "You have the best ideas," she said, giving him a quick hug. He felt it in every nerve-ending beneath his skin. Damn, but it was going to be difficult to give her up when the killer was found. He reminded himself that a relationship between them was impossible with his track record with independent women. Better to remain friends. Uh huh. He'd just keep reminding himself of that.

They bounced into the gym full of vim and vigor and crawled out again an hour later, aching and spent.

"You are so damned *fit*," he groaned, leaning against the wall as the elevator glided up to the tenth level.

She smirked. "I know. I kept count. For every one of your push-ups, I did two. For every one of your ab sit-ups, I did two. But you licked me on the pull-ups."

He choked. "Good God, woman. I should think so. I doubt you weigh more than one hundred and twelve. I'd be a pathetic specimen if I didn't carry more muscle than you." One thing was sure, Brand thought, if she met the killer face-to-face and the guy was stupid enough to give her a little leeway, she'd give him a run for his money.

But he didn't plan for Célie to meet the killer face-to-face.

They attached themselves to the phone and the Net and went hunting. Brand shoved aside the possibility of failure. Failure wasn't an option.

Two hours later Célie sighed as she crossed a name off the list. "I can't get over what the profiler told you yesterday," she said.

Brand thought Célie looked exactly how he felt. Frustrated and desperate. The clock was ticking and all they had was a list of possibles that was getting shorter and shorter.

He walked over and stood behind her. "Here," he said, using his thumbs to massage the back of her neck. "This might help."

"Oh, yeah," she whispered, leaning back into him. But her docility didn't last long. "What are you not telling me?" she asked.

"Not telling you?" Trust Célie to get to the heart of the matter. "Well, Lilah's done hundreds of hours of work on the Cliff Road serial killer, but the police budget..." He shrugged as he continued down to rub concentric circles on her shoulder-blades.

"What?" She sat bolt upright and his hands fell away. "Don't tell me they're giving up already! Are they scaling down inquiries—?"

"Not yet."

Célie glared at him as if it was *his* fault.

Doggedly he continued. "But the budget *has* restricted progress. Lilah is doing hours and hours of unpaid work and she's angry as a hornet."

Célie raised her eyebrows. "Not the dedicated sort?"

Brand grinned. "Lilah's an unusual young woman."

"Did she come up with anything else I need to know about?"

"No." He went back to kneading the muscles on her back.

"Two of them, Brand! I'm scared shitless."

Brand knew if Célie admitted that, then inside she must be a quivering jelly. He was glad she hadn't heard Lilah's cold assessment of the evidence, the way she'd spoken as if Célie's two friends were of academic interest only. He sat down beside her as she pulled a face at the computer monitor.

"From what you say, it looks as if we're still on our own," she said.

Brand tweaked the ends of her hair. "Yeah. We've got each other, and that's about all we've got. I hate this hurry, hurry pressure. I have a feeling that—"

"Me too," Célie agreed. "I'll do all the phone calls if you like," she offered.

"Thanks. First, would you telephone the bullmastiff breeder named Parlane?"

She grinned and rubbed her hands together. "Cool. His phone number's on his website. Stupid man," she added with a superior sniff. "Asking for trouble."

"He probably has heaps of puppies to sell," Brand pointed out.

"Email," she snapped. Then she blocked caller ID and dialed the number. She oozed honey. "Ted Parlane? Great! I'm trying to get in touch with Colin Parlane. Oh, he's your cousin. That's great. Look, Colin promised to find me a bullmastiff."

Brand listened and learned. Oh, she was good.

"I see. So *you* breed the puppies and Colin has nothing to do with the business." She nodded at Brand. "So did Colin pick up an adult male for me, like he promised? I'm out of town at present, but on my way back—" There was some quacking at the other end of the phone. "Oh. You only have puppies. I wonder where Colin was going to get me an adult dog? You don't know? Never mind, at least I don't have to hurry back to town now. Thanks anyway." She clicked off. .

Brand looked at her admiringly. "Butter wouldn't melt in your mouth, you liar."

She shrugged and grinned.

He turned back to the computer. "Well, that's one question cleared up. Let's keep going in the same way. You do the phone calls and I'll continue with the research." A moment ago he'd felt dispirited, but now they were making progress. Negative confirmation was every bit as important as positive information. Facts that didn't necessarily eliminate candidates still added to their store of knowledge. He and Célie made a good team.

Not that it would last, of course. Even if they got through this unscathed, in the end he would disappoint her. Marina's biting words on the day she'd left, scattering belongings down the hallway, were still burned on his brain. *Honestly, Brand. For an intelligent man you can be so stupid! Why won't you give me the space and freedom I need? You smother me.* She'd ground her teeth in frustration. *And I can't stand it anymore.* The slam of the door had echoed through the empty apartment for weeks.

And Célie was much more self-sufficient than Marina for whom "freedom" was a euphemism for "get myself into trouble and resent it that Brand has to bail me out." Célie wouldn't dream of asking for help even if she were on her last legs, so how much more would she resent his smothering? What perverse gene attracted him to feisty women? Lord, he loved women with a streak of mean.

"Brand?" Célie interrupted his musings.

"Huh? Ah, yes. Who's next?"

"Someone named Wainwright. Have you met

him?"

"Yes. He's a constable who does computer research. He's petrified of Parlane."

Célie grinned. "Who isn't?" But she could find no internet references to the unhappy constable. "Phone book," she said, diving for the thick tome on the bedside table. She ran her finger down a page. "Here he is."

"How on earth do you know which one he is?" Brand asked.

Célie stared hard at him and turned the telephone book around to face him.

"Oh!" Constable Wainwright's Christian name was Zacariah. Not a lot of Z Wainwrights in the Auckland telephone directory. One, in fact.

"But what are we going to say?" Célie asked. "I mean, he's a cop, even if he is on the bottom rung of the ladder. You can't just phone him up and say, 'By the way—are you selling information about relocatees?' He'll rush off to Parlane in a stew."

Brand thought hard, rubbing his fingers together. Then he saw Célie frown at his mannerism and stopped. "Well, the odd thing is that Parlane didn't forbid me to interview anyone. He implied that he had his own ideas and didn't care what I did. I think he was humoring me to keep us out of his hair." Exasperated, Brand bashed his fist against the window and Célie jumped. He spun around and tossed the papers on to the bed. "God, I'm slow. He sent me off on a wild goose chase to get rid of me."

"You don't think you're being paranoid?" Célie asked.

"No!" Brand snapped. "I'm trying to be logical and think intelligently."

"Don't trip over your brain on the way to the answer," she snarled.

Brand stared at her. Her fists were clenched and her eyes snapped. Her belligerent stance defied him.

What was that about?

"I'm sorry, Célie," he said at last. He couldn't think of anything else to say.

"Sorry? What for? Being yourself?" She hunched a shoulder and shuffled the papers together.

He persisted. "I mean it. Disappointment made me impatient. I'm not normally—"

"Balls. All men are impatient. Then they get violent. It's part of being a man."

Oh, hell! He stared at her in consternation. He had frightened her and she had come out of her corner fighting. He sat down beside her. "I didn't mean to frighten you."

"You didn't frighten me," she sneered.

He looked at her for a moment and she had the grace to blush. He changed the subject. "Do you want to carry on checking the list?"

For a minute she said nothing, then she nodded.

They checked through the names of the Unit's management committee again. Foster, Parlane, Ellery, a lawyer and Dr. Bob Anderson, the M.E. They tried the lawyer first.

"*Who* did you say you were?" queried the lawyer, bristling with suspicion. Brand crisped his voice up to professional level and listed his credentials before explaining their problem. But there was no joy to be had there. The lawyer had been out of town for the past two weeks, skiing on the southern snowfields. He'd never heard of Célie Francis. Or so he said.

Dr. Anderson, the North Shore M.E., was a different kettle of fish. Brand respected him professionally and he had an idea the feeling was reciprocated. No way could Brand envisage Bob Anderson disclosing secret information. The man was possessed of bone-deep ethics. And judging by appearances, Bob was financially secure. Brand phoned him anyway, because who knew what was hidden beneath a person's surface? Also, he could hear Parlane and Ellery croaking about bias if he didn't treat everyone the same. What was more important in Brand's book was that Robert Anderson M.D., PhD was an expert in forensic mental health.

Brand explained what he'd learned about the medical progress on the case from Lilah, and then floundered around, wondering how to tell Bob he was on their list of suspects. But Bob was way ahead of him. "I guess I'm on your famous list, then," he rumbled. "Good God, Turner. Don't know whether to feel indignant or amused. It'd be a turn-up for the books, wouldn't it, having an M.E. who investigated his own crime scenes?"

Then to Brand's relief he laughed. "Do you honestly imagine that between police crime-scene investigations and lecturing in my so-called spare time"—here Bob snorted at the very concept of spare time—"I would totter around leaking information to a bunch of criminals?"

When Brand explained the process they were going through, Anderson sounded amused at their attempts to play detective. Then he sobered and warned Brand, "Be careful. If someone from the Unit is leaking information, it's being done for a number of reasons, not necessarily money."

Brand blinked. What a fool he was! He had been swayed to the police equation of information equals money. He was so busy dodging bullets he hadn't thought outside the square.

"Someone wants you two dead for reasons known only to them," Bob continued. "Watch your back."

Brand clicked off the phone and walked over to the window, staring out at nothing, thinking about Bob's assessment of the situation. Bob sure had a way with words.

"What is it?" Célie crossed the room to stand beside him.

"Something he said."

Célie glanced at him then stood silently, gazing into space. Which was cause for alarm. Usually Célie waded in with enthusiasm. He watched out the corner of his eye as she wound a lock of hair around her finger like a little girl. She looked as if she were trying to make up her mind about something. Inwardly he snorted at his own imagination. Célie— indecisive? Ha!

"Brand, you said yesterday that my—my sister wants to talk to me about our father?"

At last. The whole time he'd been searching for clues about the informant, a corner of his mind had been occupied, waiting for Célie to acknowledge that startling message. She had told him so little about her family, just that they had gone off and left her when she was seven. These were deep issues for her to work through and the timing could not be worse.

"Yes. Nadine left a phone number."

"Cancer." Just one word, but it held the rejection of years underlain with something else—something that made him ache for her whilst the psychologist in him twitched its tail.

"Did my s-sister leave any other message for me?"

It hurt him to admit it, but he mustn't lie to make her feel better. "Nothing else."

"So they don't really *want* to see me. Father needs to make his peace before dying." She turned to him. "What should I do?"

Brand took her hand. "I'm a psychologist. Guess what I'm going to say?"

Célie smirked. "It's up to you," she chanted. "Do what you think you need to."

Ah yes. Those months in therapy had left their mark. But he refused to let her ride roughshod over him. "Believe me, Célie, if I could take your place, I would. But you have to make this decision yourself.

If you want to see your father, Inspector Ralston at Auckland Central will arrange it so you'll be safe."

Brand's mobile rang and he snatched it up, staring at the caller display panel. "Perfect timing, Ralston," he said into the mouthpiece.

"Oh, God, I hope Dad hasn't died already." Célie pressed her hands over her mouth.

Brand flicked her a quick glance. In spite of her bravado, she *did* care. He listened to Ralston for a minute then sat down heavily on the bed. "Thank you. I'll tell her," he muttered. He moved closer to Célie and took her hand. "Honey..."

"Dad's dead?"

He shook his head. "That young woman whose Mini was trashed yesterday—well, the Mini belonged to Nadine Francis."

Célie's jaw slackened, and for a moment she went away inside herself. Then she came out fighting. "What rubbish! How could she know we were at Sim's place? It can't have been Nadine. Maybe it was a friend of hers who borrowed her car or—" She stopped when she realized the futility of it all.

Brand stroked her hand and said nothing.

She stared into the distance as if trying to recall something. "It's terrible but I don't know what Nadine looks...looked like. How could she have traced us to Sim's house?"

"I don't know, Célie. According to Ralston, Nadine said she'd been watching you for years, against her parents' wishes. They thought it was better to let sleeping dogs lie. Then she lost sight of you. How she tracked us to Sim's, I have no idea."

Célie bowed her head and gave way to wracking sobs that tore at Brand's heartstrings. He gathered her up and let her cry on his chest. It was all he could do. There was a lot of hurt to come out about Célie's childhood, and the psychologist in him wanted to sit her down and help her work through it.

But he was a man in love with the woman in his arms and that was a different thing altogether.

Oh, hell! What was he doing to himself? Struggling uphill had always been his way, but this was his worst mistake yet. He rested his chin on the top of her head and felt like crying himself. Of course he'd seen love coming like an express train on greased rails, but he'd thought he was strong enough to resist. Now he was in for a lot of heartache, a heck of a lot more than Marina had left him. She'd pricked his pride. Célie would pierce his heart with dozens of little arrows, all of them strategically placed, knowing Célie. He smiled into her hair. She was one tough customer. She reminded him of the battery bunnies that kept on keeping on when all the other bunnies had ground to a halt.

But he was tough too. When the case was solved and she left without a backward glance, he'd smile and survive. For one thing he was older and wiser than his Marina days, and he had the scars to prove it. For another, he detected enough guilt in Ms Francis' psyche to weigh down the broadest shoulders, and he would not add to it.

"Brand? I think I should go to the hospital," she finally said, with an inelegant swipe of her hand across her nose.

Chapter Nineteen

Now she was in trouble.

If He found out what she'd done, He'd go crazy. There'd be that gut-chilling silence then the steady measured force of his fists. He didn't fight like the guys she saw on TV, with shouting and posturing. He just hammered silently.

Luckily He didn't use the maroon Mercedes any more. It was no longer registered. The last time He got the car out of the garage He'd lent it to a couple of friends. She hadn't seen the men, just heard their voices through the door.

And a day later they'd brought the car back and there had been a furious argument. He'd shouted at them and they'd sounded placatory. She knew the feeling. When He got like that it was time to back off.

But she'd done it this time. The front of the Mercedes was badly damaged. One tire was burned right down to the rim and the mudguard was hanging off where she'd rammed the girl's Mini so hard that the little car had been shunted backwards. Anyway, she'd got one of them. The girl couldn't tell any more tales.

But once He saw the state the car was in, He would come rampaging into her rooms looking for the hidden door key. After He'd confiscated the first one He hadn't checked to see if she had another. "Confiscated." That was what He called it. Sounded like a schoolteacher.

She wasn't stupid—muddled sometimes in her memory, but not stupid. She'd found the car keys hanging on the same nail where they'd always been. Men were *so* predictable, even the clever ones.

And He was clever. But she was one step ahead of him.

Now she had to find the other girl. She wasn't sure why, but she knew her life depended on it.

****

Célie thought their visit to Auckland Hospital was carried out more like a sophisticated army maneuver than a visit to a dying man.

Inspector Ralston organized two detective constables from Central to collect them from the Hilton. When he phoned, he asked to speak to Célie.

"Ms Francis," he began in his plummy tones, "I am sorry for your loss."

For a second Célie thought he was being somewhat premature, then she realized he was referring to her sister's death. She tried to shove the thought away but her stomach fluttered and burned. She drew in a breath and set her shoulders. *I'm sorry, Nadine. But you must understand I can't afford to give way just now. I have to get through this first. Please forgive me. Later.*

"Thank you," she whispered politely.

"Now—here's what I want you to do. Are you able to disguise yourself in any way?"

"Huh?" For a moment Célie wondered if Ralston had flipped. Then she realized what he meant.

"I could try," she told him cautiously.

"Do, Ms Francis, because if by some chance the stalker finds out your father is in the hospital, you can be sure he'll try to get there. He'll expect you to visit your father."

Not necessarily, Célie mused. Ralston didn't know about her dysfunctional family.

"I'll do my best. Do you want to speak to Brand?"

"Definitely."

Why couldn't the man just say "yes?"

****

Half an hour later Célie was trying on expensive wigs from the hotel hair salon. "If I don't wish to purchase one, can I hire one for a few days?" she asked the haughty blonde presiding over the reception desk.

"Madam wishes to *hire* a hair enhancement?" inquired the blonde, looking affronted.

She took a hasty step backwards when Célie narrowed her eyes and snapped, "That's what I said."

"Well, if madam would wait while I inquire..." The blonde scuttled away, casting nervous glances over her shoulder.

"You frightened her," said Brand's voice behind her.

She turned, grinning. "That was the general idea. I loathe saleswomen in beauty salons and dress shops who treat you as if you're an idiot if you ask for something outside the square."

"Old sales ploy. They put the onus on you," Brand commented. "I'm glad you don't snap at me like that."

Célie rolled her eyes and grinned. "As if you'd care. I don't frighten you in the least."

Brand said something, but he said it very quietly. She wasn't sure what it was but she thought he'd muttered, "Think again."

The blonde returned at that moment and cast an appreciative eye over Brand. Smiling widely she asked, "May I help you, sir?"

"We're together," Brand explained.

"You are?" The blonde's basilisk stare moved from Brand to Célie and back again.

She got her own back on me, Célie thought.

Then the shop assistant added, "Come this way please." She ushered them into a quiet area where, presumably, they would not taint the other clientèle.

"Monsieur Charles will be with you in just a moment," Ms Blonde trilled, casting another look over her shoulder at Brand. Then she wobbled in her butt-hugging tight skirt and ankle-snapping high heels back to reception.

Brand quirked his eyebrow at Célie.

"You didn't have to come in," she muttered. Jealousy was such an embarrassing emotion. She could taste its metallic flavor on her tongue.

"I came in to keep an eye on you."

"You could have fooled me," she retorted.

A smile spread across his face.

"Oh—rats!" she said, before she could stop herself.

He began to laugh.

"Shut up." She turned towards "Monsieur Charles" approaching with an armful of the most unrealistic looking wigs she'd ever seen. Sometimes onstage she had worn a wig just for fun. But this was more a matter of life and death. It sure took the sun out of fun.

She discarded a blue-black Cleopatra look-alike and a perky blonde Pink look-alike and stretched out a hand for a long dark brown one. Then she drew back. No. Too much like her natural style. She went for a pert, blunt-cut auburn one.

As she gazed in the mirror she had an idea. Rather than detract from herself, why not go over the top?

Sweeping out of the salon with Brand carrying the auburn wig in a box, she prowled through the arcade till she found a shoe shop. There she discovered just what she had in mind—an outrageous pair of go-to-hell black thigh-high boots with decorative silver chains that clanked like jailer's keys.

"Hell's teeth," muttered Brand's strangled voice behind her.

"What?" she asked. She sent him a wide-eyed innocent look as she clung to the salesman's arm and delved her foot deep, deeper into the boot. The salesman's eyes gleamed as he smoothed the boot up her leg and knelt down to slide the zipper upwards.

"I'll do that." Brand swept the salesman aside and eased the zipper over her taut calf muscle.

Célie laughed down at him. "What are *you* going to wear?"

"I'll be wearing a police constable's uniform."

She gurgled. "I love it. The cop and the prostitute."

"Umph." Brand's expression was pained, and she understood that the last thing on earth he wanted to look like was a cop.

As he slid his hand up her leg, she stiffened. The hand kept going way up past the end of the zipper.

"Brand!" she hissed. "Behave yourself."

"You too. The salesman's tongue is wiping the floor."

****

In their hotel room they faced each other, the call girl and the cop.

"Hmm," Brand said, circling around her. "Could you possibly get a shorter skirt?"

"Not if I want to bend over."

He scowled. "That's what I thought."

"I'd know you in spite of the uniform," Célie said, inspecting him in return. Ralston himself had delivered a crisply pressed police uniform to them.

"Close up or from a distance?" Brand asked, looking anxious.

She made him walk to the far end of the hallway and decided that from a distance he looked just like any other cop. The hideous trousers and hat were

174

not designed with fashion in mind. He looked like a complete dork. She said so.

He smirked. "Want me to say what you look like?"

There was a knock on the door and he peered through the fish-eye lens to check that it was one of Ralston's minions. Even though only Ralston and a couple of his team knew where they were, it didn't hurt to be careful.

As they drove away in the police issue Holden Commodore, Célie stared at the backs of the heads in the front seat. The men were friendly enough, but she had been startled to see the plainclothes detective checking his Glock as they pulled away from the curb. Until now she and Brand had made their own decisions, right or wrong. Now their autonomy had been taken away. Bored, cold-eyed cops who saw the scenario as just another job were in charge.

As the driver pulled into a reserved parking space outside the hospital, the other detective jumped out and dashed around to Célie's door. The driver pulled his Glock out of a compartment under the dashboard and slid it into his shoulder holster. Then he, too, got out and motioned to Brand to walk in front of him.

Célie's stomach churned. She had avoided thinking about her father for the past couple of hours. Now she couldn't avoid it any longer.

The police knew which ward to head for. Silently they all entered an elevator. Brand looked at Célie and gave her a half-smile. She felt a little better. He understood.

"Your father's room is this way," the lead detective said as the elevator doors opened. "Because he's terminal, he has a room on his own."

Jeez, a real charmer, this guy. No polite condolences. No emotional connection. A man was dying. His daughter wanted to see him. The daughter was under threat. The police would protect her. End of story. She hoped one day Mr. Hotshot Detective faced a similar situation, preferably before he escorted someone else to hospital. He needed a few lessons in compassion.

She flicked a glance at Brand and caught him surveying the detective clinically. What a fine time he'd have with Detective Hotshot's psyche!

"Here."

The squad halted outside a closed door. Detective Hotshot opened it, peered inside, then pushed Célie into the room with a hard hand on the small of her back He followed close behind.

She turned to glare at him. "I'd prefer to be alone with my father."

He glared back and shut the door in her face.

Célie peered into the gloom. The dun-colored curtains were drawn against the blue of the day, and the room smelled acrid and fusty like every other sickroom she'd been in. A bedside lamp threw a strip of pale yellow across the covers on the bed where a hand lay twitching spasmodically.

Her heart thudding, she tiptoed closer.

Ten years.

They had taken their toll.

His eyes were closed and his chest rose and fell so slowly that she held her own breath, waiting for him to inhale. His scaly skin looked dry and wrinkled, and the hairline had receded out of sight. Chemo perhaps? Tubes snaked from one arm up to two machines clicking and burbling away beside the bed.

The room was excruciatingly white and tidy. There wasn't anything in it except a locker, two machines, and a bed on which lay a dying man. The bathroom door stood ajar and she glimpsed the edges of a shower and toilet.

Nobody had sent flowers. No dressing-gown was tossed over the bed. There were no slippers underneath the bed.

Emptiness.

The hollowness echoed inside her. Gathering herself together she trod towards the bed, her sexy boots clumping on the cold, polished floor.

"Dad?"

Blue-veined eyelids flickered above the pasty face.

She waited.

Machines bleeped into the silence.

After a long time he asked huskily, "Who...? Nadine?"

"No. It's Célie."

"Célie? Célie?" The eyes widened, vacant and glassy. Morphine, she guessed.

"No. Go. You and Nadine. Go." He gasped for air, then choked.

She had expected this. She swallowed the disappointment. "I came to say goodbye."

Outside in the corridor, shuffling feet passed the door and moved away. Célie looked around for something to sit on. She refused to leave before they had talked.

She would not sit on the bed. That smacked of a cozy relationship they did not have.

There was a strange smell rather like incense that she couldn't identify. For some reason it reminded her of her mother, all those years ago. Must be because of being here with her father like this, she guessed.

"Goodbye." The voice from the bed sounded clearer this time. "I saw you once, in concert." Then the voice died away again.

Startled, she leaned over him. "So it *was* you!"

Now what should she say? What did you say to an estranged father who had turned up out of the blue to check out your show?

The faded grey eyes slitted open again, then closed. He took a shallow breath. "Keep away from her."

"Who?"

"*Her.*" He sounded irritable, as if she was an idiot not to understand his morphine-induced ramblings.

A slight movement beside the bathroom door caught her eye. She hadn't heard a nurse come in, but she was glad someone was there. She needed to talk to a member of the medical staff to find out what she should do about her father. Now that Nadine was dead, it was her responsibility to find out how long he had left, to make sure he had plenty of pain relief.

Her father's hand moved on the covers. He seemed to be reaching for her. Tentatively she laid her hand on top of his. His turned with shocking strength to grab hers, his fingers pinching her skin. "Go," he whispered. "Now!"

Célie was nonplussed. He had come to see her one-woman show, so he must have kept up with what she'd been doing over the years instead of cutting her out of his life as she had always believed. Yet as he lay dying, all he could say was, "Go."

His bony fingers bit deeper into her hand. Drawing in a deep breath he rasped, "Go now, Célie!"

Startled, she drew back. Her father's eyes flicked to something behind her and she spun around.

Too late. A heavy blanket dropped over her, and a rush of panic had her stifling in its dark, choking folds. She heard her captor breathing heavily and felt his feet grappling for purchase on the slippery floor. Hard arms hefted her up onto a shoulder where she teetered like a bird about to take flight.

Fight, Célie, fight! You're a fighter, remember. Yes, Brand. I'm a fighter.

Driving deep with the pointed toes of her outrageous boots, she kicked her captor as hard as she could and was rewarded with an agonized "Ahhh." Definitely a man. Whoever it was, she'd got them where it hurt most. Elated, she bashed her head as hard as she could against his chin till the top of her head pounded with jags of pain, and she couldn't take any more. Changing tactics, she wriggled and bounced like a demented earthworm, trying to slither out of his hold. His grip slackened.

Then a persistent buzzing sound filled her head. Oh, God. She must have banged her head so hard she was losing consciousness. Or had he doped her and she hadn't felt the needle?

She felt herself falling, and her hip and elbow cracked on to the hard floor. Footsteps pounded towards her father's bed and the buzzing sound stopped. Fighting to extricate herself from the tight folds of the blanket, she could hear a strange gargling sound and then the slither of a sliding door. Footsteps thudded towards her.

Bunching her legs as best she could, she lashed out with both feet at the nearest source of noise.

"Ouch! Shit, Célie! It's me. Brand."

"G-mmmm-ff."

She felt herself being unrolled like a carpet runner, one that had been thrown over the clothesline and beaten with a broom to get rid of the dust.

Lying prone on the cold floor, she spat out fluff and gulped in air. Conscious of several pairs of feet around her, she propped herself on an elbow. "I'm all right," she mumbled. Two pairs of feet disappeared as someone helped her up.

"Sit on the bed," Brand said. His voice was strange, and she glanced up at him, licking the blanket residue off her lips. His face was a mask she couldn't read. Running feet pounded down the corridor outside and Brand's head swiveled towards the door.

She reached out a hand. "Are you okay?" she asked.

"No. I'm *not* okay. How the hell did he get in here? What were the cops doing?"

At the head of the bed, an intern struggled to re-insert the IV line into a vein on her father's hand.

Célie watched anxiously. "The attacker was in the bathroom. My father tried to warn me but I didn't understand." She heard the intern curse under his breath and she scrambled closer. "Dad?" The sheet-white face and blue lips testified to unbearable pain.

The intern worked frantically to re-establish the pain relief line. "Someone yanked the drip right out of his vein," he hissed between his teeth as he struggled with the collapsed vein. "Who pressed the buzzer?"

"He did," Célie choked. "My father did. I wondered what the noise was. I couldn't see inside the blanket and he-he—"

"He saved your life," Brand ended for her.

A nurse scurried in. "Help me with this," the intern muttered. "Quick!"

But it was too late. With a slight, murmured exhalation, Tom Francis let go.

Célie sat holding the lifeless hand while all around her people spoke in whispers, as if that could assuage her guilty grief. His death left more questions than answers. From a distance, she heard Brand demanding explanations from the police.

"We didn't know about the new system of interconnecting bathrooms on this floor," the detective explained. "They were installed recently to ease the load of the nursing staff. The guy threaded his way through a couple of rooms and bathrooms and took the stairs to another level. Hospital security is searching for him."

"Security cameras?" Brand inquired.

"Only in public areas. Dying people like privacy," the intern answered.

Célie could understand that.

"But there are security cameras on every stair level and in the elevators," the nurse offered.

"Then he might still be here somewhere!" Brand exclaimed.

A uniformed constable poked his head around the door. "Excuse me, sir. You need to see this," he said to Detective Hotshot.

A hospital security officer dressed only in his boxers had been found unconscious in a stairwell. The security screen on that level had been sprayed over by someone wearing a double stocking mask. Impossible to tell if they were male or female, let alone get a clear description.

And two levels down, the camera showed a security officer walking away from the camera, his cap pulled low over his face, flipping the camera a two-finger salute.

Chapter Twenty

Brand kept a wary ear open for Célie. Since they'd returned to the motel she'd been brooding in the bedroom. He'd left her alone to grieve.

He flicked on the TV. Anything was better than going over and over stuff in his mind. His heart had stopped for a few seconds when that buzzer rang. Thank God her old man had cared enough to call for help. Or perhaps he had just been trying to protect himself.

One thing Brand knew for certain—Célie was amazing. In spite of the attempts on her life, each time she managed to drag herself back off the ground. Marina she was not. Marina, who had so wanted her "freedom," would have been a whimpering puddle on the floor by now, expecting Brand to keep her safe.

Charging into the room suddenly, Célie said, "I think this is about my family."

"What?" Startled, Brand turned to stare at her. "All those murders?"

"No-o-o," she said. "But I think the attempt to grab me from Sim's place, Nadine's death..." she drew a breath "...and today's stuff is all to do with my family. Somehow," she ended, shrugging helplessly. "My father told me to 'keep away from her.' I don't know if he meant Nadine or my mother, because he wouldn't have known that Nadine is dead. Well, I haven't seen my mother in twenty years, but whether she likes it or not, she's going to have to see me now. We have two funerals to arrange."

She returned to the bedroom, pulling the door shut behind her.

Brand tilted his head to one side and stared at the closed door. Was that a message saying "Come and get me?" Or what? Ah, to hell with it, Turner. Just go in and get the girl.

He eased the door open and she looked up with a half-smile. She had, in her own inimitable way, been saying "Come and get me."

"Tell me why you think this is about your family," he said, leaning against the door-frame.

"Because Nadine's death was no accident. According to witnesses, the driver revved the vehicle and drove straight at her—twice. Someone has tried to kidnap me, and now they've killed Dad. Wherever my mother is, she needs to be warned."

Brand hesitated. "But how could your family be linked to a serial killer?"

A minute's silence stretched between them while she looked down at her hands.

He said gently, "Célie, I know you don't want to talk about it, but you need to."

She pushed past him and pranced in those mind-bending boots to the sofa. Then she flung herself down and stretched out her arms. "Is that so? Go ahead then, doctor man. Tell me what I need." Her head tilted back in a challenge.

Brand damn near choked on his tongue. Tell her what she needed? Oh, boy, oh, boy, oh, boy. *Me. You need me,* he wanted to say. But of course he couldn't. She was gutsy and striking and savvy, but she wasn't for him.

When this was over he'd read about her in the papers and see her on TV. One day she'd refer to "my fiancé" during an interview, and all hope would die a natural death. The fiancé would be in show business, like her. He'd be ambitious and have loads of musical talent so he could help her with her career. He'd be outgoing and charming. And he certainly wouldn't drag her into danger.

Whoever he was, Brand hated his guts.

Shoving his thoughts aside, he gestured to Célie to move over on the sofa. He tucked himself beside her. "Tell me about your family," he urged her.

****

Célie felt everything inside her crumble. This man could coax a secret from 007 and she needed to tell *someone*. Someone like Brand Turner who wouldn't judge the dysfunctional family they'd been.

So she told him about the early years, the happy years. She flicked over the time when her mother had begun her secret drinking and become first querulous then demanding. She touched on her father's growing impatience and anger, and as she talked, she listened to the words that came pouring out. She listened and she learned.

She'd never considered her father's point of view before. After all, he had thrown them out, hadn't he? So she'd believed he was at fault.

Now, years down the track, she heard her words and wondered. Why had she never remembered the months she and Nadine had come home from school to find their mother stretched out on the sofa in a chaotically grubby house, clutching an empty bottle of whisky? Why had she buried those memories?

Brand asked mundane questions. Once he asked her, "Did your father always have work?"

"I-I don't know." Célie realized she knew nothing about her father's job. As a child, she had seen him leave the house about the time she got out of bed, and arrive home while she and Nadine were watching TV, stomachs rumbling. Their mother rarely prepared dinner because she never ate it.

When they were old enough, the sisters fended for themselves, but Célie couldn't remember making any dinners for her father.

After a silent dinner alone, her father would get up from the table and pile the dishes in the sink. While she and Nadine fought over who would have the first shower, their father washed the dishes and picked up the junk lying around the house.

Drones, he had called them. Yes.

When they were very young their mother had instructed them that men worked to provide money for their women and children. But she never mentioned that hard work and sharing was a two-way street. Célie cringed inside. They had taken him for granted, never seeing him as anything other than a meal ticket.

Now he was dead and she could never atone. She owed the man her life and she could never tell him how sorry she was for taking him for granted. "I hate myself," she wept, drooping over Brand. "What did we do to him? We were all so selfish."

Brand said nothing, just rubbed her back.

"And when they notified my grandfather that I was in hospital—"

"Hospital?" he interrupted.

She told him her tawdry little history and how Social Services had hounded her father until he'd made the minimum payments for her upkeep.

"Why do you think he was reluctant, Célie, to hand over money to his father for your upkeep? He could trust it would be spent wisely."

She shook her head. "Not always. Sometimes Poppa got phone calls from my mother and he would say he had to go out. Then he'd take some money from our stash in the coffee jar and go out for a while. I knew he went to meet my mother and give her money."

"Your grandfather probably hoped it would be

spent on Nadine."

"I guess so." She rested her head on his chest, rubbing her cheek against his sweater. It was comforting to have him listen objectively. His questions had helped her to look hard at the unhappy family the Francises had been.

Really, she knew of families with worse problems than hers had faced. Her mother had been the catalyst of most of their troubles, yet Célie could remember a time way back when the family was a happy, solid unit.

"What stressor started your mother drinking?" Brand asked.

"I don't know. Looking back, she always seemed to have a drink in her hand. Nadine might have remembered but..." She trailed off.

There was a short silence. Then Brand asked, "Dinner?"

"Uh...yes. Good idea." Reluctantly she pulled herself away. This leaning on him was getting to be a habit. Damn it all. She wanted her life back—the life where she didn't lean on anyone, where she was self-reliant and confident and happy. Of course, if she had to lean on anyone at all...

She bounced up off the sofa. "Can we eat in one of the restaurants here?"

He smiled, unfolding himself from the sofa cushions. Lord, he was tall. And hunky, and...different. Sigh. *Control yourself, Célie.* He'd made no moves on her since the other night. And she'd made the first move there. She prided herself on helping him out of the blue funk he'd been in that night anyway. And the sex had been great. No. More than just great—stupendous.

"I'll change out of these clothes." She rushed to the wardrobe in case her face showed her thoughts.

"I'd be grateful," he called out. "Not that keen on being seen with a hooker."

She grinned to herself. She wasn't that keen on looking like one either. The disguise hadn't worked anyway. Whoever was after them had been one jump ahead. Someone apart from Nadine had known her father was dying and had expected her to come and see him.

Try to forget it for a while, Célie. You're going out to a cordon bleu dinner with a fabulous guy.

They went up in the elevator to the rooftop restaurant. Although part of the view was the border of the airport, most was of a green vista of fields surrounding a ruffled, deep lake.

"What do we do now?" Célie asked around a mouthful of salad.

His cell phone rang. He listened for a moment, said "yes," and clicked off.

Swallowing a mouthful of wine, he explained. "That was the inspector. Parlane has asked to meet us on neutral territory in Ralston's office. He has something to tell us. And something to ask us, too, of course."

Célie grinned. "I'll show you mine if you show me yours."

Brand's eyes glinted over the rim of his glass. "Do much of that when you were young?"

"When I was young? Hey! I sometimes do it now I'm older. Not often, mind you. Just for special people."

There. She'd gone as far as she could.

Brand's cool hazel eyes surveyed her with amusement—and something else. A sort of yearning. Then the lids dropped, and he looked down at the table.

"Finished? Or would you like dessert?"

Oh, would she! But it didn't look as if she was going to get dessert tonight. Damn.

"Coffee?" she tried.

"Got some back in our suite."

She gave up. Rising, she tossed her table napkin on to her chair and stalked in her librarian-strength, sensible shoes towards the elevators. She was obviously no femme fatale.

Chapter Twenty-One

Parlane glared at them across Ralston's desk. His hands were propped on his thighs as if he was ready to lunge to his feet at any second. His eyes were flat and angry. Whatever had bitten Parlane's backside was a biggie.

"Anyone else coming?" Brand asked.

"No." Parlane's voice was sharper than a fleshing knife.

Startled, Brand almost gasped aloud. If Ellery wasn't shadowing Parlane as usual, then maybe Ellery was the informant! No wonder Parlane was devastated.

Beside Brand, Célie sat up straighter in her chair.

Ralston said nothing. He surveyed them all with a cool, assessing stare.

"Inspector Ralston supplied me with some...useful information." Parlane ground out the words. "His squad trawled through the phone records of everyone in the Unit. They discovered that Ellery called Mrs. Cameron from his home phone two weeks ago."

"Surely that's not all you have to go on?" Brand protested. "Mike probably rang to tell her the program had been compromised. He knows...knew her quite well. He arrested her husband last year, but couldn't make the charges stick." He was trying to needle Parlane into admitting there was much more to it than that. Unless he pushed hard, Parlane would continue with his need-to-know routine. It wasn't that Brand found it difficult to see Ellery in the role of informant. He'd tried to keep an open mind so he could envision any one of the Unit members in that role—still could. But he wanted to know what else they'd discovered.

"He's either innocent and clairvoyant, or guilty as hell," Parlane responded drily. "He phoned her three days *before* we confirmed we had an informant in our ranks." Here Parlane paused, looking as if he was chewing nails. "I believed him when he said there wasn't enough evidence to convict Cameron, and when Cameron was murdered by his associates we relocated Mrs. Cameron and closed the file. It seems Ellery has friends in low places." Parlane scowled. He mightn't like what he'd found, but he didn't make excuses.

Ralston asked, "Have you had time yet to ascertain how much information he's passed along?"

Parlane shook his head. "Difficult to say at this point. He transferred into the Unit a couple of months after its inception, so there's a huge pile of data for the analysts to work through. It's made more difficult because a lot of relocatees stop checking back in with us in spite of our instructions. They seem to feel safer that way. Some go overseas or go deep under locally. Cut all ties. Added to those, we have to review all the files on anyone Ellery brought in for questioning but released for lack of evidence. I can tell you this, though. Over the past year he's made scores of unauthorized calls hunting up unlisted numbers."

Brand kept a wary eye on Célie. As the two cops yammered on, her face darkened and her fingers twisted the leather handle of her handbag. Anxiety pulsed off her in waves and he knew she was wondering the same as he was. Was Ellery just a crooked cop or was he connected to the Cliff Road killer? And who was the second killer?

Without compunction he interrupted Parlane and Ralston's gabfest. "Where's Ellery now?" he asked.

"He's been stood down and is being watched. Unless there's irrefutable proof, we can't hold him on suspicion. He point-blank denied everything but we were able to force him to take leave on the strength of those phone calls. That's all we've got so far."

Brand wondered if Ellery had contacted the Police Union or if he'd get himself a solicitor. This whole thing would be bogged down in drama for weeks to come.

Célie spoke for the first time. "Where does my attacker come into this? Do you think Ellery knows the identity of the Cliff Road killer? Could the two of them be partners?"

Brand watched Ralston and Parlane fumble the ball. "We don't think so, Ms Francis," Parlane said eventually. "My guess is that Ellery was approached by either the killer or an intermediary and he passed over information for a fee as usual, not realizing who he was dealing with. He was in the box seat when it came to tracing you—until you and Turner took matters into your own hands."

Parlane still sounded pissed off about that. Brand couldn't care less. He'd kept Célie alive by mistrusting everyone connected to the relocation program, and he'd been right all along.

Célie got there before Brand could ask. "My dog. Did you check to see if Ellery knows someone who breeds security dogs? It's strange that Peaches didn't bark when we were in the bushland. I'm sure Peaches knew whoever was chasing us."

Parlane shook his head. "I doubt that has anything to do with Mike Ellery, Ms Francis."

Célie leapt to her feet. Uh oh. Parlane was about

to get seriously whipped. Brand sat back in his chair and watched the show.

"Bullcrap! I bet Ellery knows who the killer is. How come the killer has been one step ahead of us all along? Eat this, you cretin." Celie's voice rose to a shout. "My family has been wiped out! Get it?"

From the pained expression on Parlane's face, he got it.

Ralston smirked. "Ms Francis, I've received instructions to take over the CRK investigation. I can't guarantee your safety—nobody can—but I *can* assure you of my impartiality." Ralston's glance at Parlane was nothing short of condescending.

Brand flinched. He felt downright sorry for Parlane. If anyone had looked at him like that, his teeth would have itched. Shockingly, Parlane did not vent his spleen on Ralston. It was a measure of how devastated he was by Mike Ellery's betrayal that he could not dredge up a single, snarky retort. "It had to happen I suppose," was all he said. "I'd do the same thing in the Inspector's shoes." Then he turned to Ralston. "But don't imagine I'm going to sit on my hands while you poke around my team. I won't let this go."

"What a perfect policeman!" Ralston said, oozing false admiration.

That was uncalled for. Brand narrowed his eyes. There was something off about Ralston's attitude. Brand went in to bat for Parlane. "He is, as a matter of fact. Always got the police's best interests at heart." It didn't come out quite the way Brand had intended, but near enough. He earned a grateful but puzzled look from Parlane.

"Hmm." Ralston hummed as he began shuffling papers around. "We won't keep you any longer, Colin. Let us know of any progress you make." His offhand tone sounded as though he didn't expect Parlane to make any progress at all. Was it professional jealousy or an old score to be settled? Brand and Célie couldn't afford to be caught between two ambitious cops with axes to grind. For a moment Brand tossed up letting it go. Then he thought, to hell with it. His and Celie's lives were at stake. "If you two have a history, leave it at the door," he advised. "Ms Francis and I need you to catch these killers as soon as possible—and so does everyone else in the community."

For a second, both men looked taken aback. Ralston recovered first. "Quite right, Brand."

Parlane just grunted and stalked out of the room, slamming the door behind him.

"You can be sure," Ralston said to Célie and Brand, "that I'll review every single file of Ellery's myself. I'm curious about the exact date he applied to transfer from the burglary squad to the Unit. He might have seen it as an opportunity for advancement or there may be something else behind it. But he strikes me as more of a white collar cop than one who's used to getting his hands dirty. I can see him as an informant, but there's no way I see him as a killer."

"But the M.E. thinks there are two killers involved," Célie protested.

Ralston nodded. He stretched his long legs out in front of him and lay back in his chair. "As far as the murders go, we're back where we started. I'll order in some coffee, Ms Francis, and you and I will go through your evidence once more."

"Oh, hell," Célie muttered, sotto voce.

"Tell him about the woman, Célie," Brand urged her.

"Woman?" If Ralston hadn't been such a smooth operator, his jaw would have dropped.

Célie touched Brand's arm. "Please stay," she said.

Brand looked down at his hands. In front of

Ralston, she'd asked him to stay. She trusted him—or at least she trusted him more than she trusted Ralston. It was going to be so hard to let her go.

****

For two hours they thrashed out details back and forth. Célie got more and more uncomfortable as Ralston took copious notes, every now and then saying, "That isn't on the file."

Eventually she admitted, "Ah...I probably wasn't as cooperative as I might have been with the North Shore police, Inspector."

"Why?"

"Because at first they acted as though they didn't quite believe me," she snarked. "Especially Ellery. Look, my hands were shaking; I couldn't stop crying. Did the idiots think I'd concoct a story about being pursued by a killer for fifteen minutes of fame?" She shrugged. "There was no point in cooperating."

"Anything else you might have ah...omitted, Ms Francis?"

Célie grinned at Ralston. "Very diplomatic. There's something rather strange I can't explain."

Ralston leaned forward. "Yes?"

Wolf on the trail, Brand thought. Ralston wasn't methodical like Parlane. He raced off with a scent, his nose to the ground. Here's hoping it brought results. Sometimes instinctual experience and thoroughness like Parlane's brought better results. He knew Ralston better than he knew Parlane, but whichever way you sliced it, Ralston was still a cop and cops needed to go about things in a proscribed way. Ralston might have the wolf instinct but in the end his hands would be tied by rules.

"When I visited my father at the hospital, there was an unusual smell in his room that reminded me of m-my mother." Célie peered at Ralston through her bangs of chewed hair and Brand's heart contracted. For all her punch, she reminded him of a waif in a picture he'd hung in his office. The waif was an orphan, uncertain of her welcome at the back door of one of England's stately homes. He wanted to open that door and invite her in out of the snow and keep her safe.

"What sort of smell?" Ralston asked. He tapped his pen on the writing pad in front of him.

For a moment, Célie hesitated. "It's like candle wax," she said.

"Candle wax?" Ralston repeated blankly.

"Yeah. I guess I associate it with my mother because she liked to take long baths with perfumed candles burning on a table beside the bath." Célie shrugged.

"Our memory sometimes plays tricks on us." Ralston turned to Brand. "I guess that's something *you* should explain to Ms Francis, Brand."

"I smelled it before, recently," Célie said, her nose wrinkled in puzzlement.

Brand stared at her. "When?"

"That day on the beach when Occy and Tara and I saw the sick woman stumbling around. She was very distressed—worse than usual. We tried to talk to her but she pushed Occy aside and ran away. I hadn't thought of it before. Sorry."

Ralston looked at Brand. "Maybe this woman on the beach had been burning candles," he suggested.

Brand sat bolt upright in his chair. Stunned, he wondered if his surmise could possibly be true. "Célie, did your parents get divorced?" he asked.

"I should think so. Dad would have made sure he didn't have to pay out any more than was necessary. If Mother was free she'd have the option to remarry and let him off the hook financially. She was always on the lookout for better prospects."

Brand winced, glad he didn't have kids.

Ralston glanced at his watch. "Okay. I really

want to pursue this but I have to go. Got a meeting in five." He stood up, every inch the busy executive.

Brand opened his mouth to tell Ralston about his suspicion, but Ralston was stuffing documents into a satchel, his face remote. His mind was already on his next meeting. Ralston should have been a businessman not a policeman, Brand thought. Before this meeting he would have said he trusted Ralston more than Parlane, but something about the rivalry between the two had eroded that trust.

"Anyway, we've made a little progress today. When I leave here, I'll have a trace put out on your mother. She must be warned she's in danger." Ralston nodded to Célie as he ushered them out of the room.

And just how the hell are you going to do that? Where will you start? Not for the first time today, Brand wondered if Ralston was a step or two ahead of them—that he knew more than he was telling them.

"Same time tomorrow morning, Ms Francis, so we can wrap this up." It was an order, not a suggestion. "You too, Turner, if you want," Ralston added.

Brand wanted. Mostly he wanted Ralston to stop fiddling while Rome burned. Ralston was no improvement on Parlane when it came to preconceived ideas of what questions to ask and what bells to ring. As far as Brand could see, they had two murderers breathing down their necks while the cops played by the book. Thank God he was a civilian. He didn't have to play by the book.

Detective Hotshot drove like a maniac back to the motel, glancing several times at his watch, insinuating he had better things to do than babysit a couple of idiot civilians.

Brand hung on to the safety strap and grinned across at Célie.

But Célie had shut down. She huddled in the car seat, her fingers kneading and plucking at the outsize handbag she carted everywhere with her.

Brand put his hand over hers to still the restless movements and she snapped out of her reverie. She turned to him, twining her fingers through his. "Know what I'd like to do?" she asked, tilting her head to one side like a robin.

"No." He smiled, then grinned as she slid her hand up his arm. "Oh."

"How do you feel about that?" she asked, rubbing her foot up the side of his leg.

How did he feel? Edgy, needy and freaking uncertain, that's how he felt. He leaned across as far as he could with the safety belt cutting into him and nuzzled her neck. But Célie was having none of that. She yanked his head closer and ran her tongue around the rim of his lips. Then she set to work to show him just what two people could do, hampered by safety belts, in the back seat of a police car. God, Brand couldn't tell which way was up and when the car lurched to a stop, he raised his head and looked around dazedly.

Hotshot glared at them as, disheveled, they clambered out of the car.

When they reached their suite, Célie grabbed Brand's hand and tugged him into the bedroom saying, "I need this *now*, Brand."

Did she think he was going to object? Not hardly.

As he held her and loved her he made mind pictures for his collection, so that when she had gone he could bring them out and look at them.

****

Célie hummed as she poured coffee into two mugs. Another day being questioned by Ralston loomed, but after last night with Brand, she could face anything. Anything. That man sure had stamina. She grinned. How he'd hate to be thought of as a stud. He was so sure he was all brain—

Then she heard a scuffling sound like a large rat outside the door. For a second she froze, heart racing with fright. Shit. Brand was in the shower.

If it was Ralston outside, why didn't he identify himself?

She picked up the knife she'd been using to slice oranges. Hesitantly she pressed her face against the door. "Ralston?" When she peered through the fish-eye lens, she couldn't see anyone outside.

"Célie," whispered a disembodied voice.

She jumped, her heart bolting into her throat. She knew that voice.

"You know who I am. I have your mother. If you come with me, I'll let her go."

Célie's heart began pounding like a jack hammer. It was the creepy voice she'd heard through the fog a lifetime ago.

In the background the shower ran, water gurgling as it escaped down the drain. Brand was humming to himself. She took a deep breath. This time she wasn't alone. She wasn't in a terrified funk like she'd been on that foggy morning.

"I don't know what you're talking about," she said calmly, pressing her face against the cold door. "I'll get Brand. You can talk to him."

As she turned away a photo was shoved underneath the door. She picked it up. It was a grainy photo of an older woman. She saw no resemblance to the mother she remembered.

"It's not my mother," she hissed. "She's nothing like that."

"I have Roberta Anne at my house," the loathsome voice insisted.

Yes, Roberta was her mother's name. But anyone could have found that out.

"Who the hell are you talking to?" Brand's voice

came from behind her and she jumped guiltily, as if she had something to hide. She shushed him but it was too late. Footsteps pounded around the corner and clanged down the iron fire escape outside.

"What the hell?" Brand was naked, dripping water on the floor.

"It was him. He says he's got my mother."

"Who? What?" Brand yanked at the door, but by the time he'd flung it open, the pounding footsteps on the fire escape had died away.

Célie raced to peer out the window, but next door's sundeck jutted out, blocking her vision. Then she saw a figure running towards the carpark in the distance. "There!"

Brand squinted. "Could be anyone," he said, sounding annoyed. "Goddamit, I can't go out like this." He prowled back to the bathroom and got dressed, and Célie knew he was angry with her. "Why didn't you call me?" he demanded as he stuffed his shirt into his jeans.

"I handled it," she snapped. "Anyway, at first I wasn't sure if it was the same person who'd chased me in the fog. It sounded the same but there was a different timbre to it."

"What do you mean?" Brand eyed her as if he didn't believe her.

"He sounded sort of excited, as if he was holding himself in, trying not to say too much." She handed Brand a cup of coffee. "And in spite of what Occy, Tara and I suspected, the killer is *not* a woman. It was a man who chased me through the fog, and it was a man outside the door just now."

"But there are two of them, Célie." He clattered his coffee mug on to the benchtop and buckled his belt. For a moment her eyes strayed, then she dragged them up to his face. And got a shock. He was examining her as if she were one of his clients who had given an unexpected answer in a psychotherapy session. "You're quite sure he spoke to you, Célie?" he asked.

He didn't believe her! She tried not to bounce out of her corner fighting. But his cool assumption that the hiding and fear were changing her brain to mush was irritating. How could he? Surely he'd gotten to know her better than that.

"After all you've been through—"

"Here," she snarled and shoved the photo at him. "He says that's my mother and that he's got her."

Brand examined the photo. "It's a terrible photo. Can't see a thing." Then he looked closer and examined one corner. He stiffened. "Did you look at this?"

She stood beside him and peered over his shoulder. "What?"

"See the date imprinted in the corner?"

She glanced at her watch, then stared at the photo. "Today's date."

Brand strode to the kitchen bench and grabbed a couple of orange slices. "Here." He handed her one and chewed on his piece, brooding and distant.

Célie watched him, saying nothing. She seethed with resentment.

"Well," he said at last, "to find out where we're staying, he either followed us from Ralston's office yesterday, or a cop or one of us is passing him information." She opened her mouth to protest but he carried on. "We know it's not us, but somehow he must have found out about our meeting with Ralston."

"How could anyone have followed us yesterday? I mean," Célie shrugged, "Ralston's office is buried deep in the center of police headquarters. And there's no way Ralston would pass on information...I guess."

"One of his staff might have done it," Brand

surmised, taking another orange slice. "They may not have realized its importance."

"What about Detective Hotshot?"

"Maybe. I doubt that Hotshot knows anything about the serial killer connection. For him, the hospital visit was just a minor escort job. He may think you have gangland affiliations."

"Thanks a bunch!" Célie exclaimed.

He grinned. "Oh, I dunno. Yesterday you looked very like a Cobra's moll. Loved the boots. I have this fantasy of—"

"Yes, all right," Célie said hurriedly. "Later."

"That a promise?"

She eyed him uncertainly. Then she saw the glint in his eye. He wasn't joking.

She grinned back. "It's a promise."

He reached out and touched her arm, the touch as delicate as a butterfly's wing, as if he was afraid that if he got too close he wouldn't be able to let her go.

Good.

She turned away to rinse the knife under running water. For days now she'd been toting it around inside her big shoulder bag. The knife fitted snugly across the bottom of the bag. She felt much more secure carrying a weapon.

As their pick-up car drew up outside, Brand's cell phone rang. Célie checked the hallway. All clear. Grabbing her bag, she ran on ahead to warn their designated driver that Brand was delayed. They never spoke on the phone in the police car, just in case.

She bent down on the passenger's side to see if it was Detective Hotshot today, and the driver leaned forward and pressed the button to wind down the shaded window. "Get in, Célie," Mike Ellery said.

Chapter Twenty-Two

"What you are you doing here, M—?"

"Get in quickly and shut up." Mike's right hand was on the steering wheel. In his left hand, his police issue Glock glinted in the sun.

Should she make a run for it? Please Brand, hurry up! As she dipped her head, preparatory to getting into the Holden, she swiveled her eyes to the back seat. Detective Hotshot lay gagged and trussed like a roasting chicken along the seat. A pair of indignant, angry blue eyes glared at her. In spite of her stomach-chilling fear, she almost laughed. She must be crazy, wanting to laugh at a time like this.

"Get in *now*!" Ellery flicked the safety catch off.

She barely got her feet inside the door before he accelerated. Her door banged shut with the force of the drag away from the curb. Mike gunned the car into the heavy commuter traffic and Célie automatically pulled on her safety belt. God knew why. If Mike was one of the Cliff Road killers, she wouldn't be alive for much longer. What did a car crash matter?

At least she was in a better situation than poor old Hotshot who kept rolling back and forth on the back seat every time Mike braked or accelerated. A car cut in front of them and Ellery stood on the brakes. Hotshot crashed to the floor.

Célie was amazed at Mike's calm concentration. He focused on his driving, dealing with the early morning crush of traffic. He didn't look at her. His cool competency sent her nerves skittering. He had a plan and he was carrying it out with passionless efficiency.

She said nothing. In every movie she'd seen, all captives did was yammer, yammer at their kidnappers. She wouldn't give him that satisfaction.

Ellery fiddled one-handed with the safety catch, then put the Glock in his lap. He didn't seem to be as familiar with the pistol as he should be. She'd always imagined a cop would cherish his gun like a lover.

He clicked on the indicator and changed lanes, heading north. Why was he taking them back to his jurisdiction? It would be sensible to stay well away from where he'd be recognized.

As the car climbed the rise to the harbor bridge, Ellery checked in his rearview mirror. At the same time Hotshot booted the back of Mike's seat with both feet.

Ellery quirked an amused eyebrow at Célie. "Your companion seems to be a tad upset," he said.

Yes! He'd spoken to her first. He didn't like being ignored. In his eyes he was in control and she should be terrified of him. Of course she was, but she had no intention of showing it. She feigned indifference by hunching one shoulder and staring out the window at the iron struts zipping past.

"Tell me what you're thinking, Célie," he coaxed. "Are you scared?"

Ha! "I'm thinking you must have spent weeks training Peaches, that's what I'm thinking. How the hell could you spend all that time with an animal and then kill him?" Anger drove the fear away, even though her inner voice urged caution. "You're a monster."

But he didn't seem fazed. He grinned. "You want to see a monster up close, baby? I'll show you a monster."

What the heck was he talking about? She eased her handbag into a more comfortable position on her lap. Brand's kitchen knife lay heavy on the bottom.

"And 'Peaches' as you call him was almost trained when I bought him. Bet you thought Parlane had sent him, didn't you? Quite a stroke of genius on my part, setting up that little red herring."

Célie didn't bother to reply. She didn't see any "stroke of genius." All she saw was an amoral, vicious killer.

Detective Hotshot thumped with his feet on the back of the driver's seat again.

"Do that one more time and I'll roll you out on to the freeway," Ellery said, taking a hand off the wheel to rub the small of his back.

"Huh! I doubt it," Célie said over her shoulder to Hotshot. "The bridge ramparts are studded with security cameras. Right now nobody knows where we are. The instant he raises his head, they'll be all over him like a rash."

She spoke as if Mike Ellery were not in the car.

"Smart mouth you've got there, Célie," Ellery commented. A slight edge to his voice warned her that he was more dangerous now than ever before. "But you're quite right. How about I put a bullet in his head instead?" His cold amusement was nothing like Brand's amused patience when she'd tickled him with one of her tough comebacks. With his eyes on the road, Ellery leaned to one side and brushed the muzzle of the Glock against her mouth.

Fear crept through every nerve ending and slithered across her skin.

Brand, she prayed. *Find us.*

****

As Brand grabbed his jacket, he checked caller ID. Ralston.

"Turner?"

He'd never before heard Ralston so agitated.

"Yes?"

"I'm paging a call through from Parlane. He's got some news."

Colin Parlane's voice was cold and malevolent, the sound of a hunter. "Turner? We've made a connection between Ellery and Cliff Road. He owns a house two streets away. And—" Parlane was still talking, but Brand stuffed the phone in his pocket and raced for the door. The elevators were all occupied and he blitzed the stairs three at a time. Crashing through the hotel doors, he raced across the courtyard to the carpark.

The unmarked police car was gone.

And so was Célie.

Oh, please, God, no.

His heart climbed into his throat and threatened to strangle him. He took a couple of deep breaths and hit redial on his cell phone.

Ten minutes later, Brand and Ralston rocked from side to side as the squad car, siren screaming, wove through heavy commuter traffic towards the harbor bridge. Parlane was already positioned around the corner from Ellery's house. They were working on the assumption that, like a rat, Ellery would head for his bolthole. But Ellery hadn't shown up with Célie yet. Everyone wondered if she had become victim number six.

Brand prayed he'd see her again—that cheeky grin when she'd bested him, the rats-tail hair and those cool, assessing silver-grey eyes. By God, he bloody well wasn't prepared to have some half-baked psychotic cop take her from him when he'd only just found her. He slipped his hand inside his jacket and touched the Colt as if it were a talisman.

"Keep the radio lines open and your computer on," Ralston advised Parlane. "The Armed Offenders' Squad is standing by."

As the vehicle approached the harbor bridge, Brand heard a strange sound over the police radio. It sounded like someone laughing.

"Ellery," he said to Ralston.

"Huh?"

"That was him laughing."

"At us?" Ralston sounded pissed off.

"Maybe. Maybe he just feels happy." The worst possible scenario, Brand thought.

"God Almighty."

While Ralston juggled with his cell phone, the squad car radio, and the onboard computer system, Brand eased the old Colt out of its holster. Ralston didn't notice until Brand checked the magazine.

"Shit, Turner! You're a civilian! Put that away. Someone could get hurt."

"Someone will," Brand answered grimly. "Ellery."

"Leave it to us."

"You haven't been successful so far."

The young driver took his eyes off the road for a second to watch the stand-off.

"Keep your bloody eyes on the road!" Ralston screamed, too shaken to worry about Brand for the moment.

Brand agreed. They had just reached the summit of the harbor bridge and gusty winds buffeted the car about. The needle on the speedometer hovered over the 100 mph mark as they accelerated down the other side.

****

Three police cars using a moving block challenged the Holden as they roared along the coast road. But Ellery maintained his speed, shunting the squad car in front of him off the road. The car crushed a barrowload of fruit outside a fruit shop before plunging through the shop window, shattering glass in a spectacular array of splinters in

206

the morning sunshine. The other two cars in the block dropped away. Animated voices squawked over the police radio.

"Shut up," Ellery muttered beneath his breath, and flicked the cut-off switch.

There had been no sudden impact so the airbags hadn't engaged, but Célie's shoulder burned where her safety belt had dug in and rubbed. Her handbag slithered to the floor and she cast a quick glance down to make sure it hadn't burst open. Ellery didn't seem to be affected at all. She screwed around to look at Hotshot. Rolling unchecked on the floor between the seats, he looked pale beneath the gag.

Ellery braked suddenly and shot down a side road. Célie glanced at the street sign. Alfriston Grove. She'd run down here a time or two when she'd lived in Cliff Road. She might have to run down here once more if she could engineer an escape. Thank God she wasn't wearing her come-get-me boots with spiky heels. She'd be crippled before she'd run twenty yards.

Ellery cruised past a squad car parked by the roadside. He peered at the driver and chuckled. The hairs on the nape of Célie's neck stood up.

"The cavalry's come to rescue you," he said to her.

"Cavalry?"

"Your mate, Parlane."

"Oh." She hoped Parlane had at least one other cop with him. Or two. Or three.

Ellery slowed the car, preparatory to doing a U-turn.

Célie stretched her hand towards the door handle.

"It's locked."

Ellery's voice sounded calm and amused again. It grated on her nerves.

They eased past the squad car. Parlane was

yelling into the radio phone. He began to open the car door.

Ellery pressed the button to wind down the window. He picked the Glock off the dashboard with his free hand and readied it.

Célie dived for her handbag with one hand, and with her other punched Ellery's shoulder as hard as she could. Their vehicle cannoned sideways into the squad car, grinding alongside the driver's door. Ellery jabbed the brake and his Glock shot out the window and thunked onto the roadway. He cursed long and loud. As the two cars meshed and crunched together, from inside the squad car someone stifled a groan.

Ellery threw back his head and laughed. Célie shrank away from him into the corner of her seat, scrabbling to open her handbag.

Ellery laughed and laughed as if what had happened had been the funniest thing he'd seen in a lifetime.

Then he turned and punched Célie.

Chapter Twenty-Three

Semiconscious, Célie felt herself being dragged out of the car. She was jostled and thumped until she hung over Ellery's shoulder like a sack of potatoes, her head hanging down his back. Her face throbbed but not enough to rouse her fully. Something cut into her arm. Her handbag?

She came to with a start. Handbag equals protection, her fuzzy brain computed. She struggled to unzip the fastener, but at that moment Ellery began descending some steps and she swayed around like a trapeze artist. She grabbed the bag in one hand and used her other to clutch Ellery's coat.

Coat? When she had last seen him he'd been wearing a suit—a rather nice one. Now he was wearing an old gaberdine raincoat like a bag lady.

Raincoats flashed through her mind. A person in a raincoat waiting at the top of the hill that she and Brand had jogged up. A woman wearing a flapping raincoat as she rushed along the beach towards Occy and Tara and Célie.

Ellery stopped to open a door, and as he stepped inside she clung frantically to the architrave over the door jamb.

"Bitch!" He just kept walking until her arms and body were stretched out like chewing gum and her bruised fingers lost contact with the wood.

His comment pissed her off. "*You* oughta talk," she snarled.

He ignored her. Nobody ignored Célie Francis. Not anymore. They might have ignored her when she was a helpless kid, but she wasn't helpless now. As his footsteps echoed on bare floorboards, she hooked the handbag over her neck and hung down his back to pummel her fists into his kidneys. At the same time she wriggled a leg free and booted him in the balls—at least she hoped it was the balls. Her aim was a little off as she slid all over him trying to keep her balance.

Ellery cursed and dropped her. Hard. As she scrambled to her feet he doubled up, clutching himself, mouthing words she hadn't heard since she'd tossed Giorgio out on his ear. Good. She'd scored twice in three days. Those *cojones* must be plenty sore by now. Snatching up her handbag she unzipped it, but she was too slow. She never would have thought Mike Ellery could move so fast.

"Carrying, are you?" One hand still cradling his injured balls, he used the other to snag her bag, yanking it away from her. Brand's big kitchen knife clanged to the floor, lying sinister and silver between them. Célie stamped her foot on it before Mike could get there.

Silence hung between them. They stared at each other from a distance of two yards, hunter and hunted.

How long would she last when he stopped playing with her and really started hurting her?

He eased backwards. "Well, well, well," he said softly. "Like mother, like daughter."

What was he burbling about?

Then he laughed. "The joke is on you, Ms Francis. Come and meet your mother."

With a flourish he opened a door to their left, and Célie peered inside, wondering what he meant. In the gloom a hunched figure rocked to and fro.

Ellery gave Célie a shove but she stood firm. No

way would she leave that knife behind.

"If you're concerned about your knife, you'll find your mother is well equipped. It's her weapon of choice, you might say," Ellery said.

Célie pointed. "That is not my mother," she said.

"Oh, yes it is. Célie, allow me to present Roberta Anne Ellery."

Célie spun around. "*Ellery?*"

Mike's smooth, sophisticated face creased in distaste. "Unfortunately for me—yes. For ten long years. For the last eight of them, she's been like this."

Lost in her own world, the woman sitting on the sofa ignored them.

Suddenly Ellery lost patience. "Get in!" he yelled, shoving Célie so hard that she shot into the room like a rock from a catapult and landed on her knees in front of the woman. The door slammed behind her.

****

"Nadine?" queried an unused, feathery voice above her.

She looked up into expressionless, silver-grey eyes. She swallowed hard. It was the woman from the beach.

And it didn't take her two seconds to recognize those eyes close up. They were the same color as the ones that looked back at her from the mirror each morning.

But how...?

She scrambled to her feet. "Who are you?"

The woman drew back in fear.

"Sorry." Célie stretched out a hand in reassurance.

But the woman drew even further away and pulled her feet up onto the sofa. She wrapped her arms around her bony knees and began rocking again. This time she talked to herself. "Not Nadine.

Not Nadine. Can't be Nadine."

"Nadine was my sister," Célie said.

"No sister."

"Yes. I'm Célie."

But the woman shook her head.

Célie hesitated. If this woman *was* her mother, she was nothing like the mother Célie remembered. Célie's mother had had long dark hair that twisted and curled on her shoulders and her skin had been clear. Célie could recall good days when Roberta had taken them to the zoo, and evenings when their father had rushed in the door, waving tickets for a special première at the movie theatre where he worked on weekends. But during their last two years as a family, Roberta's eyes had become glazed with alcohol and she had rarely moved further than the sofa, and the good days had become few and far between. For many years now Célie had done her best to forget both the bad days and the good ones.

"Mother?" she tried tentatively. Roberta had instructed the girls to call her "Roberta," but sometimes they had forgotten and called her "Mother."

To Celie's shock, the woman spat at her. A globule of spittle landed on the floor at Célie's feet.

"Hey!"

"You!" The woman sprang to her feet and pointed at Célie.

And with that one movement, the buried memories came flooding back—Roberta jumping up from the sofa swinging a whisky bottle and pointing at her daughters. "You two! You've turned him against me. Shoulda had boys." Then, unable to maintain her balance, she had fallen back on the sofa, shrieking with laughter. "Too damned drunk to stand! Just watch his face when he comes in." And she'd pulled a sour, disapproving face. "This is how he looks, isn't it, girls?"

Nadine and Célie had beaten a hasty retreat, because the next stage was maudlin tears of self-recrimination culminating in a screaming match with their father.

And there was the unforgettable day when Roberta had sent her off to school, knowing she'd be gone before Célie got home again. "You!" Roberta had said, pointing her finger at Célie's chest. "You'll be fine. Maybe."

She felt the same despair she had back then when her heart had sunk into her little black school shoes. At the time she hadn't known what her mother meant, only that it did not bode well for her.

She swallowed bile. This broken down old woman who shambled along the beach was *her mother?*

"Did you go to the hospital to see Dad?" Célie blurted before she could stop herself.

Roberta looked wary. "Hospital? I'm not going to any hospital. He said I didn't have to!" she shrilled.

"No. Not *you* in hospital. I meant Dad in the hospital."

The woman stared at her blankly. The suet colored skin crumpled into folds and wrinkles that took away all animation. The eyes were quite dead.

Célie wondered if something else besides alcohol had turned Roberta into such a wreck. She glanced around looking for pill bottles or ampoules of drugs, but the room held only the sofa and a TV. No knick-knacks, no books.

Célie edged to the far side of the room. She had no idea what to expect, but if Roberta had done what Ellery hinted, then Célie was in grave danger.

Two killers, and one of them her mother!

Her thoughts darted around as she tried to think of a way out. She would have to save herself—somehow—because Parlane was injured. Pray God he'd had enough strength to contact Brand and

Ralston. And with a bit of luck, the patrol cars from the roadblock had followed them.

"You!" Roberta snarled, beginning to sound more aggressive. "I watched you."

The idea of being stalked by Roberta made the skin on the back of Célie's neck crawl. A trickle of sweat ran down her back, dampening her T-shirt.

"D-did you come to one of my shows, like Dad did?" she croaked.

"Shows? Shows?" Roberta's voice rose with every word.

Sweet heaven, *please* let me out of here, Célie prayed. She edged nearer to the door, keeping a close eye on her mother.

Roberta prowled towards Célie. "I went to get rid of you but you'd gone," she said, as if she were discussing laying down rat's bane. "So He said He'd take care of it. He fixed the others but He didn't get you, did he? You always were a difficult child."

So she knew who Célie was after all. Célie shoved her chin in the air. "And you were a bloody difficult mother," she snapped.

"Oooh. It bites." Roberta giggled inanely.

"Why did you leave me behind?" Célie blurted. Damn and double damn. The very last thing she'd wanted to say.

"Because you could look after yourself. The other one now—she needed me. And I found her useful for a while."

"For a while?" Célie's heart sank.

"Mike told her to go away. And she did. But then she came back and said I should go to hospital. And she kept on and on about wanting to see you. She found your name on the...the..."

"Internet?"

"Yeah. In the papers, too. Done all right, like I knew you would."

Roberta laughed suddenly, a shocking, cracked

sound. "Couldn't have her contacting you. So He told her where you were and I settled her hash."

"You mean you...killed Nadine? Your own daughter?" Célie's stomach heaved. A mist swirled around her head and she pressed back against the wall, the only security in a world gone mad.

Oblivious, Roberta stood swaying in front of her, her odd assortment of clothes swinging with her movements. "He says I've killed lots of people. Maybe. Sometimes I remember things..." Her voice faded away and her gaze turned inward as she reflected on a picture only she could see.

Célie's stomach churned again. Poor, poor Nadine.

"You're next," Roberta said, her face lighting up with anticipation.

Oh, shit! Brand, where the hell are you?

Célie shuffled along the wall against the wainscoting and reached out a hand to try the doorknob. Locked. Of course it was. Okay. New plan.

Roberta spun around and dived for the sofa. Delving beneath the sofa cushions she produced a lethal-looking carving knife. Her mouth curled in the rictus of a smile, and her face was frightening in its intensity.

Célie swallowed. She was loath to fight her mother, but it was a question of life or death—hers. She had no choice.

On the edge of her consciousness, she heard the thud of pounding feet outside the house, but she didn't dare take her eyes off Roberta.

Suddenly the small window on the seaward side of the room exploded inwards.

Célie hit the floor and covered her head as shards of glass tinkled around her.

"Célie?"

Thank God.

Roberta turned in surprise, her knife held aloft

like an avenging demon.

Brand slithered through the small space and rolled. He scrambled to his feet and strode across to Roberta.

Roberta's mouth opened, but she said nothing. She just stared in amazement.

"Careful, Brand," Célie warned.

"I know. Been here before. Thank God you're okay," Brand murmured, never taking his eyes off Roberta.

He'd done this before? Psychologists must lead more exciting lives than she'd thought.

"Hi, Roberta. I'm Brand Turner. It looks as though you're feeling upset today. Can I help?"

Upset? He thought her *mother* was feeling upset? What the hell did he think Célie was feeling? Chirpy?

Roberta lowered the knife and surveyed Brand with her head tilted to one side. Célie was reminded of an inquisitive cobra.

"Brand," Roberta said experimentally, like a toddler trying out a new word.

Brand smiled. "Yes. Let's sit down and you can tell me—"

Then they all froze as something thudded against the door and the key scraped in the lock. Roberta dropped her knife and huddled behind Brand.

"Keep Him away. He'll be angry. He's always angry," she whispered.

Célie's heart twisted at the terror in her mother's voice.

Not bothering to spare a glance at Brand, Ellery staggered into the room, bent double under the weight of Parlane's body. He dumped the bleeding body on the floor and Célie heard the hiss of Parlane's indrawn breath. Strips of shirt and skin hung off the side of his torso. Forgetting about escape, she scrambled across to Parlane and dropped to her knees beside him. One of his feet lay at an awkward angle. The ankle was either dislocated or broken. A steady stream of blood wept from the injuries on his side. She struggled to stem the flow with the tail of her shirt.

"Careful, Célie," Brand warned.

However Ellery showed his utter contempt for them all when he turned his back on them and strode to the doorway.

But when Brand reached for Roberta's knife, Ellery spun around, snarling, and yanked out his Glock.

The nagging wail of sirens carried on the breeze. Too late.

Ellery laughed inanely and Roberta shuddered and clutched Brand's jacket in a death grip.

What the hell had taken them so long? By the time the cops were stationed around the house, Célie knew they'd all be dead. Ellery was going to win after all.

He'd blame everything on Roberta. She'd take the rap for every single murder, attempted murder, assault, burglary, download of pedophilia and anything else he could pin on her.

Facing the Glock clutched in Ellery's unsteady hand, Célie's mind spun like a top, running through her options. There weren't any. She was closest to Ellery, so she'd go first.

She shuffled her feet a little and Ellery frowned. He juggled the Glock as if it was a remote control and Célie remembered how awkwardly he'd held the weapon in the car. Brand had once commented on Parlane's scorn for Ellery's lousy test shooting. All well and good, but he wasn't going to miss her at such close range. Even the newest, most nervous police cadet could manage a shot like that.

"Keep still," Ellery growled at her.

Good. She was making him nervous. If she could distract him enough... With that one shuffle she had gained half a yard and changed the angle of her body. She looked across the room at Brand. "Love you," she said.

Brand smiled and drew a deep breath. Then he nodded. Ellery stared at Brand and sniggered, his attention diverted. "How sweet." His lip curled.

Célie launched herself and bashed hard into Ellery. He skidded sideways. Off balance, he fumbled to release the jammed safety catch on the Glock. The muzzle pointed at the ceiling.

"Bitch!" Ellery splayed his legs to steady himself and raised his free arm to smash it down on Célie's head but she'd darted behind him. She rammed her arm up between his legs. He bucked, startled, as she grabbed him by the balls. Gritting her teeth, Célie thanked her lucky stars that a life spent fighting her way uphill had taught her how to play dirty.

Frantically Ellery tried to drag her hand away, but Célie increased the grinding pressure, gouging with her long, piano-playing fingers. Ellery screamed. The Glock clattered to the floor and Parlane swiped it away with his uninjured foot.

A sound like rolling thunder presaged a crash as the door flew open and Ralston burst in, followed by a flurry of uniformed cops.

"About freaking time," Célie snapped.

Chapter Twenty-Four

Brand grinned and shoved the Colt back in his armpit holster when Ralston muttered, "Put that thing away. I never saw it."

Célie stalked up to Brand. Her face was a study. "Did you have that all the time?" she demanded, ignoring the cross-conversations behind her.

He nodded.

She poked him in the chest. "Were you going to use it?"

"Only if you couldn't cope."

She grinned weakly. "Correct answer." She leaned against him. He knew she'd feel the fear still trembling through his body. For two minutes he had been within a hairsbreadth of losing her forever. He had gambled on two things—Ellery's ineptness with firearms and Célie's determination. Even as she'd pivoted behind Ellery, Brand had released the Colt's safety catch.

"Anyway," Célie said perkily, "Confucius say 'man with balls in rat-trap forget gun in hand.'"

Brand choked with laughter. She was still on a high. Thank God he'd held back for that millisecond, because she had needed so badly to take down Ellery herself. But Christ...the nerves in his stomach were still jumping.

Dry skin scraped his hand and he looked down. Roberta Ellery, big-eyed, was watching her husband lying prone with a constable kneeling on his back, handcuffing him. Clutching Brand's hand, Roberta suddenly laughed. "He wanted to be promoted," she snorted.

Brand patted her hand. "We'll look after you, Roberta. Look at me," he urged her, but the transient glimmer of light in the eyes had dimmed.

"You'll be all right," he promised her.

Roberta hunched her shoulders and stared at her feet. She looked as though she was trying to disappear within her own skin. Brand knew that all these people invading her space had sent her back to her own private world. He cajoled her into sitting on the sofa and jerked his head at Ralston to remove the knife lying on the little table. Then he sat down next to her. Ralston wanted to question Célie, and Brand wasn't going anywhere without Célie.

"At least *you* can go back to your old life," Ralston told Célie. "Some of the others on the program—the Crown witnesses to crimes—they'll have to be relocated yet again, thanks to Ellery."

As Parlane was loaded on to a stretcher, Brand asked him, "Colin, when did you start suspecting Ellery? Was it the day I came to your office and handed over my notes?"

"Yeah. I could see you thought it was me, but I knew it wasn't so it gave me an advantage. Everyone else checked out, so..." Parlane shrugged. "As his wife said, he won't be getting promoted now." Parlane paused for a moment to grimace as a paramedic checked his abrasions. "His wife!" Parlane continued. "We never knew he was married. He didn't cite it on his application and he's never once mentioned her."

"He's ashamed of her," Brand said quietly.

"Damn fool. Why didn't he get medical help for her?"

"Don't run away with the thought that Roberta committed all the murders, Colin."

Colin Parlane stared at Brand for a moment then looked down at the sheet covering his legs. "Oh, God Almighty, I hope he hasn't... Surely not. Perhaps the man is sick," he mumbled, refusing to meet Brand's eyes.

"I'm not so sure about that," Brand replied.

Colin Parlane swallowed hard. "Are you saying he calculated all the risks and—"

"Yes. I am."

"Sweet Jesus." Parlane looked gobsmacked.

"Let's face it, Colin. With Ellery drawing red herrings across the trail all the time, you were unlikely to solve the case. It was worth the risk because he could hold Roberta as insurance for a while. Then if the investigation stalled, he'd no doubt kill Roberta and dump her body. Even if her body was discovered, it would be difficult to trace her. She'd be just another Jane Doe. Ellery made sure she slipped off the radar some years ago. On the other hand," Brand went on, "he might have continued killing. He seems to have developed a taste for it."

Parlane surveyed Brand's face for a few seconds. "I want you in on the interview, Turner." Then he lowered his head on to the stretcher. "Please," he added as an afterthought. "You seem to be able to read him." He screwed himself around to face Ralston. "Unless, of course, you decide to run the whole show, Ralston."

"We'll see," Ralston chirruped. His barely suppressed cheer showed he was enjoying the implosion of the North Shore Unit. Brand had never seen him so chipper. What was it between these two?

A constable approached them and reported that he'd found a battered red Mercedes in the garage adjacent to the house.

"Did it have an *M* on the numberplate?" Brand asked.

"Yeah."

Parlane gave him a thumbs-up as he was carried away.

Roberta was being escorted to an ambulance by two minders and Célie hovered behind them. "Where are you taking her?"

"Well, not to the Marriott, lady," one of the attendants answered.

"What did you say, you cretin? That's my mother there. If you can't keep a civil tongue in your head, I'll fix your tongue for you."

"Ah, Célie? Time to go home," Brand intervened. She was still running on adrenaline, but anytime soon she'd wind down and the crash would come. He wanted to get her back home—wherever that was for both of them at the moment—as soon as possible.

"Just a minute, Brand. I need to know where they're taking her."

"I already have that covered, sweetie. Let's go." Brand raised his voice.

Célie stopped harassing the medical attendants and looked at Brand. "What's with the orders?"

Hmm. He hadn't thought it would be long before she went back to being her old, confident self. He wouldn't be needed much longer.

He squelched down the unhappiness and turned to Ralston. "Three o'clock do?"

"Ah, yes. Of course." Ralston was trying to subdue a grin. "See you both this afternoon."

"Célie?"

"All right, *all right*, I'm coming," she grumbled, following him along the passageway. "Where are we going? I don't have a home at the moment."

"Cut the Orphan Annie stuff, Ms Francis. We'll collect our stuff from the motel and go back to my place."

"You called me Ms Francis. I can be Célie Francis again! I've found myself! Not that there's anything special about being me but—”

“There’s a lot special about being you,” Brand said, but she didn’t respond. Casting him an enigmatic look, she flounced out the door.

****

An hour later he carried a tearful, fretting Célie into his house in the hills. He looked down at the woman in his arms. As he’d anticipated, reaction had set in.

“All those years,” Célie wailed. “All those years when I hated her, she was sick. Poor Nadine. She had to cope on her own. And then Ellery made things worse by...what exactly did Ellery do to make her that way, Brand?”

Brand set her down on the sofa, tucking a rug around her. He sank down beside her, spent. “My guess is he withdrew her abruptly off alcohol and didn’t provide any supportive treatment. I found rohypnol pills in the medicine cupboard. I think he’s been dosing her with those to keep her docile. One of the worse things he could do.”

She bounced back up again, dislodging the rug. “But you knew just what to do, how to handle her.”

“It’s my job. I’ve seen psychoses in many forms. She needs gentle understanding and medication. But you need to face facts, Célie. She’ll never improve.” It was better to be brutal than to have her hanging on to a futile wish that her mother might recover.

“Did you hear what she said about leaving me behind?”

“No. I guess about that time I was chewing my knuckles as we detoured through back streets. They’d blockaded the junction of Cliff and Alfriston and we couldn’t get through. I had to run the last half-mile.”

Célie’s brain rattled on in overtime. “What happened to Detective Hotshot?” she asked.

“Uh...I’m not sure.”

She snorted with laughter. "Poor old Hotshot. And we still don't—"

"Célie, honey, stow it. My nerves aren't as tough as yours are. I need a drink." He reached into a cupboard and pulled out the first bottle his hand touched. Bourbon. Good. He drank straight from the bottle.

"Hey! What about me?" Célie demanded.

"You? You're tough as old boots. You're still firing on all cylinders. You don't need this stuff to make you fly."

"Oh, don't I just," Célie retorted, grabbing the bottle from him. "I don't intend to end up like my mother, but if ever there was a time to drink, it's now." She gulped a mouthful, then spluttered and gasped. But she went back for more.

Brand laughed and Célie grinned sheepishly. "It's terrible. What is it?"

"Cheap bourbon. A Christmas present from one of the relocatees."

She dumped the bottle on a table and collapsed back on to the sofa. "I wonder what will happen now."

"Ellery will be a hard nut to crack. They have some evidence against him, but he'll fight to the last to blame Roberta for everything."

"Brand," Célie said quietly. "It was incredible of you to stand back and let me deal with Ellery. I needed the satisfaction after what he's done to my family. But what if it had gone wrong?"

Yeah. What if? The control he had exerted to hold himself back had been the hardest thing he had ever done. Having the Colt ready had been the only thing keeping him sane. "Nothing went wrong. I knew you could do it," he said, refusing to raise the lid on a basketful of seething fears. "Parlane won't be happy that I let you make the first move. He'll demand my resignation. Just as well, I plan to quit."

At last he'd admitted what had been on his mind for weeks.

Célie's jaw dropped. "But you mustn't, Brand! You're the only person the relocatees can talk to. I ought to know." She stared earnestly into his face. "Parlane has no people skills. Anyway, he'll be on sick leave for a while. Ellery is gone. That leaves—who?"

"John Foster."

"Oh, no. Way too intellectual for frightened people starting fresh lives. Relocatees need sensible, useful advice, not convoluted buzz words."

Brand raised his eyebrows. Only Célie could come up with a reason for him to continue to work in a sphere where the cops tried to make him feel inadequate because they considered his people skills to be too touchy-feely. A warm glow suffused the pit of his stomach. Or was it his heart? She believed in him. Stumbling over the words he murmured, "We'll see." But he knew she was right. He *had* built up a good rapport with most of the relocatees and Foster seemed to respect him. Which only left Parlane...and who knew what Parlane thought?

Then Célie added, "With you at the helm, people like me stand a better chance of getting back to our real lives."

'Real lives.' Yeah. He was an interlude, a throw-away relationship she would leave behind when she went back to her real world. And when her real world collided with his real world, she would move on.

Chapter Twenty-Five

Three hours later, Inspector Friedman and Parlane, his foot propped up on a stool, left Brand in no doubt that they wanted him to lead the Unit from now on. Amid the buzz of chatter from a roomful of strangers, Parlane gestured to him.

"You're the one we want," he said, his foghorn voice raised above the babble.

"I know that, but do you?" Brand challenged him.

"Just said so, didn't I?" Parlane trumpeted. "I'll continue with the police end as usual, Foster can concentrate on the research and you can correlate the whole thing and see to the relocatee's ah...psychological needs."

The room quietened. Everyone was listening. Ralston elbowed his way through the crush. "Tell him the rest," he said to Parlane.

"Oh, yeah," Parlane added as if he was having a tooth drawn. "You'd have final say on all policy decisions."

Brand's mind reeled in shock. They *had* come a long way in a short time today.

Parlane grinned reluctantly. "Okay. I admit it. I'm not fond of psychology per se, but I can differentiate between what you do and who you are."

Brand's eyebrows shot up. His mind raced. How much work could he cram into a day? What about his private patients?

"You're ideal. We need someone like you—someone who thinks on his feet but has the human touch," a cool voice said from the back of the room. The owner of the voice stepped forward. He was tall and lanky with a shock of grey hair.

Brand rose to his feet and held out his hand. "I'm sorry. I don't know you." He felt awkward taking praise from a complete stranger.

The man shook his hand with the iron grip of an amateur golfer and handed him a card. "Detective Superintendent Nate Allingham," he said.

Well, well. In his sharp, neat suit, Allingham seemed more like a businessman than a cop. It looked as though Ralston was aping his boss's style. Ready to step into the boss's shoes perhaps?

"I've read your file. Your past experience shows us you deal well with the press," Allingham continued, "and the next few interviews are not going to be pretty."

A sacrificial lamb, Brand thought. That's what they were looking for. They wanted him to act as a buffer between the press and the cops. His abilities were only part of the reason they wanted him. He looked Allingham in the eye. He had nothing to lose. "Mistakes happen in any institution. It wasn't as if Ellery was crooked when he began police work so you don't need me to paper over the cracks." He handed the business card back. "I'll consider the job but I'm not going to be your press scapegoat." He turned to leave.

"Wait!" Nate Allingham grabbed Brand's elbow. "That's not what I meant. You're the best person to run the Unit. Otherwise it might be disbanded and become reabsorbed into Central's jurisdiction again."

Brand glanced at Ralston, whose feral grin stretched from ear to ear. The guy's enjoyment irritated Brand and hardened his resolve. Okay, Ralston had recommended Brand for the North

Shore Unit, but over the past few days Brand had seen another side to Ralston, a side he didn't like. He'd come to prefer Parlane's tell-it-like-it-is style of policing.

He studied his shoes. *Face it, Turner. Without you they wouldn't have caught Ellery.* Or if they had, they would have been too late to save Célie and others like her. North Shore needed him, for a while at least.

"Okay. You've got yourself a deal." He leaned forward to shake hands with Colin Parlane. He wasn't interested in anyone else in the room. He and Parlane would be the ones in the hot seat for the next couple of weeks.

Parlane eased back in his chair, looking relieved. "Shit, Brand. I thought for one moment there you were going to walk out," he muttered.

"Nearly did."

"What stopped you?"

"Ralston's smug face. One day you must tell me what lies between you two."

Parlane grinned. "One day." Then he grimaced as he leaned forward to pick up the crutch beside his chair. "Let's get Ellery's initial interview over and done with."

****

By design, Brand and Parlane interviewed Ellery in a newly constructed room so that nothing was familiar or comfortable. The room smelled woody and sharp with the tang of building glue.

Parlane, his face pale and weary, seemed unable to grasp why a cop, a man he'd trusted, would murder innocent people. "The guy was covering up for his wife," he kept saying. "There's no way he would have murdered in cold blood."

But Brand burned to prove that Ellery was responsible for what Roberta had done. No matter how Ellery twisted it, it was his mistreatment of

Roberta over the years that had set her off on her murderous rampage. If Brand could prove that, then Célie could take her place in the world again without any stigma attached to her name. He might not be a part of Célie's future, but he intended to make sure she did not suffer because of Ellery's callous machinations.

Ellery took the initiative. "You were quick off the mark, Brand," he began in a conversational tone, as if they were three buddies, just chewing the fat.

Brand waited, his face impassive.

Ellery clicked his tongue as if he couldn't believe Brand was that dumb. "When you jumped in through the window," he explained, looking as if he was re-assessing Brand's intelligence.

"Oh, that. Yeah." Brand shrugged.

"I misjudged you. Or did I misjudge your attachment to Ms Francis?"

Ellery's voice was calm, but the hairs on the nape of Brand's neck rose. If Ellery had discovered earlier how Brand felt about Célie...

"That time in the bushland when you took a swing at me, well...I thought that was just a reaction to being taken out of your comfort zone. Didn't know you could pack such a wallop. Damn near laid me out." Mike grinned at Brand as if they shared a private joke.

Parlane's eyebrows rose. Brand hadn't told him about grappling with Peaches' murderer since, after all, the guy had got away. And at that stage, Brand had been unsure about Parlane's involvement.

Ellery grinned again. He rubbed his thumb and forefinger together. "All I had to do was crook my finger and she came running," he said, his voice as smooth as cream. "Don't you love it how I set you up?"

Brand struggled to suppress the hot anger welling up inside. He picked an imaginary piece of lint off his cuff. "Why the bike?" he asked casually, looking down at his notes.

"It was the only thing available at the time," Ellery responded, grinning. "Hell, that girl can run! I knew I'd never catch her on foot, and good ol' Octavius Newton kept a rickety bicycle outside his back door."

"So you put the fear of God into her by whispering that you knew her. Was that to keep her quiet, or was it because you enjoy sticking it to people?" Brand allowed a shade of contempt to creep into his voice.

And waited.

Sure enough, Ellery's savoir faire deserted him in a rush. He leaped to his feet. "Stuff you, you smart little shrink!" he yelled. "Think you know it all, don't you?" He mimicked Brand's voice. "Do you enjoy sticking it to people?" he parodied, sounding like a pissed-off teenager.

"Sit down!" Brand barked.

Startled, Ellery subsided. He stared at Brand for a moment then glanced at Parlane. "How come he's taking the lead on this?"

Parlane didn't answer. He examined Ellery's face as if he had discovered a disgusting beetle in his picnic sandwich.

Ellery gabbled, "It was all for Roberta. I had to cover her tracks. Shit, I wouldn't have had to do any of this if it wasn't for that crazy bitch. *Do you understand? I did not instigate any of this!*"

Brand noted that his histrionic outburst was leveled at the recorder. Who would have thought Ellery had Thespian skills?

He must have realized he hadn't impressed Brand. He searched Brand's face, trying to gauge his mood. "You saw how she was. Hell, at first I didn't even know she had another daughter. She and Nadine never mentioned Célie. It was sheer bad luck that Célie came to live close by. I guess in a country as small as New Zealand, their paths were bound to cross sooner or later. No such thing as six degrees of separation in New Zealand. But we would have been safe if Roberta hadn't gone sniffing around people's backyards, peering through windows. Seeing that girl set her off worse than ever."

Yes. He was angling to blame Roberta for everything. *Not on my watch*, Brand thought. "How did Roberta's psychosis come about?" he asked Ellery, his tone mildly curious. He lay back in his chair as if he had all the time in the world.

"She was beautiful when I met her, you know," Mike Ellery muttered, staring off into space. "Okay, she was a lush, but I was sure if I took her off the stuff cold turkey, that would fix her. But Nadine kept interfering—kept saying we should send her to a detox centre. In the end I gave in to her nagging. But when we brought Roberta back from the health spa she was a shambles. Restless and demanding. Tried to throw her weight around. I managed to get my hands on some good drugs that kept her quiet. And I made sure she was safe. Kept her away from people. Did a lot of reading about dependent personalities."

He pronounced this throwaway line as if Brand's ten years of handling disturbed patients amounted to nothing. Brand knew that was what Ellery wanted. He was playing him. So he just said, "Hmm, looks like you took a wrong turn there somewhere, Mike. She faces life in a sanatorium."

Ellery shrugged.

Ever the loving husband, Brand thought with disgust. He had already contacted a couple of colleagues who specialized in the field of psychosis triggers. They'd confirmed that Ellery's "treatment" had aggravated Roberta's psychosis, which was now irreversible. Brand was going after this lousy excuse for a human being with all the ammo he had.

"How did you feel having to cover up what Roberta had done?" he asked.

Right on cue, Ellery sneered. "Ohhh...don't you love it?" He turned to Parlane. "Isn't he predictable? The shrink's perennial question. How did you feel...?"

Parlane just looked at Ellery as if he'd never seen him before.

Ellery snorted and turned back to Brand. "You want the truth, psycho boy? It made me feel strong, that's how it made me feel! I was a winner either way. If the crimes were never solved, I'd be able to laugh about it for the rest of my life. And if it didn't work out the way I hoped—then Roberta would take the rap for the lot. And she will," he ended. "You won't get me for any of those murders."

Brand looked at his watch and said, "How about a break?"

"Getting frustrated, psycho boy?" Ellery asked, grinning.

Brand looked up and smiled. "Oh, no, Mike. Got a *long* way to go yet."

Ellery's face fell.

****

Brand and Parlane met Célie in the canteen. She threaded her arm through Brand's. "Any progress?"

Brand grinned. Ever the optimist. He echoed his words to Ellery. "Got a long way to go yet."

Dr. Anderson joined them, Lilah trailing after him. "I think we've linked your mother to the first two crimes, Ms Francis. Would you be prepared to give us her hairbrush or toothbrush for DNA testing?"

Célie nodded. "I've got some of her stuff in the car. I'm going to talk to her doctor when she's settled in at the hospital."

Brand knew she had no qualms about assisting the police since Roberta would never stand trial. Célie trusted them to lay the blame squarely where it belonged—on Ellery's shoulders. Brand prayed he could continue to play on the man's ego and get the truth out of him before he clammed up and got himself a lawyer. Which was a puzzle in itself. Any cop knew to get himself a lawyer pronto even before charges were laid. But Ellery's ego was telling him he had nothing to worry about.

Lilah said, "We have nothing viable yet from the crime scenes of the old man and the girl."

Brand felt Célie stiffen at the profiler's cold way of wrapping up the lives of the two people she had loved most. He put his coffee down and pulled her close.

"Neat way with words, Lilah," Parlane commented.

"Takes one to know one," Lilah snarled back.

Célie shook with laughter, and Brand grinned and released her.

Swallowing a mouthful of coffee Célie asked, "By the way, what happened to Occy's old bicycle?"

"The squeaking noise in the fog," Parlane murmured.

Célie grimaced. "It sounds funny unless you were there. But I remember that morning the stalker didn't wear gloves because I saw him—" she broke off to glance at Brand—"rubbing his fingers together as if it was a habit."

Parlane stared at Brand and muttered, "Huh?"

Célie continued, "Ellery was in charge of that part of the investigation, so I bet he wiped his fingerprints off the bike, but you never know. Maybe he was so confident..." She shrugged.

Brand glanced around the circle of faces and saw hope etched on each one.

Parlane fumbled to pull out his cell phone with

his sore fingers. "Shit!" He thumbed a number awkwardly with one hand. "Here's hoping he slipped up," he said, his eyes keen and excited.

His white coat flapping behind him, Dr. Anderson rushed back to his lab, talking on his cell phone as he went.

A constable sidled up to Parlane and handed him a note. Parlane read it and grinned at Brand. "Well, here's one of your problems solved at any rate. A neighbor found Brian Robinson hanging around your property. She cornered him with a shotgun. Brian wet his pants. He reckons the woman's unstable."

Brand snorted with laughter. "*Brian* thinks someone is unstable," he chortled. "Christ, she must be bad. Who was she?"

Parlane looked down at the piece of paper. "Says she's called Dolly Macklin."

Brand groaned. "She was probably gunning for me, but got Brian instead. Poetic justice. Brian finally found someone he couldn't con." He walked over to the door. "I'll carry on interviewing. This gets more and more interesting." He allowed himself a small—very small—upswing in confidence as he strode back to the interview room.

****

"Got a lot of patience, that guy," Parlane said to Célie as the door shut behind Brand.

She smiled. "Yeah. I know."

They sat in the empty canteen, surrounded by the smell of burnt coffee, waiting for the crime scene team to phone. After jiggling her knees for a few minutes, Célie got up and strolled around, examining the wall posters of off-color police cartoons and notices exhorting the readers to retrain for various specialist teams.

Colin Parlane slid down in his chair and rested his chin on his chest, his eyes closed. Dropped from

234

nerveless fingers, his cell phone clattered on to the table. The pain-killers had caught up with him.

Célie paced, praying she hadn't set them on a false trail about the bike. If this didn't bear fruit, where would they go from here? Brand might winkle some information out of Ellery, but without cold, hard evidence, the amoral prick might only go down for unlawful disclosure.

When Parlane's cell phone buzzed, she grabbed it and thrust it under his nose. Parlane roused himself. "Uh huh. Hmm."

Célie danced with impatience.

"What? What?"

Obviously forgetting his sore ankle, Parlane tried to surge to his feet. He dropped back on his chair, wincing. "Got him! The arrogant bastard hid the bicycle at his own place and filed a report saying he'd been unable to locate it. The cheeky swine said he didn't believe there ever *had* been a bike, that it was your imagination. He cleaned it, but not well enough. There are three magnificent sets of prints on it—one of Octavius Finlay's and two of Ellery's."

They grinned at each other.

"What happens now?" Célie asked.

"Now the team examines both of Ellery's properties with a fine toothcomb. We might also have to go back to Finlay's house and maybe to your old place. We'll dig and dig in case there's a shred of evidence that's been overlooked. More importantly, we'll try to trace those two goons-for-hire. Without Ellery's red herrings, we now have a base to work from. It's a matter of building the case block by block. It's almost over, Ms Francis."

And so was her time with Brand, Célie thought. It had been a terrifying experience, but in the middle of all the mayhem, she'd met a man for the long haul, one she wanted to spend the rest of her life with. He'd protected her and laughed with her and loved her. But he was meant for bigger things than to be tied to an entertainer who had to rebuild her career. He wasn't meant for her, a woman of limited education with a notorious mother who'd need ongoing care and a stepfather who was about to go down for murder.

****

"Brian who?" Ellery asked, grinning.

"Come on, Mike." Brand examined his fingernails and looked bored. "The whole Unit knows about Brian."

"Little psycho," Ellery said. "I knew where he'd hole up. Same place as he did last time. So I left him a message."

Yes, Brand had known that Brian would flee to his sister's place to pick up his stuff. But he had accorded him with more intelligence than to hang around there. Anyway, it had been a police matter. It wasn't up to Brand to chase absconders from juvenile detention. Mike had been admirably placed to stir the pot by using Brian's pathological hatred for Brand.

"You set him on to me to provide a little diversion from the Cliff Road crimes and to muddy the waters," Brand commented.

Suddenly, the air was thick with aggro. "I didn't *need* to provide a diversion, Turner. I was doing fine." Then Ellery stopped. Brand could see him going back over his words, checking to make sure he hadn't said more than he'd intended.

Brand's cell phone rang. He turned away from Ellery and flipped it open. "Uh huh?"

Parlane rapped out just one word. "Yes."

Excitement fizzed through Brand's veins and he had to force himself to keep calm. "What did you find?"

"The bike, plus his DNA all over Tara Smith's clothesline wire where he'd spun it around.

Remember, he was never called to that crime scene." Parlane sounded both elated and weary at the same time.

Brand took a deep breath. Célie and Roberta were home free.

Where did that leave him?

Chapter Twenty-Six

As they emerged from North Shore police headquarters, Brand shivered. The night had grown cold. Icy stars wavered in an inky sky and a raw wind blustered through the streets. Only a few hardy people lingered at the local bus stop, their hands buried deep in their coat pockets.

He glanced at his watch. "Hell, look at the time! We've spent all day listening to that—"

"Evil, sadistic moron?" Célie suggested.

"For want of a better phrase," Brand said, grinning. "So long as none of my clients hear you say that."

"Anyway, it wasn't quite all day," Célie said.

Brand glanced down at her. How callous could he be? She'd been kidnapped, fought off Ellery and faced up to a mother she hadn't seen in twenty years. Then she'd waited, hour after hour, while he'd tried to unravel the skein of Mike Ellery's life. Compared to Célie, he'd had it sweet.

"Okay," he said. "What comes first—a drink or dinner?"

"Both."

He grinned. That was his Célie. He sobered instantly. He'd damned well better get over thinking of her as "his." Soon she'd go back to her real life and forget about the boring psychologist she'd been forced to spend several horrific weeks with. If she was to recover quickly, getting back to her old life would be the best thing for her. As long as he hung around, she would find it difficult to get over the fear. Cue for Turner to move on out. He'd begin right now to lay the groundwork.

As they sipped a crisp Riesling, he put out feelers to see what her plans were. "What will you do now, Célie? I guess your first priority is to find a new place to live." He tried to keep it distant, cool, as if he was only mildly interested. Doctor to client. That's what she was—a client.

She stared at him and licked a drop of condensation from her wine glass.

His stomach contracted.

"I'm not sure." She ran her finger around the rim of the glass, making it sing. "I'm more concerned with where I sleep tonight." She sounded doubtful, as if she was testing him to see what he thought. But he wouldn't fall into the trap of making her decisions for her. Nope. Ms Francis would soon be herself again and then she'd castigate him for daring to make up her mind for her. He was damned if he was going to repeat the mistakes he'd made with Marina.

"I've got a lot of stuff back at the hotel," he said carefully, "so I have to go back there tonight. The budget will have to spring for another night at the Hilton."

"Are you—do you want me to come back with you?"

She sounded uncertain. That was a good thing. He would *not* beg her to stay.

Deep down he knew he was an idiot. Would life be so bad if Ms Francis ran rings around him forever? It would be infinitely better than having no Célie at all.

"If you want to," he heard himself say.

"That wasn't what I asked," she snapped, startling the waiter as he placed a bowl of mussels in front of her. "I asked if *you* wanted me to come back with you."

Brand tried to smile. "Didn't think the real Célie would lie down for long," he said.

She exploded. "Oh, for Christ's sake, Brand!" she yelled, jumping to her feet. Twenty pairs of eyes swiveled in their direction. The other diners and a couple of waiters watched in open-mouthed fascination as Célie reached across the table and grabbed Brand's tie. "Answer me, damn you! And be honest. If you want me out of your life, I'll go right now." Then she shoved him back in his chair. His jaws snapped together and his teeth clacked like castanets. He smoothed his tie, thinking quickly as Célie leaned over the table, her perky breasts jutting over the mussels.

"For heaven's sake, mate. Answer her so we can all eat in peace," a joker at the next table called out.

Red-faced he muttered, "I'll answer that later when we're alone. Eat up. You must be starving."

"Feed the beast and it'll keep quiet, right?" she snarled. She attacked a mussel, viciously prizing it out of its shell with a silver fork. "I'm just a case to you, aren't I?"

Then she set down the fork and looked up. To his horror, two huge tears rolled down her cheeks. "I'll try to change, really I will," she sniffed. "I know I'm not in your court when it comes to intelligence and I'm as abrasive and annoying as hell, but I can change."

"I wouldn't want you to change, you idiot," he said lovingly. He stretched across the table and stroked her hand. "Finish your dinner and we'll get out of here."

"I'm not hungry any more."

He sighed, looking at the mussels. "I am."

She gestured to him to finish his meal and then sat cracking her knuckles while he scooped up the last mussels on his plate. He was wiping the juice off his hands when a shadow fell over their table.

"Hey, mate," said the joker from the next table, "I'll take her off your hands. I reckon I could tame her. You don't look like you've got the right technique." He laughed a loud, braying neigh that blasted beer fumes into Brand's face.

Brand finished wiping his hands and stood up. He was a good three inches taller than Smartass. "Piss off."

Smartass reeled back. "Or what?" he demanded.

Someone at his table called out, "Give it up, Frank. Come and sit down."

But Frank was three glasses past common sense. "C'mon buddy. Show the little lady what she's worth, huh?" He swayed and made a grab at Brand's sleeve.

Brand sighed. He wondered if this sort of thing was going to happen every time he took Célie to a restaurant. They'd better eat at home in future.

"Take your hand off my sleeve, Frank. Now."

"Or you'll lay me out, huh?"

"Probably."

Frank brayed again like a jackass. "I don't think so. You're talking to a real pro here, Suit. I'm used to getting my hands dirty. Let the little lady have a real man."

Brand slugged him. Frank lurched backwards across the nearest table and crashed sideways into the credenza holding the restaurant's cutlery and crockery. Big oval dishes teetered and serving spoons jangled in sympathy. The nearest waiter, with presence of mind, held the credenza steady while Frank dragged himself up using a chair.

"You caught me by surprise," he grunted. "Let's take it outside."

"Let's not," Célie said, coming up behind him. She bashed him over the head with her plateful of mussels. Mussel shells skittered across the floor smearing juice, and a couple rained down on Frank's bent head, anointing him with a crown of shells. He slithered down the side of the table and came to rest in the corner. His eyes rolled up and he fell sideways.

"Sorry." Looking stricken, Célie apologized to the waiter. Her lip trembled. "All my fault." She began picking up mussel shells to an accompaniment of slow hand-clapping from the remaining diners.

"Well done," someone called out, and the next minute Brand and Célie were surrounded by people trying to buy them drinks. The management took the fiasco philosophically and left Frank where he was.

"Obnoxious creep," their waiter said to them. "Comes here every week and creates a scene. This is the first time anyone has belted him though."

Célie looked appalled. As he rubbed his sore knuckles, Brand couldn't help grinning at the expression on her face when she realized what they'd done.

"I'm sorry," she said. "Things just—happened." She spread her hands to indicate her helplessness.

"They often do around you, my sweet," Brand said. "Let's go home before we get into any more trouble."

He grabbed her arm while she was still docile and hustled her towards the cashier's desk.

She muttered to herself all the way to the car. Then she sat in the car holding her head in her hands. "I've done it again, haven't I? No wonder you don't want me to live with you."

"I wasn't aware that was the issue," Brand cut in. "I thought you just wanted somewhere to stay tonight."

She squirmed in her seat and looked at him, then sighed. "I'm no good for you," she said sadly. "I try, but—"

"What utter bullshit," Brand broke in. "You're the best thing that's ever happened to me. But eventually I'll bore you. That's why it's best if we—"

"Bore me?" Célie snorted. "I can't keep up with you. How could you bore me? Not for the next forty years or so, anyway. By then I might have a handle on it."

Brand inhaled sharply. He took her face in his cold hands and brushed her lips with his own. "Really?" he said. Bubbles of anticipation surged through his blood as a bright future unfurled in his mind's eye. He rested his forehead against hers. "Oh, Lord, the Hilton is too far away. So is my place. Let's take a room at the Towers. It's only a block away."

"Too far," Célie muttered, throwing her arms around his waist and leaning into him. "But it'll have to do."

Reluctantly he disentangled himself and with his pulse thudding an urgent drumbeat, managed to get them to the Towers in one piece. The receptionist pursed up her lips and handed him a key-card with the tips of her fingers. At this time of night the foyer was deserted, which was fortunate because Célie had plastered herself against him and refused to be unstuck. They entered the elevator like Siamese twins. Célie's dexterous fingers had unzipped his pants before he discovered what she'd done. Shock and excitement warred with one another as she dropped to her knees in front of him. The elevator slowed. "Célie! Quick! Get up!" He pulled her to her feet and draped an arm across his stomach.

The elevator doors slid open and an elderly couple got in. The husband avoided looking at them, but the old lady's eyes roved over the pair of them and she smiled. "Have fun," she said as they all exited on the same level.

Célie giggled as they rushed along the hallway.

"Well, she was a good sport. But did you see his eyes? They almost popped out of their sockets."

"Know the feeling," Brand muttered. His hand shook as he struggled to slide their plastic card into the door-slot. He grabbed Célie's arm and dragged her into the suite, slamming the door behind them. Then he threw her on one of the beds and jumped on top of her.

Célie laughed and wriggled. "Boring?" she queried.

Mortified by his lack of control, Brand held her close and tried to slow down. He knew Célie understood his fervor. She was no fragile flower to be startled or upset. That was what he loved about her. "I love you," he muttered. "Love you, love you."

Célie, being Célie, had all the answers. "I know that," she snorted. "And you're not getting away. Love you, too."

She tried to wrench his tie off at the same time as he pulled off her sweater and they morphed into a crazy tangle of arms and legs. He leaned down to kiss her breast but she was bobbing around so much, he swiped his tongue along her shoulder.

"Mmm," she murmured. She pulled his zipper down again and, not bothering with the niceties of foreplay, he shoved aside her panties and plunged into her again and again.

Locking her ankles around his neck she yelled encouragement. "Yes, Brand. Hurry!" She urged him on like a racehorse and he muffled a snort of laughter.

"What's funny?" she panted.

"Racehorse," he groaned.

"Roll over," she commanded. "Let me ride."

Brand gasped, "Too late."

"Never too late." She rolled them right off the bed on to the carpet and pretended to lash at him with a whip. Brand came in a painful rush but Célie was still on a pinnacle, desperate to fall down the other side. Crushing her to his chest, he snaked his hand down between them and pressed the magic button. Whimpering, she followed him down, both of them bucking out of sync till they lay supine on the carpet.

****

Ten minutes later, Célie lolled back against the side of the bed and smiled at Brand. "And just what was that all about?"

"That was a sample of what you're in for if you're determined to stay with me," Brand said, watching her face for any signs of hesitation or, worse yet, revulsion.

"Great. Wouldn't miss it for anything," Célie said enthusiastically. She hugged him and smoothed a hand down the side of his face. "Love you. Thank God we didn't give up on each other. We're sort of mismatched, but we'll manage. We've faced more problems in three weeks than most couples do in a lifetime."

Brand lay back and curled an arm around her. He looked forward to a life with Célie, fraught with misadventures and mayhem. "We trust each other. That's the main thing."

"Uh-huh," Célie murmured. She was half-asleep but Brand knew if she'd been wide-awake she would have said, "Well, duh! Goes without saying."

He smiled into the darkness, gathered her against his side, and closed his eyes.

Thank you for purchasing
this Wild Rose Press publication.
For other wonderful stories of romance,
please visit our on-line bookstore at
www.thewildrosepress.com.

For questions or more information
contact us at
info@thewildrosepress.com.

The Wild Rose Press
www.TheWildRosePress.com

To visit with authors of The Wild Rose Press
join our yahoo loop at
http://groups.yahoo.com/group/thewildrosepress/